ENEMY WALKS

A JESSIE RICHTER NOVEL

STEPHEN EAGLES

CONTENTS

01

SLIP STREAM

September 21, 2020
Palo Alto, California

J essie Richter rolled to the side of the bed and sat up, holding the edge of the mattress as tremors pulsed through the body she now occupied. She took several deep breaths to slow the heart rate, allowing her consciousness to sync with her new host. She willed the eyelids open. They fluttered briefly, and she squinted at the harsh contrast of light and dark in the huge bedroom as it cut into her vision with laser-like precision. She blinked away the few involuntary tears that always seemed to spring up every time she transferred to a different body.

Sit still, she thought. *Relax. This only lasts a couple of minutes.*

And it did only take another minute before she settled into the body of her target: Robert Andrew Kore, CEO and heir-apparent of Kore Microsystems. The shakes dissipated and her vision acclimated to his eyes. She glanced back at the naked, fit female body lying in the bed.

Her body.

She reached over and pulled up the sheets just enough to cover her bare breasts. *A lady should always be modest,* she thought, smiling at the irony. There was nothing modest about

1

the intense tryst she'd interrupted a few minutes ago when initiating the slip-stream and taking over Kore's body.

She watched the gentle rise and fall of her chest and shivered. She'd never get used to seeing herself through someone else's eyes. After ten years of slip-streaming, she knew exactly what to expect. But it still felt insane each and every time. And Jessie loved it.

She reached out with Robert's fingers, gently removing strands of thick, black hair from her body's peaceful face. How she could always maintain the deep state of meditation necessary to control the body of another person used to amaze her. Even early on in her late teens, she learned her ability stemmed from simple human bioelectricity. Not the barely perceptible sparks of life that allowed the human heart to beat. No. Something inside of her produced more power than all seventeen of the Hoover Dam's turbine generators. At least, it felt that way. To wield the power with effect, however, had taken years of training and no small measure of finesse. She related slip-streaming to being the pilot of a remote-controlled military drone, and like a remote pilot, if she lost the connection, she lost control of the drone. Another harsh shiver ran through her. The same shiver she always felt at the beginning of a new mission, keenly aware of her physical body's vulnerability during the streaming stage.

Her gaze drifted to the digital clock on the nightstand.

It's 7:55 a.m. Shit, she thought, *I gotta get moving.*

She closed Robert's eyes and concentrated. Riding the immense wave of energy that stemmed from her consciousness, she probed his mind. She had to make certain *his* consciousness remained secure within her bio-electrical prison. She put Kore on lockdown, right on the verge of his sexual release.

"Come out, come out, wherever you are," she whispered and then shuddered at the sound of the man's voice. The first of her words to pass the lips of a target always gave her the heebie-jeebies. She shook it off and stood up on unsteady feet.

Robert's body swayed ever so slightly as Jessie flowed through him, feeling for his presence. Careful not to push too hard, she knew that some host bodies were more fragile than others, and bad things could happen—*had happened*—to her hosts. Bad things like death.

"There you are," she said, a smile rising on the edge of Robert's mouth. Not feeling any resistance, she relaxed. She sniffed the air around her and identified the musty scent of sex coming from his body. She thought it a pleasing smell. Once she had access to all his senses, she'd be ready for the next phase: to walk in the man's skin. To be the man. She only needed a few more minutes to acclimate.

She involuntarily snapped her head to the side, feeling the vertebrae in Robert's neck pop. She had seen Robert perform the action dozens of times before, especially when he started his CrossFit Workout of the Day. Although two months had passed since she had initiated the mission to infiltrate Robert Kore's life, she thought about the ease in which she'd seduced the man within minutes of showing up to the Box, what Crossfitters called their gyms. She had beaten his WOD time by a full minute. The man had about tripped over himself with desire even before the coach called time, ending the workout. He was putty in her hands, and like any good spy worth her salt, she had him in bed by sunset on the first night. But nothing about spycraft was easy, and it had taken more time than she had anticipated to get to this point in the mission.

Since Robert had the head of Kore Security sweep his house for bugs randomly each month, some aspects of preparation had been overlooked, mostly because Jessie didn't need listening devices when she could *be* the target.

She tucked away her thoughts, leaned forward, and fished a small sling-pack from beneath the bed. She measured the weight in Robert's hand, marveling at how much lighter it felt when hefted by someone with twice the muscle mass. She unzipped the main compartment and dumped out the contents. She moved the Glock 43 9mm pistol and emergency medical supplies to the side and picked up a small, black case containing a pair of wireless earbuds and an encrypted Iridium satellite phone. She unfolded the phone's antenna and waited for the unit to connect with the nearest orbiting government communications satellite. She shoved the gun and other items back in the bag.

After a series of clicks, the phone connected. After one ring, a female voice answered, "Angel-one, go ahead." Jessie had not heard the voice of Crue Intellis communications specialist Taina Volkov, a former Russian Interpreter and her regular mission specialist, for months.

"Walker-one, I'm in," Jessie said, following with, "Lima-niner-charlie, echo-two-bravo." The confirmation code validated her identity as the real Jessie. Her boss, Jon Daly, had insisted this protocol be followed even though they had yet to find anyone anywhere in the world who could do what Jessie could do.

"Copy, Walker-one. You're running about an hour behind schedule," Tai said.

Jessie smiled and fought off the slight tingle of arousal at hearing the woman's soft and sexy accent.

"Yeah, I know," Jessie said, and thought how hard, how *really* hard, it was to set up the target when pinned face first to the bed, ass in the air. "Couldn't be helped."

"What's your ETA?"

"I still need to run a function test and then take a shower." Jessie looked at the nightstand clock again and shook her head. "I'll hurry. Should be rolling through the gate in about forty minutes."

"Copy that. Sat-phone is loud and clear. Let's test the earbuds."

"Copy." Jessie laid the phone beside her and plucked the tiny communication buds from their case before pressing them deep into her ear canals. She held her index fingers in place until the crisp *beep* sounded off in her ear. The devices were short range, only good for comms less than a quarter mile. "Testing one, two, three," she said.

"Great signal." Tai's voice seemed to emanate from deep inside Robert's head. "Comms sound good to go. Power down to conserve the batteries."

"Will do. See you soon," Jessie said.

"See you soon. Angel-one, out."

"Hold on," Jessie said.

"I'm still here."

"Is Falcon on overwatch?" Jessie assumed the protection of her physical body would be handled by teammate Eric 'Gunny' Ramos. She also assumed he had heard her now. Eric came up from the enlisted ranks of Marine Corps Force Recon to Warrant Officer Huey Cobra helicopter pilot, but he always took on the duty of sniper overwatch when Jessie slip-streamed. He also happened to be her CrossFit workout partner and sometimes lover. As such, she trusted Eric more than anyone to protect her body while she streamed. She couldn't count the number of times he had already saved her ass, but she hadn't spoken to him in two months. She missed Eric.

A masculine chuckle reached her ears, shaking her out of her thoughts. "Yes, ma'am. Falcon is on overwatch and in position," Eric's voice whispered. "Were you expecting someone different?"

"Just making sure." Having him talk to her elevated her confidence. "It's nice to hear your voice."

"Well, I can't say I feel the same way," Eric said. "Be careful."

"I'm always careful," she whispered. "Walker-one, out." Jessie smiled. Ever since that terrible day, over ten years ago, when she had been recruited by Crue Intellis—and her sister had been held hostage by a maniac—her teammates had become incredibly protective of her. She meant more to them than just another one of the intelligence company's most valuable assets. After working missions all over the world and spending most of her down time with the Crue over the past ten years, they had become family.

She powered down the sat-phone, but kept it out, and stuffed her sling-pack beneath the bed.

"Okay, enough chit-chat. Time to run you through a flight test, big boy," Jessie said. "Time to be the *Walker*."

She leaned over and snatched Robert's Under Armor briefs from the floor, clumsily sliding them on as she stood. Dizziness —something that always accompanied the first moments of walking in another's body—slowly subsided, and she took a wobbly first step toward the large open area in the center of Robert's bedroom. She stumbled on the next step, then spread her stance a little and stood still. Like da Vinci's Vitruvian man with boxers, she raised his arms out to the side and waited for *her* internal gyro to synchronize with her new body. Keenly aware of the time slipping away, she tried to ignore her building impatience. Each host was different. Some took seconds for her consciousness to acclimate, and others, like Robert, forced her to wait it out.

Then it clicked. The connection felt and sounded like the buckling of a seatbelt.

It's kind of like riding a bike without help for the first time, she thought. *Once you find your balance, away you go.*

By the fourth step, she and Robert walked in absolute bio-sync. Now for a little motor-function test. She couldn't afford any mistakes once she walked in front of Robert's employees and co-workers. The best test, she found, was to perform a simple, yet dynamic karate kata. The movements would shake out any delays in synapse to muscle responses.

She glanced back at the clock, sighed, and shook her head. She had to get moving, but she also had to move with confidence.

She stopped in the middle of the room, stood with feet shoulder width apart, and launched into her favorite *Uechi-Ryu* karate kata called *Kanshiwa*. Although a beginner's kata, it happened to be Jessie's personal favorite, the simple but powerful movements forced Robert's body to synchronize with her mind's instruction without hesitation.

"Hite!" Her kiai, or inner power, flowed through her as she moved through the tightly flowing blocks, strikes, and kicks. "Hite!"

She returned to a standing position, closed fists crossed at the wrists, and bowed deeply to her body lying in the bed. Now she was ready.

"Nice form, for a Walker."

The sudden but familiar voice in her ear startled her. She hadn't shut down the earbuds.

"Hi honey," Jessie said, grinning, as she hurried to the bathroom.

"Ugh," Eric groaned, apparently not amused. "You really know how to creep me out."

"You're creeped out?" Jessie joked. "You're the one watching me, remember?" Jessie knew Eric had the thermal scope on because the window blinds were closed. A sly grin raised on Robert's lips. "I miss you," she said, quickly covering Robert's mouth to suppress his laugh. She could just picture the twisted look of disgust on Eric's face, hearing the very male voice coming onto him. "You know, baby. I can stay in Robert if you like. We can..."

"That's enough. Stop." Eric snapped. He paused, listening to Jessie chuckle. "Still, a nice kata. Powerful."

Jessie thought about how it had taken Eric a long time to get over what she could do, and her process for doing it. He had been her first demo-target, quite by accident and quite by necessity. Where passion served as the most sure-fire trigger for Jessie to slip-stream, her first time in Eric came through violence. It was the day she had been officially recruited by Crue Intellis. The day a stalker had tracked her sister, taken her hostage, and then shot her. Rage had flowed through Jessie, igniting power on a level she hadn't experienced since, and Eric hadn't known what hit him. Eric's skills, hyperawareness, and keen senses had flowed through her like a locomotive. It was also the first time Jessie had killed a man. The memory itself amped up the power within her now. It felt good, almost like a drug.

Eric knew better than anyone that she reigned as the only known person in the world who could slip-stream. He also knew she loved her job too much. Some parts more than others. So she kept Eric at arm's length, their relationship loose and their private time spontaneous. It had to be enough for now.

"Thanks," she said, not wanting to waste any more time with idle chatter. "And thanks for having my back. I gotta get moving. Catch you later."

This mission had been both physically and mentally demanding. Everything about Robert Kore was intense. Especially the sex. Jessie felt certain that any other female spy, no matter their porn-star skills, would not have garnered any more information than she had at this point in the game.

"No sweat, it's what I do," he said, then added, "Darling. Falcon, out."

Jessie sighed, looking forward to some one-on-one time with Eric. She would never admit it, being tough and all, but she needed the reassurance as much as he did. She powered down the earbuds.

Covered in a thin sheen of sweat, she turned on the shower,

tested the water temperature, and stepped in. She slowly cranked the temperature knob to as hot as Robert's body could handle: the edge of scalding. The intense heat helped strengthen her mental connection to his body. She quickly lathered up and rinsed down. She then gripped the water knob, took three deep breaths, and braced herself. If a weakness existed in the connection, this act of self-torture would break it. She slammed the water knob to cold.

"Hol-ee-shit!" she howled. She stood in the frigid stream until the shock dissipated, shut the water off, and stepped out, breathing hard.

"No breaks there," she said, her voice quavering. "Locked in su...su...solid."

After toweling off, she stood in front of the vanity mirror and leaned in to get a closer look at the glowing-red eyes staring back at her. The bioelectricity enabling her to slipstream required an immense amount of power. As the energy flowed, it coursed through the host's body, fluorescing in the optic nerve, illuminating the irises from inside the eyeball. The color never changed for the bodies she slip-streamed into. To her, the glow reminded her of a fresh Hawaiian lava flow, bright red beneath an undulating black crust.

She leaned back, retrieved a contact case from her toiletry bag, and inserted brown lenses onto Robert's eyes. She leaned in close again, inspecting the edges for light leaks.

"Lookin' good," she whispered. She sensed Robert stir from somewhere deep inside. She jerked his body upright, glaring at his reflection in the mirror. Jessie drew his shoulders back, concentrated, and mentally dug deep. She felt no resistance.

"Fucking traitor," she said, daring Robert's consciousness to leap forward and say, "Fuck you." But as usual, nothing came forth from the bio-prison holding him. "You're strong," she said, "but not that strong."

She relaxed, turned away from his reflection, and headed for the stainless-steel valet stand in the corner of the bedroom. She ignored the freshly pressed suit hanging there, slid open his mirrored closet door, and pulled out a zippered clothes bag from inside. She opened the bag and removed an identical suit to the one hanging on the valet, complete with matching shirt and tie. Robert would dress himself in a couple of hours. When Jessie had picked this suit for him to wear today, she had procured an identical outfit. He paid attention to details and would notice the suit had already been worn. Wrinkles weren't part of the process. This had to be seamless.

Jessie dressed quickly, re-installed the earbuds, and headed downstairs. When she reached the front door, she paused. She pressed her index finger into one ear, waiting for the power-on beep. "Walker-one, coming out," she said.

"We're clear." Eric's voice sounded so crisp he could have been standing next to her.

Jessie stepped out the front door and walked to her Jeep, paused, and waited.

"Still clear," Eric's voice said.

Using her keys, she unlatched the back seat, raised it up, and retrieved her version of Robert's light brown, leather Maxwell Scott briefcase.

"Nice suit," Eric said.

Jessie didn't reply. She moved back into the house, and just as Robert always did, she double locked the door behind her. She walked into the small kitchen, cleared counter space, and quickly opened the briefcase. She checked the contents, dropped the Sat-phone inside, and snapped the latches closed. She plucked the fingerprint ID key-fob for Robert's car from the hook it always hung on and opened the kitchen access door to the garage.

She flicked on the overhead lights and couldn't help but grin at the wicked looking black and red, carbon fiber-bodied, Audi R8 squatting like some alien bug on the polished concrete floor.

She pressed Robert's finger to the built-in scanner on the key fob and smiled as the car roared to life. The driver side gull-wing door slid up, beckoning her to get in. A moment later, a loud click followed by a quiet humming sound startled her. She had forgotten about the air circulation system, scrubbing out the carbon monoxide, pumping in fresh air. Robert spared no expense for his car. She climbed into the seat, pressed the garage door opener, and gripped the wheel. She drummed her fingers over the steering wheel and giggled.

"Did you just...*giggle?*" Eric asked.

"Yeah," she said.

"I've never heard Kore actually giggle," he said.

"I gotta get me one of these."

"One of what?" Eric replied, his voice crisp through the earbud.

Seconds later, the car launched out of the garage and into the street. The backend fishtailed, adding to the already numerous black tire marks in front of Robert's house, but Jessie stopped the car abruptly. After pausing for effect, she revved the engine a few times and couldn't hold back.

"One of these." she said. "Fucker would never let me drive it!" She howled with laughter just before dropping the clutch, slamming the gas pedal to the floorboard, and speeding off through the Palo Alto neighborhood.

02

MISSION

Fifteen minutes later, Jessie drove past the Sunnyvale location for NASA's AMES Research Center and the Headquarters for NOAA, the National Oceanic and Atmospheric Administration. Within another five minutes, she arrived at the employee parking lot of Kore Microsystems, located on the northwest corner of the Moffett Field airstrip. Kore's facility sat on the opposite side of the runway, overlooking the huge WWII dirigible hangar called Hangar One.

Jessie glanced at Robert's Rolex watch. It read 8:45 a.m. Jessie had visited Robert's office twice over the past month, always after dark. The entire area looked different. She cursed under her breath at not arranging a daytime visit.

"Security reasons. You're not vetted," Robert had said. A background check into Jessie's alternative identity would have resulted in her being cleared for up to Top Secret, but other than to ooh and ahh over the drone locked away in the hangar, she couldn't come up with a good enough reason to try and convince him to vet her.

She had hoped that his desire to show off would prevail, but that seed never germinated. He sneaked her in at night anyway, a total breach of security protocol, no doubt providing a rush of adrenaline for the bad-boy scientist, but she never got farther than his office, and although she'd extracted quite a bit of information during those two visits, most of her time had been spent being screwed on his desk. Hopefully, she'd bagged enough intel to get the job done.

Stopped at the parking entrance, she feathered the clutch and tickled the gas pedal, giving onlookers throaty growls as the sleek coupe crawled through the lot. Jessie guessed this would be something new for the employees because Robert told her he always used his private entrance on the airstrip side of the hangar. She slipped the car into the farthest yellow stripped, no-parking zone, knowing Robert would have done the same thing if he'd had to park out there. She performed a quick tie and teeth check in the mirror and winked at Robert's reflection.

"And away we go," she said, unfolding Robert's Varvatos-clad, six-foot-two, two-hundred-twenty-pound frame from the vehicle.

Everyone in the vicinity stopped in their tracks, staring slack-jawed at the spectacle of their CEO, the big boss man, walking among them. Robert had told Jessie he didn't feel it necessary to be around the labor employees except on big occasions. Most labor employees had never seen him this close. Today, Jessie planned for Robert to be "one with the people".

She relied on Robert's deeply ingrained muscle memory, confident that his long strides looked as natural as they felt. She measured the distance to the security checkpoint to be less than a hundred-yard walk. A robust security station, it consisted of an open-air checkpoint, an X-ray machine, and a step-through magnetometer. Robert had intentionally placed the checkpoint a hundred feet in front of the main entrance of a retrofitted World War II hangar. During her private tour, Robert explained that he got the idea for the isolated security checkpoint layout from the Israelis.

"They are much more security-smart than we are," he'd said. "They learned the hard way that it is always better to stop the bombs *before* they get into the building."

Can't argue with that, she thought.

As she turned towards the huge hangar looming before her, thoughts about her mission and what she knew so far flooded her mind. During the research into KORE, she had learned that Robert had purchased the huge hangar directly from the government once his company scored their first contract with the Department of Defense (DOD) for a portable, Sensitive Compartmental Information Facility, or "P-SCIF".

As a potential government vendor, Kore Microsystems products had to pass rigorous field trials and inspections. Kore had sent three of the custom units to Fort Bragg, North Carolina for evaluation. Her employer, Crue Intellis, a Private Military Company specializing in the collection of Human and Signal intelligence, also known in the business as HUMINT/SIGINT, had been contracted to conduct the field tests of Kore's SCIF-units just about the time she had come onboard. She had been part of that inspection team her first week on the job and thought the work boring. Had it not been for the fun she had at Fort Bragg, getting her honorary jump wings, loadmaster school, and all the attention she got from the hot soldiers, male and female, she may have thought the job with Crue Intellis wasn't for her after all. But then her boss, Jon Daly, had sprung the jack-in-the-box. Robert Kore's traitorous world had been uncovered, and with it, the man's true soul revealed.

Listening devices made from tech no one had ever seen were found embedded in the walls of Kore's P-SCIFs. This led to a breakneck paced investigation using all available resources to find out what Robert was up to. The DOD, in their great wisdom, went ahead and purchased ten of the corrupt KORE manufactured units and set into motion a worldwide campaign of disinformation to root out the culprits. Within weeks, the joint CIA T-FAD/DOD investigation revealed that Robert had made a deal with the devil. They followed the money to an almost mythical branch of the thousand-year-old Chinese crime syndicate called The Benefactors. They also uncovered Robert's twenty-five-year-old motive.

Regardless, Jessie didn't feel that Robert's father committing suicide over losing a government contract was a strong enough excuse to cause a brilliant man like Robert to sell out to the Chinese. For Jessie, there was never any reason worthy of being a traitor on any level. She also didn't think the taxpayers needed to foot the bill for the long disinformation campaign just to string the guy along as an unwitting double agent.

Jessie had kept that opinion to herself.

She shook her head and rolled her eyes at the complexity of the whole thing. None of that administrative spy-craft mattered at the moment.

It's my turn now, she thought.

"Good morning, Mr. Kore."

Jessie glanced to her left at a casually dressed male worker, saw the Kore Microsystems ID badge on a lanyard around his neck, and sighed.

"Good morning," Jessie said, "and thank you."

The young man chuckled, "For what, sir?"

Jessie pointed at the badge. "I left mine in the car. Thanks for the reminder."

"No problem, sir. Have a great day."

Jessie spun on Robert's heel and headed back to the Audi. She located the badge in the center console, thankful that Robert had stashed the badge there. She slung it around her neck and started back to the security checkpoint.

That could have been a costly mistake, she thought. *Focus, Jessie.*

She picked up her pace.

Six months ago, General Henry T. Evans, co-chair of the Defense Advanced Research Projects Agency (DARPA), had conducted a briefing to propose a mission against KORE. She'd learned that KORE Microsystems had answered the DARPA's Request for Proposal (RFP) for a new Block-6 Generation Drone Weapons and Navigation system to update future unmanned aerial attack systems. Considering everything already known about KORE Industries, it stunned the DOD when Robert entered the bid race.

"If it's up to the superior technological level of their SCIF Surveillance system," Evans had said, "we need to know what else these 'Hōn' folks want Kore to make. KORE Microsystems doesn't have the 'need-to-know' that the Stealth Fighter Drone program has been axed. So, we've been keeping that intel under wraps until we've completed this mission."

Jessie's question as to why the DOD didn't just take Kore down ten years' prior earned her a grin and what didn't sound like a simple answer.

"It's a reverse flim-flam," Henry said. "Kind of like what the Chinese did to the Russians back in 1995, when the starving Russians sold the rights of assembly for their advanced heavy SU-27 Fulcrum fighter." The General had chuckled at the blank look on her face. "The Chinese took the plane's plans, reverse engineered it, and created their own version, the JU-11, and then stiffed the Russians for about three-billion dollars. Of course, what the Chinese did was illegal, but no one cared because who likes Russia, anyway? So basically, we're doing the same thing to Kore, with the official Chinese government as allies to keep it out of the revolutionist's hands."

It all sounded much too complicated and 'administrative', but she could only guess they had dug in too deep with the whole SCIF thing, and to shut Robert Kore down, without a demonstration of the evidence, would end in Congressional Oversight Committee hearings.

Enter Crue Intellis, take two, and Jessie Richter.

"No Mission Impossible or James fucking Bond antics," Evans reminded her. "I need easy in, easy out."

"That's not going to be an issue," Jessie said.

Snapping back to reality, Jessie made a point to greet anyone within striking distance with a smile and as much warmth as she could muster. Two women stopped short of the guard station, making room for Robert to pass.

"Good morning, ladies," Jessie said with a smile and an outstretched gentlemanly hand, encouraging them to move ahead. "Please, after you."

"Good morning, Mr. Kore. Thank you," they said in unison, smiles huge and faces deep rouge. They scurried past him and placed their bags on the X-ray machine's belt. Jessie overheard the two women whispering ahead of her. "He's so handsome."

As planned, Robert's presence at the security checkpoint had caused a stir among the employees. Jessie smiled broadly as folks glanced back, whispering to each other. The word spread fast. The big man was on campus. *Also according to plan.* Jessie suppressed a laugh as she noticed the frightened looks on the faces of two security guards screening bags. Until she handed the older of the two men Robert's security badge.

The man swiped it once and smiled nervously at Robert. After a third attempt, the man's face turned beet red. He moved from around the console and leaned forward, speaking quietly.

"I'm sorry, Mr. Kore, but your identification has expired." The guard tried to be discreet.

Are you fucking kidding me?

"Really," Jessie said calmly. "How embarrassing. I'll head to HR and get that fixed right away." Jessie hoped the smile on Robert's face painted a natural look. She ran the building's construction blueprints through her mind, trying to remember the location of the Human Resources Department. Although tempted, she knew activating the earbuds would be obvious. Workers were stopped now, and the line for security started backing up. Jessie felt Robert's temperature rise.

"No can do, sir," the guard said. "I've already alerted the command center. I do apologize for the inconvenience, but if you can just wait a couple minutes, we'll get this fixed, and you can be on your way. Company protocol."

What? "Wait, what protocol?"

"Well, *your* protocol, sir."

Jessie reached up to wipe at the single bead of sweat rolling down her temple and tried to keep her cool. *So much for easy as pie.* "Okay, look, it's no big deal. I'll get it fixed now," she said and moved forward.

"No, sir, you can't. I'm sorry. Someone is coming now." Jessie felt Robert's face turn red. The older guard leaned in again and quietly asked, "Sir, if you wouldn't mind, can you please step back here with me? We need to get the others through."

Jessie did as requested, understanding that doing anything other than leading by example would cause a problem. Only seconds away from aborting the mission, she saw an older, tough-looking man stroll toward the checkpoint from the main building. Jessie knew this man to be the Director of Security, Charles Derry. When he reached her, his smile seemed forced.

"Good morning, Mr. Kore. I understand there's a problem with your badge. Let's get that fixed for you."

Derry looked at the card, then at Robert with a serious expression. Jessie had never seen Robert yell at anyone, so even though she felt the urge to yell "hurry the fuck up", she kept her tongue in check. The man scanned the card again and smiled.

"Expired," he said flatly.

"Yes, I've just been told."

"It happens, sir," Derry said, leaning in to whisper, "a little more often than we'd like, but it happens."

Jessie didn't miss the admonition underlying Derry's cordial tone. She opened her mouth to speak when Derry punched numbers into a keypad at the security station and glanced up at his boss. *Bread crumb number one. Got to be more careful.* She also thought that even if Robert had been on time, he would still be going through the same embarrassing shit. The issue was, Jessie didn't need attention from security.

"Are you okay, sir?"

Jessie caught herself and nodded. "Yeah, just pissed off at myself for such a simple oversight. I've been putting in long hours lately. Like you, right Charles?"

Derry's grin slid away to a look of uncertainty. Jessie considered that she might have just posed a question that could end up being a trap and didn't press the man for an answer.

"Ah, okay. I think we're set." Derry reached over and swiped the badge across the scanner again. As soon as the LED light turned green, Derry handed Jessie the card. "Have a great day, Mr. Kore."

Jessie nodded, clipped the card to the lanyard, and picked up the briefcase. As she moved forward, she stopped and turned around.

"Oh, and Charles?" Jessie waited for the man to look at her. "Please ensure these two get an on-the-spot award today. Excellent security mindfulness."

Before Derry could reply, Jessie marched off toward the building's front doors.

03

INSIDER INFORMATION

Once inside the building, Jessie beelined it straight to a large, modern, stainless-steel elevator embedded in the WWII era wall. She pressed the button and took a couple of steps back to admire the several huge wooden placards hanging above. Too poorly lit to see during her night visits, she admired these hand painted renditions of shoulder patches representing WWII, Korean War, and Cold War era Navy squadrons that once filled the hangar. When the door slid open, she stepped in and pressed 2.

Focus, she thought. *No more mistakes.*

She did her best not to glance up at the elevator's high-resolution security camera and mentally cross-checked the locations of other cameras she had identified on her last visit. The video sensors in the cameras were hyper-sensitive, able to see past the thin colored contacts. If that happened, there would be all kinds of explaining to do by the time Robert returned to the office in a couple of hours.

A moment later, the opposite door slid open into a large, contemporary-furnished waiting room where an older, modestly dressed receptionist sat at a white lacquered desk. A backlit "Kore Microsystems" sign glowed on the wall behind her. The woman looked confused as Jessie walked forward.

"Good Morning, Mrs. Bartlett, you look exceptionally beautiful today," Jessie said.

"Thank you, Mr. Kore," the older woman said hesitantly.

"Something on your mind, Mrs. Bartlett?"

"Yes, sir. I'm sorry. I'm just not used to seeing you come in through the main elevator."

Perfect. "I decided to come in with the employee's today," Jessie said, smiling. The woman seemed to accept this unexpected answer.

"Oh, well, it is your company after all, sir," she replied. "You have several messages, and coffee will be ready in a few minutes." She handed over a small stack of old-school paper messages, which Jessie took, knowing Robert didn't like dealing with the voicemail system and still carried an older BlackBerry phone.

"Could you bring the coffee when it's ready?"

"Of course, Mr. Kore," she said.

Jessie ran the plan through her mind as she moved around the faux wall, took a left turn, and walked down the long hallway toward Robert's office. She glanced at the doors as she passed them and realized there were no name plates.

Shit, she thought, *which one is his?*

She retrieved Robert's BlackBerry and scrolled through messages while discreetly glancing from side to side.

"You've got to be kidding me," she grumbled. She wanted to kick herself for not paying better attention to that detail during her after hours visits.

"How long have I been doing this?" she mumbled under her breath. "Two years of the hardest training in my life, and eight years in the field. Didn't I learn anything? Mother Mary and Joseph, what a stupid, stupid mistake."

She recalled his view of the hangar bay being fairly close to the end hangar door and proceeded to the end office. She moved to slide the badge across the scanner and stopped. She glanced back at the office door she'd just passed and gritted her teeth. She closed Robert's eyes and visualized the construction blueprints and what she remembered from her last visit. She shook her head. She remembered seeing windows from the outside of this office when they reconnoitered the building. Robert's office didn't have end windows.

"Stupid, stupid, stupid," she mumbled and walked the twenty paces back to the other door.

She took a deep breath and pressed the badge up to the RFID pad. The retina scanner embedded in the wall didn't activate. She tried again. "Fuck me already," she whispered. She accessed the contacts on the cloned BlackBerry and looked up Charles Derry. She pressed the call button, held it to her ear, and made a conscious effort not to look at the camera adjacent to Robert's office door.

"Yes, sir, Mr. Kore?" Derry answered.

"My card-key isn't working."

"I'm sorry, you're…"

"Card, key, isn't, working." Jessie didn't need to play the part to express her building anger, mostly at herself. Now she only hoped she stood in front of the right door.

"I apologize, sir, hold on.

"Thank you." Jessie took a deep breath. The short, twenty second pause felt like an eternity.

"Okay, sir, I reset it. Please try it again."

She scanned the badge and the round lens on the retinal scanner lit up. "There, it's working now."

"Sorry for the inconvenience, sir."

Jessie checked her anger at the door.

"If I had my badge updated to begin with," she said in a calm voice, "it would have worked. I appreciate your assistance." The pause before the reply took a few seconds too long for Jessie's liking. She felt the hair raise on the back of Robert's neck.

"No worries, sir. Have a nice day."

Jessie hung up, sensing strongly that Robert would not have apologized. Doing so may have just left bread crumb number two.

Another stupid rookie mistake, she thought.

She leaned in, presented her right eye, just as Robert had on their previous visits. Back at home base, she had tested retina scanners with even more sophistication than this one to see if they would work during slip-streaming. If anything, the colored contacts reduced some of the glare, her occupation of the other body didn't change the pattern of the vessels measured by the scanner.

The door lock clicked open.

She entered, closed the door behind her, and locked the deadbolt. She glanced around the office. "Looks bigger in the daytime," she said.

Matching mahogany furniture filled the room. Robert's huge desk had been positioned a few feet off a back wall made entirely of slanted observation glass. On the far left, a buffet butted up to the private bathroom wall. To her immediate left on the interior wall hung a large credenza with a huge LCD TV. On the right, two framed, identical etchings of Salvador Dali's Leda and the Swan.

One, Robert had bragged, an original Dali, and the other a masterful copy painted by a young, African American street artist he had run into while visiting San Francisco.

"Which one's the authentic Dali?" he had asked her. She chose wrong intentionally and learned of the safe encased in the reinforced wall behind the original.

Moving quickly to the desk, she pushed his high-back leather office chair out of the way and ran fingers along the inside edge of the desktop. Once she found the sensor, she held his right index finger in place until she heard a click. A panel cut out of the desktop lowered and slid silently into a hidden recess. An ultra-wide computer screen quietly unfolded from inside, revealing the keyboard as it filled the space. The computer booted up without prompting. While waiting, she turned around and stepped up to the slanted windows. The wicked looking US Navy X-47A Pegasus drone lurked directly below in the hangar bay, being retrofitted with Robert's A.I. combat, navigation and weapons deployment solution: KAGI-6.

"And that's the reason we're here. Right big boy?" she whispered.

The official and final test of the KAGI-6 for the Joint Chiefs of Staff and DARPA procurement had been scheduled two weeks out, and her team back at Camp Summit itched to get their hands on the new program. A lot of work had yet to be done before the flight test. Her time had expired. It had to be now or never.

Jessie turned her attention to Robert's computer. She sat in the oversized leather chair, positioned her briefcase on the desk, and unlocked it. Removing an encrypted WIFI data-drive from within, she plugged into the available port, reached up, and pressed the tiny button on the encrypted communicator in her ear.

"Walker one, testing," she said.

"Copy Walker. We were getting worried about you," Taina Volkov said.

"Yeah, so much for easy in," Jessie said, then added, "Oscar-Lima-Whiskey, Echo-Two-Charlie." Changes in the password were mandatory with each verbal check in.

"Problems?"

"Nothing I couldn't handle," she said, but she should have handled it long before today. *Complacency can kill*, she thought. "I'm hooked up. Standby," she said. Jessie took a deep, steady breath and closed Robert's eyes, concentrating. A short jolt of pain zipped through the center of Robert's head. The full second delay between her body, which lay in deep meditation several miles away, and Robert's actions were jolting–a side effect she would never get used to. *I've been farther, settle down.* She continued to press into Robert's memories until the pass-code came to her. She squinted his eyes at the throbbing in Robert's head, opened his jaw, and rubbed at his temple a moment before typing in the code. "OK. Are you ready to receive?"

"Da."

Jessie watched the tiny red LED light blink for a moment then suddenly switch to a blinking green.

"We've got it. It's transmitting," Taina said.

"OK, heading to the safe. Standby."

As the processor worked on the data transfer, she moved to the office door, checked the deadbolt, and walked up to the two Dali etchings. "Now that I can see it in the daylight, the copy is pretty damn good," she said and turned to the real one. Taina didn't reply. She ran her fingers under the lip of the frame, found a button, and pressed it. With a loud click, the frame swung open.

Behind it, a sixteen-inch, square steel door and another RFID reader. She held Robert's access card to the beam, and a box-like object with hundreds of tiny hexagonal holes folded out of the wall on a hinge along the bottom. A red LED blinked in the upper corner of the panel. She leaned in close and exhaled.

The LED turned green and the grid pulled back into the wall. The bigger metal door hissed open to reveal a digital-dial safe on the other side. Jessie pressed deeper into Robert's mind, searching for the combination. The first number, seventeen, materialized in her mind and then, *pop!*

"Shit." Jessie felt the warm ooze of blood run down Robert's clean-shaven upper lip.

"What's up?" Taina asked.

"I'm going to have to go manual. I pressed too hard. Give me a minute." Jessie moved around the corner to the full bathroom on the other side of the wall, grabbed tissue, and crammed it up her nose.

That will have to do, for now.

She returned to the safe, unclipped the BlackBerry, and

popped open a compartment in the holster. She peeled four sticky electrodes from inside and placed them around the onyx combination dial in the center of the door. She powered up the phone and located the safe-cracking app developed by her team.

"Safe Cracker? Really?" she said sarcastically. "I thought you guys were supposed to be the creative types." She shook her head and pressed the screen.

"Quiet, we're working over here!" She only just heard the male voice calling out in a fake, New Jersey accent. It belonged to Marc Samuelson, another hacker type, and not only a former US Air Force computer systems programmer, but also Taina's husband. Rounding out the hack team was Army Intelligence Officer Chip Rasher, who played driver today. She surmised the surveillance van had to be parked close by.

"Okay, I'm spinning up," Jessie said. The earbuds went quiet.

In seconds, the app synchronized with micro-transmitters embedded into each of the sticky-pads. Tiny yellow LEDs lit up on the pads and the phone's display confirmed the system checked out on-line.

According to Robert, Jessie only had one attempt to get it right—any error in the number sequence would activate the security system. The office doors, as well as every other access point in the building, would automatically lock down until Charles Derry, and the armed guards she just gave a bonus to, arrived. Jessie put her fingers on the dial and let go.

"Fuck this," she said, and probed Robert's mind once again. It wasn't that she didn't trust the technology, but yeah, she didn't trust the tech. The usual zap of pain shot straight up through the middle of his head, but this time she got the code. "Let's give it a whirl," she said, and spun the dial three times.

With earbuds in place, she instinctively cranked Robert's neck to the side, popping the vertebrae. She concentrated and carefully turned the dial to the first number, seventeen. The sticky-pad LED blinked from yellow to green. She let out a breath she didn't realize she'd held and dialed in the next number. Fifty-three. The light turned green.

"So far, so good," she whispered. She dialed in thirty-two, five, and then eased the dial into the final number slot, forty-five. Once the sequence locked in, all the pad LED-lights flashed in sync. She twisted the handle, opened the door, and reached in.

"Fuck me," she said. She reached up and touched her earpiece. "Angel-one, you on?"

"Yes, I'm here. We're almost finished with the transfer from his computer. It looks like what we expected to find on his office computer. The original contract, some specs, but not the operating system. What's most valuable here are huge money transfers into his accounts that I don't think we've seen before. We're ready for the system files transfer."

"Yeah, well about that…"

"What's wrong?"

"The hard drive is not in his safe. It's empty." A week had passed since Jessie's last visit to Robert's office. She watched him put it in the safe.

"This is a custom built safe for that very purpose," he had said.

"Shit. We didn't really discuss a plan B," Taina said, worry in her voice.

At that moment, the sound of a key in the door's manual lock seized Jessie's attention. The deadbolt thumb latch began to turn.

"Oh shit, gotta go." She slammed the safe door shut, ripped off the electrodes and spun the dial just as the door swung open.

Shit, shit, shit!

She stuffed the wires in Robert's jacket pocket, closed the painting, and hustled behind Robert's desk. She whispered "standby" when Maria Ricardi, Kore Microsystem's lead config-uration manager, backed in through the threshold, notepad and two steaming cups of coffee balanced precariously in one hand. She closed the door with her foot and spun the deadbolt locked with her free hand. The actual door lock needed a key when secured from inside the office. The woman having a key to Robert's office added to Jessie's suspicion that the two might have more than a working relationship.

"Good morning, Robert," Maria said.

The greeting lacked the expected professional tone. She walked to the credenza, set the cups and pad down, and grabbed the remote for the huge Sharp television. Jessie leaned over the desk and saw the led on the Wi-Fi drive transmitter blinking solid green.

Finished, thank the gods.

She unplugged it, dropped it in Robert's open briefcase, casually closed the lid, clicked the latches shut, and turned the locking tumblers. She let out a long, slow breath and leaned back in Robert's chair, then, remembering the wad of tissue rammed up her nose, tugged it out and dropped it in the waste bin under the desk.

Maria turned on the television, selected the Bloomberg channel, and set the volume up just a little too high. She spun on her heel and sported a lurid smile. With each step toward Robert's desk, she popped open a button on her blouse. The smile on Jessie's face hid her frustration. She'd have to have a discussion with her team about this. How could they miss that Robert and the A.I. System's Configuration Manager were screwing? But now wasn't the time. Jessie couldn't control the arousal in Robert's body as Maria squeezed her breasts together and licked her lips with each step toward her.

Oh well, Jessie thought. *I guess I'm going to have to take one for the team.*

04

TRANFERENCE

Maria stopped in front of Robert, raised one leg, and planted her stiletto-clad foot on the arm of his chair. Her silk, flower print skirt rode up her thighs to reveal garter clad stocking legs, no panties. Jessie smiled up at the woman, reached out, and laid her hand on the woman's ankle and her fingertips up the silky-smooth leg.

"I couldn't wait," Maria said. "I haven't seen you in months. I'm a little jealous over that young tart you're fucking. Is she really that good?"

Jessie dropped the smile. *On another planetary level, lady.* "Maria, we don't have time for this right now. Maybe later. But I'm glad you came..."

"I haven't, yet, but I intend to," she said.

Pulling her blouse aside, she squeezed her ample breasts together and bent forward, pressing the display closer to Robert's face. She stopped short, leaned back, and scrunched her nose.

"What happened? You get a nosebleed?"

Jessie pushed Maria's foot off the armrest, causing the woman's ankle to twist, dropping her to her knees as she tried to regain her balance.

"Sorry, sorry," Jessie said, pulling open a desk drawer, then another until she found a small pack of wipes next to a box of condoms. "Yes, I did. Must be allergies," she mumbled, and pulled out a few too many towelette's, wiped her nose, and smiled.

Maria smiled back. "Well, since I'm already on my knees." She shimmied toward Robert, reached between Robert's legs, rubbed the growing member through his pants, and flicked her tongue across his lips. "You might not have time, but your cock is telling me something different."

Holy shit, this woman's hot, Jessie thought. She couldn't control the primal response from Robert's body. *How can I? I'm turned on too!*

"I'll make it fast, Robert. I'm really horny this morning." Maria crouched in front of him and tore at his belt, working it free of the buckle.

From the distance of Robert's Palo Alto bedroom, seven miles from the office, the familiar electrical charge cranked up from Jessie's deep place in response to Robert's quickening heart rate as this wanton woman knelt before her. Jessie clenched her jaw and fought to shut down the lightning generator deep inside.

"Maria, hold on a minute." Jessie struggled not to give in to the moment. *Stay focused!* Maria stopped tugging at his zipper and looked up at him with big, brown, expectant eyes. Jessie still wasn't sure of Maria's involvement in the program deception, but this gave her an opportunity to find out. "I need your help with something project related."

"It can wait," Maria said, reaching again.

"No, it can't." Jessie grabbed Maria's wrists just a bit harder than she intended to. "We need to get to the mainframe. I need to do a full program run-through with you, with the system connected to the drone."

Maria's brow furrowed in thought. She stood up in a huff, not attempting to cover her breasts or her frustration. "Why?" Jessie wasn't quite sure how to answer the woman's straightforward question. "Seriously, Robert, you've been working on this project for six years, and we've tested it a million times over the past three months. It's as ready as it will ever be."

Jessie doubled down and concentrated. She probed Robert's mind in an attempt to seed him with a memory of what would happen with Maria later, not what happened right now. "I'm sorry, just got struck by a monster headache."

Maria slowly put the girls away and straightened the front of her blouse, "You've been working, like, a hundred hours a week, Robert. I don't get to see you as often as I'd like, and now you're worrying me. You're stressed, I can see it."

"You're right," Jessie said. "Let's just get this last bench test completed, and I'll make it up to you. Tonight."

Maria smiled, then frowned. "What about your little gym-princess?"

Jessie smiled, snatched Maria by the waist, and pulled her in for a deep, passionate kiss. She then pushed the breathless woman away. "Don't worry about her. You going to help me or not?"

After a moment, Maria nodded, licked her thumb, and reached up to wipe lipstick from Robert's mouth. "Sure. The mainframe?"

Jessie smiled. "The mainframe."

THEY TOOK THE EXECUTIVE ELEVATOR DOWN TO THE HANGAR. The few workers in the area paid no attention to Robert and Maria as they entered the mainframe room. Maria walked to the center console, with Jessie quite literally on Maria's ass. Jessie squeezed Maria's butt cheek, eliciting an enticing groan from the smoldering woman. She watched as Maria entered her access code and made a mental note of it.

"Hold on," Jessie said. "Which is the best port to connect with for a fast file transfer?"

Maria frowned. "You want to transfer the file? Why? To what device? It's a monstrous program."

"Maria, it's best if you don't ask questions. Where is the port?"

Maria stepped to the right, opened an access panel, and pointed to a SATA connector. "This is the A-port. I would say that it's the fastest. It's fully compliant, even RIBM." Jessie knew this meant Reflective for IBM, necessary for high-output data transfers. Jessie moved to plug it in, but Maria stepped in front of the panel. "You need to tell me what is going on. What have you done? You're scaring me."

Jessie stood up straight and moved close to Maria. She wrapped an arm around her waist, pulling the woman's hips into Robert's. "Maria, there's nothing to be scared of. This is so I can create a full back up of the working system. I'm concerned the other drive is corrupted."

"See, you're losing it," Maria said, a look of challenge on her face. "I picked the portable drive up with the program matrix a couple days ago and cross-checked it with mainframe. It's fine. How could you forget that?"

"Don't worry about it," Jessie said, pissed that she, nor anyone from her team had anticipated the Config Manager.

Maria's concern gave way to anger. "How can you say that? Don't worry? What's worse than this being a fucking federal offense, Robert, is what The Benefactors might do if you get caught. You know this!" She looked at the drive in Robert's hand. An even more quizzical expression crossed Maria's face. "What is that? There is no way, even compressed, that drive can hold the brain of KAGI-6." Then she recognized the device. "That's a transmitter. You're..." Maria took a step back, shocked. "Robert, you're going to get us killed. I can't..."

Jessie moved in fast, slammed Maria against the mainframe and kissed her roughly. Maria did not melt. Instead, she struggled and reached for the keypad on the terminal. Jessie grabbed Maria's arm, hooked a leg around Maria's ankle and drove the woman to the hard, concrete floor. Maria yelped on impact and tried to scream and defend herself, but just a bit too late. Anger and fear had already flooded into Jessie, the slip-stream energy at full power and pulsing through her like a locomotive. Jessie had never transferred from one target's body into another that wasn't her own. This would be a first. Jessie readied herself and released Maria's arm.

Just as Maria's ineffective punch connected to the side of Robert's head, Jessie reached up and touched both sides of the woman's face.

A flash of light blinded Jessie as the tell-tale crack of a whip filled her ears.

Time and all motion stopped for the familiar two thunderous beats of her heart. She waited for it.

Thu-thump.

Thu-thump.

Then time resumed, slamming into her, pulling her into the vortex of energy that turned her upside down and around until parts of her own consciousness snapped like twigs in a storm. The expected invisible force grabbed her spine and pulled her inside out. The scream that always came, the one she could never release, caught in her throat as the souls of Robert, Jessie, and Maria scraped against each other, sounding like the world had cracked in two.

Nausea, more powerful than the first time she had slip-streamed some ten years ago, overwhelmed her. The pain and pleasure jolted her body. Maria's face, Robert's face, then her face, flashed before her. It was like looking through the slots of a Victorian-era Zoetrope. An intense vibration unlike anything she had experienced before threatened to shake her apart.

Jessie thought that maybe, this time, she had gone too far. But then it stopped.

As Jessie's vision cleared, she couldn't breathe. Robert's unconscious body lay on top of her. She shoved with all her might, rolling Robert off to the side. She clambered upright on unsteady feet, gripping the mainframe's structure for balance.

"Fuck me sideways," she said, Maria's voice jarring to her ears.

Once the dizziness subsided, she squatted down to take Robert's pulse. She nodded at the slow, but steady pace which clocked in at about thirty beats per minute–faster than her own body's rate during the stream. This was new. She felt a defiant lag in the time her thoughts resulted in action. She didn't have time to worry about this, not being sure how long she could maintain the dual connection. A sense of urgency screamed at her from somewhere deep in her mind that she needed to hurry. She gently dug Maria's fingernail into Robert's ears and plucked the communication earbuds from his head.

Shoving them into Maria's, she started talking, still breathless from the unusually agonizing slip. "Walker-one, India-zula-alpha," Jessie paused, gasping for air, "one-foxtrot-alpha. Fuck... is that right?"

"Shit, Jessie, what happened?" Taina asked.

"You have got to work on following protocols, woman," Jessie croaked. "I had to improvise, standby."

"Are you okay? Don't sweat protocols, your earbuds are encrypted. Besides, we've got full ECM deployed. I checked, no one's tapping in. So, you're in the Config manager? What happened to Kore?" Panic crawled along the edge of Tai's voice. Jessie didn't need to hear that right now.

Then Marc Samuelson cut in. "Jessie, are you alright? Can we help in any way?"

Marc's deep, even voice soothed her. He was with Tai in the van to monitor the coming download of information, and Jessie knew he would keep Tai's panic in check. God only knew Jessie was on the brink, too.

Jessie leaned down, picked up the Wi-Fi transmitter off the floor, and retrieved the proper SATA plug from Robert's pocket.

She connected the drive to the PFFT port and waited until the small LED light blinked yellow.

"We've got connection, Jess, ready to receive," Taina said.

"You guys tapped into the phones?"

"Yes. Once you initiate the data transfer, we have the challenge code ready for the call from Security Operations Center. If they call."

"OK. Great. I had to slip into the Config manager before she entered the proper authorization codes. Standby." Jessie struggled to hold on.

She sensed Robert's consciousness stirring, and Maria felt even more powerful than Robert. She reached toward the terminal when movement caught her eye. As her hand moved, so did Robert's. She raised and lowered the left hand, then the right. So did Robert. She wasn't consciously controlling him because she concentrated on keeping Maria going.

How strange. She wondered if her hands were moving back in Robert's bedroom.

"I'm stretched thin here, guys," she said, "trying to keep it together."

The Crue Intellis team in the van knew what Jessie could do and how she did it. They did not know if she had ever streamed through two separate bodies before and were wise not to ask any questions. With this problem, everyone, Jessie included, understood the precariousness of her position, like walking on a tightrope over a gator pit.

Jessie dropped to her knees next to Robert, held out her hands, and focused her power once again. Maria's eyes rolled into the back of her head, and small, silken threads of light sprang to life off Maria's fingertips. She directed her energy at Robert's consciousness first, reaching down, keeping her fingers an inch or so from his face. The little strands of light danced and sizzled on Robert's cheeks. She found him quickly and locked on, settling Robert back into her bio- electric prison.

Standing up, she mentally probed Maria's mind with as much force as she dared to use in this situation. Jessie didn't hear herself moaning during the effort.

"Walker-one, your status."

"Standby for data transfer and be ready." The voice emanating from Maria's mouth sounded slow and slurred.

"Ugh. If I lose these connections, there is going to be some serious shit hitting the fan down here," Jessie said. "You might want to prep for an extraction."

"Hang in there, Jessie. We're a go. Standing by." Taina's voice seemed calmer now.

Jessie resumed her probe. Pain charged through Maria's head, and Jessie yelped involuntarily. Like a Jack-in-the-box, the codes she needed sprang forward into her mind. She backed off enough to allow the dizzying feeling to subside and typed in the code.

Dozens of LEDs on the mainframe lit up, and the server's fans whirred to life. Jessie glanced down at the ghost drive she'd installed. The LED turned hard green.

"Data incoming. Looks like we've got...thirty minutes for full upload," Taina said.

"Jessie." Mark Samuelson's voice again. Calm but firm. "Are you going to make it?"

Jessie paused at the question because, honestly, she wasn't sure. "You're damn right I will. But we've got some time. I need to meditate for a couple of minutes. Just call me when it's done."

"Copy that. Speaking of a call, the SOC is dialing in right now about the data breech."

"Imagine that," Jessie said, and walked over to the computer access door to flip the deadbolt closed just before she dropped to the floor. She forced herself to maneuver into the Lotus Pose. The forty-something woman took great care of herself and had a flexibility that impressed her. Jessie adjusted Maria's feet high onto the thighs and straightened her back before resting the backs of her hands on her knees. She took three deep breaths, formed a circle with her thumbs and middle fingers, and slowly released the low Om vibration from deep inside Maria's chest.

Now settled into Maria's body, while she maintained her connection to Robert, she retreated into her own mind to recharge.

And plan my way out of this fucked up mess.

Intrigued by the side effect of mirrored movements from Robert's body. She felt calm enough, strong enough, to try a little experiment as she waited. Like hanging from a cliff's edge, with the safety rope only just within reach, she stretched her mind from Maria back to Robert. Slowly, his body's eyes opened, and for a minute, Jessie saw two images, overlapping one another. Holding the yoga pose, she concentrated.

She pressed Robert's body up into a sitting position, kicked off his shoes, and managed to get him into the same yoga pose, facing Maria.

This is so freakin' bizarre, she thought. She extended Robert's right hand as she extended Maria's…she brought them back to her lap.

"Okay," their voices said together. "Time to remember my piano lessons." She took a deep breath as both bodies exhaled in unison. Maria's right hand reached out to touch Robert's left. She did it again and held fingertips together. A small thread of electricity passed between the fingertips. She lowered their hands.

"Holy crap," she said.

"What's wrong."

"Nothing. I've just discovered something new."

05

VAMOS

Jessie glanced at the R8's radio and swore under her breath. The trip to KORE shouldn't have taken two-and-a-half hours. It increased her chances of getting busted once she slipped back into her own body. *I'm going to have to make it worth it,* she thought.

During Jessie's experimentation with both Robert and Maria, controlling both of them simultaneously, she dug deep and made some mental impressions that would no doubt drive Robert and Maria nuts. Maria would only remember getting pinned against the mainframe KAGI-6 computer and thoroughly screwed from behind after running the tests. She would remember having an earth-moving orgasm and being satisfied. Jessie left her only slightly disheveled and grinning when they exited the computer room.

Robert's story, on the other hand, had to be different. He wouldn't have any memory about the morning, especially fucking Maria. And that was going to be a problem.

He's going to freak the fuck out, she thought. But she also knew his big ego would not allow him to admit the memory loss. Running this scenario quickly through her mind, if this happened, he'd run his own investigation, review the cameras, see everything. She did the best she could by seeding deep memories that he worked too hard, that he felt stressed out by his illicit dealings with The Benefactors. And if that didn't work, and Robert ended up thinking too hard about that morning, she'd planted a spike of pain that would rivet him to the floor.

41

After that, whatever happened, happened, because in the next few hours she'd be long gone.

She knew the other team members had most likely warned Jon and General Evans of the distinct possibility the DOD would have to scuttle the flight tests and just take down Kore. Although Jessie had been learning the new flight simulator, and had been chosen to test the drone's security, she still believed the entire facade to be an exorbitant waste of taxpayers' money and an unnecessary risk.

Regardless, Jessie planned to push even harder to muddle Robert's recollection of the morning. Worst case scenario? She shuddered at the implication. Pushing too far could be fatal. *The man might be a traitor,* she thought, *but I'm not an assassin.*

As she approached Robert's townhome, she pressed the garage door button built into the visor, slowed her speed, and glided into the space. She shut down the car, popped open the trunk to allow air circulation around the engine, and grabbed one of Robert's microfiber towels and a bottle of Meguiar's quick detail spray to wipe down any smudges on the door. She performed a quick polish of the car's exterior, closed the garage door and opened the kitchen door to allow the colder inside airflow into the garage. Before she had left for Moffett, she dropped the AC to 65 degrees. The engine needed to cool down for at least thirty minutes–her 6 a.m. trip to Starbucks was four hours ago, and any sign of a warm motor would not fly under Robert's radar. She stripped off clothing as she climbed the stairs to Robert's bedroom. *So far, so good.*

She walked to the edge of his king-sized bed and stripped the sheet off her naked body. Her shoulder-length black hair lay draped over the pillow. Her breathing, only barely perceptible by the slow rise and fall of her breasts. Seeing herself from an outside perspective, she thought her body looked like some kind of Michelangelo sculpture. A trickle of sweat rolled down the left side of Robert's face. She reached up to collect the bead in his fingertips and rubbed his thumb and forefinger together. *Stress.* This morning's fiasco with Maria had pushed it too far. Sometimes this happened. If she stayed in a body too long, or she ended up being overly stressed, the host's body would over-heat and sweat profusely. The company doctor called it Hyper-hidrosis. Streaming through two bodies at once most certainly counted as abnormal, and the sweats were coming on fast.

She stuffed her identical copy of Robert's clothes into her large, overnight bag and slid it under the bed. She looked at Robert's Rolex once more, unbuckled it, and wiped it down before returning it to the top shelf of his valet. *Everything's ready.* She walked to the thermostat and tapped the digital display-still at 66 degrees. She slipped off his skin-tight boxers before climbing back in bed next to her body.

Her connection to Robert, to any other body she had slip-streamed through, was always a two-way street and much deeper than just a drone-like control of his body. She felt what he felt and could access some of his deepest, darkest memories. If she stayed in a host too long, however, things went even more sideways than the sweats. On a couple of missions, she had spent too much time inside and almost lost her own mind. The host's memories had mixed and muddled with her own. She shook her head and shivered. *Sure glad I won't have to go through that again,* she thought. Now she had to concentrate.

Jessie ran Robert's finger over her own supple, warrior fit body. Her abdominals were etched into her skin like paver stones, the vascularity in her hips tapered toward her smoothly shaved mons-pubis. *Thank you, CrossFit,* she thought. Robert's body responded, as all her target's bodies responded, with immediate arousal. Jessie had snatched him up before he could get off this morning, and she had also held off while banging Maria on the floor. This wouldn't take long. She didn't need to look, she felt the heavy hardness, erect and ready for service. She spread her body's legs apart and moved into the same missionary position they were in before she slip-streamed. *Nope,* she thought, *this isn't going to take long at all.*

For Jessie, sex had zilch to do with romance. She did what she needed to do to complete her missions. No different than any other spy worth their salt in the field. For her, she called it "sport sex". She'd picked up that term from a prostitute she met while on another mission a few years ago, and it fit. Long ago, even before being recruited by Crue Intellis, Jessie had gotten over the weird, close-to-rape feeling of having sex with her own body. As a teen, sex and fear were the only two emotions she'd known could ignite what she called The Little Generator inside her. The whole process of slipping into, and then streaming her consciousness through, another body had been an accidental discovery. But she had to admit, in the early testing phases, experimenting with other bodies, men and women, turned out to be a lot of fun.

No time to reminisce. Time to get back to work.

Because of the time she had already lost, she decided to give Robert the bonus package, and pray his meticulous attention to detail would be lost to the lascivious performance she resigned herself to deliver.

ROBERT STOOD IN FRONT OF THE FULL-LENGTH MIRROR AND adjusted his tie.

"Goddammit, Lisa, I can't believe it's almost noon. Why didn't you say something?"

"Because it's difficult to say anything when I have your big dick in my mouth," Jessie replied from the shower. "Besides, you started it by coaxing me awake in your special way, so it's not my fault."

"I swore that was at, like, 7 a.m.," he said, looking at his wristwatch. "What is it with you and time?" he asked.

Jessie called out from the shower. "No, sweetheart. You left at close to nine, came home before lunch time, and woke me up. I looked at the clock. I think at 11:30 or so. Not that I couldn't take more."

"What? No, I didn't go to work, you're crazy. I'd remember going to work. I remember you and me. That's…" he paused, "…wow, I don't think I've ever had a headache like this."

Not sure he'd bought into the lie or would stop testing the erasure of his memory, she tried a different tactic. "Aww, you're so sweet! When you got home, you said something about having completed all your tests and had time to play. Are you sure you can't take the rest of the afternoon off?"

"I don't remember any of that. My head is *pounding*. Fooling around usually cures my headaches."

"Baby, I do not call what we do 'fooling around'. With you, it's all business…and I love it." Jessie peaked out from the bathroom door, displaying her half naked body. "Do you have to go in, really? I have something better for you to do, and I bet I can cure your headache," she said.

Robert glanced her way and grinned, but Jessie saw the smile didn't reach his eyes as he made a monumental effort to mask the pain without slowing down on his tie.

"Damn, you're sexy," he said as he buckled on his Rolex and glanced at it a third time. "I am late. Why don't you stick around? I should be home around eight," he said.

Jessie understood his faux invite to stay as a dismissal and felt relieved that she hadn't killed the man outright. She watched. Close. He hadn't left the doorway, yet, it might still happen. He could drop to the floor dead from the mother of all aneurysms.

"We'll see," she said. "I planned on an afternoon WOD at the Box. I think it's 'Fran' day." Crossfitters named their workout-of-the-day after women or soldiers: the "Fran" routine consisted of twenty-one, fifteen and nine repetitions of fifty-pound barbell thrusters, followed immediately by pull-ups, repeated until three sets were completed as fast as possible. Unprepared athletes were sometimes left on their hands and knees, puking. Jessie smiled. An afternoon round of "Fran" would be a fitting end to a successful mission.

Robert walked into the bathroom, gave her a peck on the cheek, and turned to leave.

"See you tonight?" she asked.

"You bet. I'll call if anything comes up," he said and reached for the door, but missed. He stumbled, ramming his right shoulder into the door jam.

"Robert!" Jessie rushed across the room and held him by the waist. "I'm not sure if your passing out after our romp would be a compliment," she said. "Come sit on the bed." Robert stood up straight and rubbed his temples, groaning. He resisted Jessie's light pull toward the bed.

"No, it's passing. What the hell? I've never felt like this." He turned and kissed her on the cheek once again and exited the bedroom.

Still naked, Jessie walked to the window and opened the blinds an inch or two. She watched as Robert Kore slowly pulled out of the driveway and crawled the wicked Audi down the street at well below the speed limit.

Yeah, that's what I call pain. Fucking traitor, she thought, and then she flipped his ghost the middle finger. She waited just another minute, then retrieved the sling-pack once more from beneath the bed. She activated the sat-phone and looked around the room while the phone went through the ritual clicks while encrypting the signal. She realized there wasn't a piece of furniture or countertop she and Robert hadn't had sex on. But this wasn't the movies. She didn't need a cleaner to come in because Jessie wasn't an assassin. Not intentionally, anyway. Not yet.

"Joe's Pizza." Jessie rolled her eyes and almost laughed at the sound of Marc Samuelson's horrible attempt at a New Jersey accent.

"Alpha-Alpha-Charlie, One-two-Alpha," she said. "He's out. I'm showering, then leaving in about thirty." She had showered a few minutes ago but felt the need to really scrub down now her part of the mission was over. "Marc, we're…"

A sound, like some ultra-high-pitched squeal reached her ears. She turned, looked behind her, eyes darting around the room. "Hold on, Marc." She lowered the phone, then listened. Nothing. She brought the handset up and rested it on her shoulder as she sorted through her other backpack for something to wear.

"We're going to have to have a debriefing about my trip to KORE," she said. "I'm not happy that we missed the ID expiration, and Robert's relationship with Maria."

"We're already talking about that, Jess. The consensus is we just didn't have the time to dig as deep as we normally do. This whole thing was short notice."

"OK, well we made it through," she said, as she headed once again for the shower.

"Barely. On our end, we weren't sure the AI program was going to fit in the storage we had on the van. It did, but I don't think there's a single gig of space left."

"Yeah, well, it was no cake walk on my end either. I'm going to have to tell you guys about streaming through two bodies simultaneously. It was crazy."

"Well," Marc finished, "at least you didn't die."

06

CAT...

Tano watched the video feed in disbelief. Robert had showed up for a lunchtime quickie, not an unexpected behavior for Kore, and mounted the unconscious woman. His eyes narrowed as Robert positioned the woman's legs, masturbated to a full erection, then buried himself into her. Tano gasped. He wondered if, in fact, Robert had drugged the woman, certainly that hadn't been necessary, certainly...

And then Robert reached out to touch the woman's face. She suddenly sprang to life and met each one of Robert's thrusts with lustful abandon, as if she had been actively participating the whole time. To him, it appeared obvious that Robert had orgasmed quickly. The woman jumped up out of the bed, apparently well rested, while Robert staggered and almost fell into the bathroom.

What the hell?

He played the video back, and again, before leaning back in his chair and rubbing at his eyes. For the first time in his life, Tano felt lost. Confused. He did not understand what he was seeing on the tape and still wasn't sure he'd witnessed anything at all. He shook his head, put the cameras on real-time, and then kicked back to watch. *How much stranger can this get?* he thought.

Within another twenty minutes, Kore finally made it out the door. Tano got up from his chair, preparing to visit Robert at his office, but then it happened. The girl, still naked, moved to the bedroom window and leaned against the wall, watching. Then she flipped Robert the bird and pulled the same backpack from beneath the bed that Robert had handled earlier. He sat back down in his chair.

"What have we here?"

The girl activated what appeared to be a sat-phone. Tano tweaked the microphones in the bedroom to maximum sensitivity. He pushed too hard. The quick squad of feedback caused the woman to look back over her shoulder, then at her phone before continuing her conversation.

Tano picked up his own encrypted cellphone and dialed a number, but he had no intention of calling Chen. He didn't need the man's permission for everything.

"This is Tano. How fast can I get a live bird on station?" he asked, speaking Chinese.

"Xiānshēng, wèixīng zhèngzài xuánzhuǎn." *The satellites are in rotation, sir.*

"Zhè gàosù wǒ shénme, duōjiǔ?" *How long before I can have access?* Tano replied, then added, "Nǐ huì shuō yīngyǔ ma?"

"Yes, sir, I speak English, although not well."

"Well enough," Tano said. "So how long?"

"Exact coordinates?"

Tano looked at the Google Earth program on one of his other screens. "Thirty-seven, thirty-eight, double zed, by negative one-twenty-two, twenty-four, sixteen west."

"Standby."

Tano drummed his fingers on the table.

"Command and control advises six hours until in range for live feed."

"No wonder the Chinese are in second place," Tano said.

"Excuse me, sir?"

"Never mind."

Tano hung up, checked the video feed from Robert's room, and saw the female appeared to be packing her things. She was rabbiting, and Tano had to make a decision. He stood up, entered the nearby storage closest, and pulled a grey, all-weather case from the top shelf. He rushed downstairs into the kitchen, opened the box, and removed a medium-sized commercial drone. He unfolded the wing assemblies, inspected the small propellers, and checked the battery. He guessed that a full battery would give him about thirty minutes of flight time. What he had in mind wouldn't take more than ten minutes tops. But time ticked away. He needed to get the drone over the woman's jeep before she left.

He plucked one of six discs out of the foam material lining the drone's case. The little GPS tracker looked exactly like a half-dollar coin, but in order to have enough power to last, it had been built twice as thick to support room for the battery and magnet. Attaching the magnet to any metal surface automatically activated the little device, which would transmit its location by pinging off cell towers. Any wi-fi signal within range would charge the battery indefinitely. The more towers it passed, the more accurate the location. Tano carefully taped the little disc to the landing foot of the drone, magnet down, and hoped it wouldn't fall off. He hoped even further that it would mount properly and have enough juice to give a strong signal. He had no other options. He rushed out onto the back deck of the house and, using his phone to control the drone, he launched it.

As the little drone rocketed skyward. Tano capped off the altitude at about three hundred feet and had the unit hover overhead. He maneuvered it directly over Robert's house, and within seconds, he locked onto the image of the woman's jeep. Taking a risk, he dropped the power on the drone and held his breath as the jeep's image filled the phone's screen in a matter of seconds. At the moment before impact, he regained control and spun the camera around for a view of Robert's front door. With a flick of the switch, he dropped the drone into the Jeep's open bed. The image on his phone jolted a little when the magnet held one drone foot in place. "Shit." He powered it up slowly, but the drone did not move. Giving the stick a little nudge of juice, the drone jerked up to about six feet above the jeep.

"No, no, no!" he hissed, seeing the front door creep open. He reduced the power, flew the drone backwards, and lowered it on the opposite side of the jeep, inches from the ground. "I can't see her, damn it." He had no idea if the woman had spotted it or heard the propellers. He took another chance and flew it as slow as possible on a horizontal path directly backwards, with the intention of getting far enough away to set it down without being noticed. The camera's angle showed nothing but the side of her Jeep, and just as she came into view, the camera's angle tilted, and leaves came into focus. He had no idea where the drone was, but he guessed in the bushes of Robert's nosey neighbor. He tilted his head to straighten out the cockeyed image coming from the camera. He raised an eyebrow as the woman climbed in and looked behind her to back out.

Tano hurried back to the monitor room, switched to the outside camera of Kore's garage, and watched as the woman backed out of the driveway. He let out a long, slow breath and activated the GPS tracking app on his computer console and selected the proper code to access the tracker's signal. Then he waited. After the first blip on the screen, he let out a breath he hadn't realized he had been holding. There was another. And then another. "Got you, woman," he said.

Tano understood the possibility existed that he might be chasing the rabbit down a hole. He pulled his cellphone off its belt clip, cleared the screen, and activated the mobile tracking app. After punching in the code, his phone showed what the computer screen showed: Miss Laina Main heading east.

Tano's next step would be to interview Robert, in detail, about Miss Main, about his lunch trip home, about hiding the suit, and more importantly, about his time at the office this morning. But that had to come later. Now, however, he had to retrieve that drone.

Thinking he might be able to wait until after dark to get it, he looked at his watch. Still several hours before sunset. He wondered about its visibility from street side and, after a moment, shook his head. *I'm going now.*

He snatched up the controller, activated the camera gimbal, and upon spinning the lens a little to the right, he had a clear view of the empty street, which meant whomever ended up in front of that house would have a clear view of the drone laid up in the bushes. Maybe. He had to get to it before anyone else did.

He went back into his room, pulled on a pair of hiking shorts and a t-shirt, and stopped at the front door to slip on a pair of Zori sandals. He kept the controller and his phone by his side, hoping that any Portola Valley neighbors who saw him would think an amateur had just lost his toy drone.

07

AND MOUSE

An hour after Robert departed once again for the office, Jessie pulled her Jeep off the road at University Ave and the Bayfront Expressway. She retrieved an older model Nokia flip phone from the outer pocket of her sling pack and speed dialed Robert Kore's personal cell number. As expected, the call went straight to voicemail.

"Robert, I'm sorry, babe, but I just got a call from my father a few minutes ago. My grandmother's not doing well. She's in the hospital so I'm heading to Reno to help out. I know you're super busy. I just wanted to let you know what's going on. I'll call you later and give you an update. Muah!"

She ended the call but left the phone flipped open in her lap. She turned right onto Highway 84 and proceeded onto the Dumbarton Bridge. At the halfway mark over the bay, she pulled the jeep into the emergency lane. She glanced into the rearview mirror and then ahead of her for any sign of police. Not seeing any, she stood up in her seat and looked over the rail for any boat traffic that might be heading under the bridge. With the coast clear, she prepared to flick the little phone out and over the concrete wall…when it rang.

She glanced at the Caller ID and frowned. Eric. The sight of his burner phone number gave her a sick feeling in her stomach. Eric would never break protocol if there wasn't a reason. She pressed the answer button and put the phone to her ear.

"Hello?" she said as natural as possible.

"Is this…Sheila?"

In all the missions she had worked with Eric, there had never been a need to call and code-talk.

"I'm sorry. You have the wrong number," she said, per the script.

"Oh crap. I'm sorry. This is the *second time* I called her today at this number, and now I'm just figuring out that she probably gave me the wrong number. I do apologize. Have a great day," he said.

"Not a problem," Jessie replied. "You too."

Something had gone wrong to cause Eric to launch this protocol. With his emphasis on the words, 'second time', she knew to scrub meeting at the pre-planned rendezvous point and to meet Eric, alone, at a secondary pre-selected point along the route to her real destination: Beale Air Force Base near Sacramento. The others would have been called already and would also meet at different locations, then all together as the original plan outlined. She couldn't shake the feeling that something else she had done during this mission had fucked everything up.

She stood up in her seat once again, looked both ways for the police, and flicked the phone out and over the concrete wall. She watched it glide, helicopter-like, as it descended the eighty-five-foot drop into the bay.

After driving another hour-and-a-half northeast on Highway 80, Jessie turned onto the Alamo Drive exit and into the parking lot of a new, veteran owned and operated Black Rifle coffee shop. She snatched up her sling pack that contained her pistol, her iPad mini, and encrypted sat phone. Plan A was to call Jon Daly, CEO of Crue Intellis and her boss, and let him know the band was back together and they were on their way to the waiting company AC-130 cargo plane.

Eric's call meant plan B was now in effect. She knew he couldn't be more than thirty minutes behind her. She parked, hopped out of the Jeep, grabbed her pack, and went into the shop.

The older female barista smiled as Jessie stepped up to the counter.

"Welcome to Black Rifle. What would you like?"

"I'll have the Nitro Cold Brewed with Sweet Cream, please," she said.

After collecting her coffee, she found a table nearest to the back exit and, as per Plan B protocol, she waited. After her second cup of coffee, and almost an hour later, Jessie caught a glimpse of Eric's Ford pickup truck from the corner of her eye. She went back to reading her well-worn copy of *Clive Cussler's* book, *Sahara,* knowing it would be another ten minutes or so before Eric cleared the area of any threats. If he did find something out of place, he would activate Plan C via her instant messenger program on her e-reader. Or she would hear the gunshots.

Eric came through the door and barely glanced at her, an unreadable expression on his face. *What the fuck's that about?* she thought. Without closing the paperback, she watched as Eric ordered his usual black coffee and carefully slid into a chair across the table from her. Jessie looked into his eyes, and fear pulled the starter cord of the little generator deep inside her mind. Her power sprang to life.

"What happened?" she asked. She tried to force the tension from her eyes, force the fear from riding the edge of her voice. Force the little generator to quiet down. Jessie closed the book. "First it was my badge, then Maria, and now what?"

Eric glanced around the room and let out a deep breath as he leaned closer.

"We're not sure, but we think you've been made," Eric replied quietly, sipping at his coffee, his eyes darting around the room. Jessie almost choked on her own drink. This was not what she expected. Her thoughts ran more along the lines of how maybe she had pushed too hard and either Robert or Maria were injured. It had happened before. But made? No way.

"How?" she asked, concern etched on her face.

"We're not sure, and we could be wrong, but we've got to look at your Jeep. Now."

"My Jeep?" The look of confusion on Jessie's face was evident for all to see had the coffee house patrons been paying attention. "What's my Jeep have to do with it?"

Eric leaned forward and lowered his voice.

"I was in the wooded lot up on the hill across from Kore's house. Right when you came out the door, I saw a drone."

Jessie's brow furrowed. "You saw, a what? A drone?"

"Yeah. A drone. A little commercial model. I'm thinking it might have been a Mavic or Parrot, some type like that." Jessie said nothing, took a sip of her coffee, and nodded. Eric continued. "I was just getting ready to leave, when I saw a flash in the corner of my optic. I focused on your jeep, and just as I was about to give up, the drone popped up out of the cargo area, then flew out and low to the ground. I couldn't see where it went because of my limited angle of view."

"When did this happen?" Jessie asked.

"Like I said, right when you came out the door."

"I didn't see anything. Or hear anything."

"Neither did I after that, until about ten minutes after you left. I decided to stay still and wait it out. That's why I'm late." Eric pulled out his cellphone, chose a photo, and slid it across the table. "This is what I got."

Jessie reached toward the phone and frowned, treating it like some kind of poisonous thing. She reached tentative fingers out and turned it over. The image appeared to be of a very tall, very muscular light-skinned man with white hair cropped into a military style haircut, holding what looked like a drone controller.

Eric continued. "The man walked around looking for the

drone, holding the controller out and playing with it. Once he passed Kore's house, he spotted it in the bushes of a home right across the lawn from Kore's, and he retrieved it.

"And what makes you so sure he didn't accidentally lose it?"

"I'm not," Eric said. "But we're going to find out right now. Ready?"

Jessie nodded.

They left the coffee shop and walked out into the lot where Jessie had parked. Eric had already parked alongside her Jeep and immediately began to unload her stuff into the bed of his truck.

LESS THAN AN HOUR LATER, JESSIE PLUGGED THE SAT-PHONE INTO her iPad, activated the conferencing app, and dialed. Jon Daly answered on the first ring, a concerned look on his face-time image. "Hi, Jess. How are you holding up, young lady?"

Jessie smiled at the genuine concern on his face. A memory from over ten years ago flashed through her mind of how Jon had rescued her from an almost fatal error in judgment and then coaxed her into confiding in him. He'd recruited her after that. If she thought of the Crue as her family, then Jon Daly was the closest thing to a father she'd ever had.

"We've got a problem," she said.

"I heard about drone guy. I take it you found something?" It always amazed Jessie how calm Jon could be in stressful situations. She had a bit more trouble getting through this one.

"Yes, sir." She tried to keep her voice steady. "We're pretty sure he's onto me. We found a small GPS tracking device in the bed of my Jeep. Transmitting photos...now." Jessie paused, then added, "I'm sending a PDF file of the anti-bug scan readout. It's got a lot of data I'm sure David will be interested in." Jessie thought about David West, the former Air Force Computer programmer turned surfer, who happened to have married Jessie's sister a few years back. She thought to ask how they were doing but put the idea on the back burner. For now.

"Okay. I think I have everything," Jon said. "Wow, that is one big boy."

"Tell me about it," Jessie replied. "I know we were all planning on heading home, but I think we need to play this out. Find out who this guy is and how much he knows."

The line was quiet for a long moment. "It's risky," Jon said quietly. Jessie envisioned the man rubbing his chin, brow furrowed deep in thought. "It might be safer just packing it in, hedging out bets that what we have is what we need."

Jon didn't see Jessie shaking her head. "I don't think so, Jon. This guy either knows something about me or saw something that tipped him off to a problem. I have no idea what that might be. Although we've found out information about who is funding Kore, we had never seen him with or tracked him to any Hōn operators. None that we have identified, anyway. This is an opportunity to catch an even bigger fish, Jon. I'm thinking we should let this play out."

"So, you're giving up your seat for the takedown?"

Jessie thought about this. She had worked hard to obtain the information needed to investigate Kore's latest project and had been offered the chance to be part of the flight training as a co-pilot to the AI system. David West and Northrup/Grumman had already created a flight simulator very similar to the drone of the X-47B unmanned combat aerial vehicle, or UCAV drone, sitting in Kore's hangar bay.

"I'll do what I have to do," she said, and rolled her eyes knowing the force of her words didn't hide her disappointment.

Silence on the line, again. Jessie almost spoke when Jon's words cut her off. "Okay. So, the rest of the team heads to Beale Air Force base. They'll pack and head home, but I guess you should go ahead to Reno. That's what we told Kore. Right?"

"Yes, sir."

"I want Eric to run overwatch on you. He doesn't think he was made."

"I don't think he was made either, but I want him loose. Very loose." Jessie glanced back at Eric, who busied himself putting her things back in the jeep. "I'm concerned that if they see him, they'll bolt." Although, what Jessie was really thinking was that if they saw him, all hell might break loose in Reno.

"That's your call, Jessie. He's there with you. You're calling the shots. Fill him in on the plan. Do you have a plan?"

"No, sir. Not yet. I'm thinking drone boy took a chance to plant the tracker. They're not going to wait too long to make a move. I agree with you. Reno is the best place to regroup. It's a difficult location to run a surveillance on," Jessie said.

"Let's just hope it's not at a distance through a rifle scope."

"I'm sure Eric's counter surveillance will catch that," Jessie said, and then thought, *I sure as hell hope Eric catches that!* "Do we have a dad in place?"

"Yes." Jon chuckled. "It will be Steve."

"Good choice," Jessie said, thinking that former LAPD Homicide Investigator Steve Walters, who was around Jon's age, would be perfect as her dad, although, he didn't have any of Jessie's exotic features. She also liked Steve as a choice because he was single. No wife, no kids, parents long passed. *In case it all turns to shit.* "Tell him I'll see him in Reno early this evening."

"Will do. He knows others will be watching. He'll be ready. Have a safe trip."

"Will do. Catch you on the other side," she said, and then pressed the end button on the phone.

Jessie had no idea what path this giant of a white rabbit intended to lead her, but she had to play this out as normal as possible. She turned and watched Eric load the last of her bags, then she approached him.

He turned toward her only to have her shove him into the

side of his truck, jump up onto his chest, and wrap her arms around his neck, her legs around his waist. "Hey, what's this ab…" His words cut off as Jessie's mouth pressed tight against his.

"I've missed you," she said, reaching around him to pull the back door of his truck open. "We've only got a few minutes, let's make the most of it."

08

RENO

S teve Walters had already been sitting on the porch swing, sipping a glass of lemonade as Jessie's jeep pulled up to the front of the house nestled on the outskirts of the Mt. Rose Wilderness area, just outside Reno. Jessie hopped out of the Jeep, sprinted up the flight of stairs, and hugged him.

"Good to see you, Jess." Steve's voice sounded somber and serious. "How you holding up?"

Steve had come on board with Crue Intellis a few years ago, within a week of retiring from the Los Angeles Police Department as a Detective Captain. A long-time friend of Jon's, he had jumped at the chance to join when approached. Jessie figured the reason Jon chose him to play the role of her father had to be the mix of Steve's age, about fifty-five, and the man's uncanny ability to sniff out trouble.

"I'm pissed, but fine," she said. "Jon fill you in?"

"Yes, while you were on your way over. Which, by the way, I was starting to get worried; you're about an hour late."

"Yes, Dad. Sorry. I got hung up for a bit outside Sacramento."

Steve raised an eyebrow. "How's Eric?"

Jessie blushed. "He's fine," she replied, her grin confirming to Steve what he already knew. Jessie reached over, plucked several ice-cubes from the canister, and poured herself a glass of the tart yellow. "I'm not really sure what to do next."

"We wait."

"But how long?"

"Well, I'm imagining that if they're just tracking you to see what you're up to by location, there won't be anything to worry about. You'll be able to leave the Jeep here, fly to White Sands, and train on the simulator until the takedown." He took a long draw from his glass. "That's the plan anyway."

Jessie frowned, took her own sip, and hoped like hell Steve was right. "This is really good."

"My grandmother's recipe," he said. "She liked it tangy."

So do I, Jessie thought. *So do I.*

TANO ZOOMED IN ON THE SATELLITE IMAGE OF WHERE THE GIRL'S Jeep had been parked over the past several hours. He immediately located the address of the two-story home and completed a records check of its owner. Steven Main. House purchased in 2000, an extension added to the house, a small observatory, complete with rotating sky port, in 2008. As Tano scanned data from his computer, frustration set in. He slammed a fist onto the table, pushed his chair back and stood up. This was too much work for not enough reward. Despite all outward appearances, his instincts told him there had to be more to this woman than met the camera's eye. Other than wasting time with research, he needed to speak with Kore. He felt the time slipping through his fingers like fine sand. He had to move on his hunch, now. He plucked his encrypted phone off the desk and dialed.

"Nǐ hǎo?"

"I need some assistance," Tano said, not caring about responding in the same Cantonese dialect on the other end of the line. "Someone with research and…" he thought about what he needed, "surveillance capabilities. Good fighting skills, too."

"Qǐng děngdài." *Please standby.* The line went silent a long moment. Tano knew what *that* meant. A few minutes later, Chen picked up.

"What seems to be the problem, Tano?"

"No problem, sir. I'm…"

"Then why are you calling for help?"

Tano took a deep breath. He had never once called for assistance of any kind on any other project he had been tasked to work. He closed the box on his ego and thought carefully about what he needed to relay. "An anomaly has come up that I sense needs investigation. I am wasting time, your time, and your money by performing cursory research when I need to refute any suspicion, quickly. Shall I go into details, sir?" The phone was quite a long moment. Tano's sense of direction regarding any task had always been valued in the past. He counted on that recognition now.

"Do you anticipate problems with the live testing?" Chen referred to the upcoming tests of the KAGI-6 AI combat system, the Hōn's secretly funded pet project for the past several years. Being honest with himself, Tano was not sure if there was a threat or not. However, he always leaned on the side of caution.

"At this moment, there is a question in my mind I would like to have answered, sir. There is something about this situation that garners my attention to ensure a smooth event. I plan on talking to Kore as soon as possible."

This time, Chen did not hesitate. "I'm sending the twins. They are already in San Francisco. Will that suffice?"

"Shì de xiānshēng. Xièxiè." *Yes, sir. Thank you.*

The only response to Tano's thanks was a dead phone line.

Tano smiled. The Twins were coming. Bolin and Bohai Sòng, were more than capable. Tano had worked with them since they were young men, and he had watched them grow into talented and lethal assistants. Identical in every way—dress, mannerisms, hairstyles, and expressions—Tano could only tell the men apart by their style of combat. Tano thought about the boys who had been street urchins, abandoned as infants and somehow able to survive the mean streets of Hong-Kong on their own. That is, until they were caught stealing from none other than Lai Chen, one of the Seven, a chairman of the ancient crime family, The Hōn. Impressed by the children's aptitude for street crime, Chen adopted the boys, and after a few years of in-house training, he had sent Bohai off to a Shaolin monastery while his brother Bolin trained locally, learning to navigate the criminal empire of Hong-Kong, street style. Ten years later, the brothers were reunited and had since become inseparable. They rarely spoke unless spoken to and were sent to University together where they mastered the ways of computer programming, hacking, and other black hat functions. Tano estimated that the boys were now twenty-eight, and both had become as lethal as they were computer savvy.

A motion sensor alarm from Kore's house sounded off. Tano quickly returned to watching both the live satellite feed of the woman, Laina Lane's house near Reno, and the camera images from Kore's residence. Robert had arrived home early. Another irregularity.

Tano studied the man's actions as he entered his house, tossed his keys on the counter, dropped his briefcase on the floor, and uncharacteristically stripped out of his clothing, leaving one piece at a time in a trail from the kitchen to the back yard deck, where he quickly threw off the cover to his hot tub. The camera images were so crisp, Tano clearly saw the water bubbling and swirling as Robert climbed in naked. Tano leaned closer to the screen as the man sat still as stone, hunched over to rest his head in his hands. Robert didn't move for the better part of an hour. Something had to be wrong. He had never seen Kore behave this way. If Tano had to guess, he would say that the behavior the man exhibited looked like pain. As the man slept, Tano pulled up an updated satellite image from the woman's house near Reno and observed only the Jeep, still in the driveway.

Tano drummed his fingers on the table, then moved to a third screen, launched the DVR, and called up a video clip of the woman as she had pranced around Robert's bedroom naked. He had seen women as unabashed as this one, but never had he seen such a physique. He paid close attention when the woman rushed to Robert's side as he virtually collapsed into the wall. There was something there. He felt sure of it. He scoured the tapes from the day of his arrival a little more than a week ago. His instructions had been to keep a watch on Robert. Step in only if he appeared to be in jeopardy of missing his deadline for the flight tests. After three hours of viewing every moment this woman had interacted with Robert, which consisted mostly of uninhibited sex, the motion alarm from Robert's deck sounded off. Tano switched back to the live camera feed and watched as Robert toweled off, then without shutting off any lights, without rinsing the undoubtedly heavy amounts of chlorination from his body, Robert crawled into bed and apparently passed out. Tano marked the time: 7:15 p.m. Another red flag. Even on the most inactive of evenings, Kore never went to bed before 11 p.m. and always arose at 4 a.m. to be at his favorite CrossFit Gym for the 5 a.m. WOD, or Workout of the Day. Robert's life operated like clockwork. The Kore clock appeared to be broken, and Tano didn't like it.

He reset the bedroom camera's motion sensor to activate an alarm should Kore get out of bed. He stood up and stretched, annoyed that he was so, well, *annoyed* at the unsettled feeling he had about this woman. His inability to pinpoint why frustrated him most. Now, while the opportunity presented itself, he had time to exorcise some of his angst by getting in a couple hours of work in the dojo.

Only an hour into his Japanese Kenjutsu sword katas, Tano heard the motorcycles well before they pulled into his driveway. He paused only a moment, the slightest of smiles rising on the edge of his mouth, then resumed his forms. Within minutes, the red lacquered dojo door quietly pushed open, and two Chinese men, dressed in traditional garb, their long hair tied into braids, bowed deeply, then entered the dojo. Silently, they moved to a corner of the room and, standing relaxed next to a rack of martial arts weapons, watched with interest as Tano continued. After another twenty minutes, one of the twins, Bolin, silently walked to the corner, retrieved a Chinese broadsword, and smiled at his brother who followed and collected a weapon of his own, a long, wooden bō staff.

Tano finished his kata, returned to his relaxed stance, and swiftly sheathed the razor-sharp katana.

"Your form's looking good, old man," Bohai said, stepping out onto the floor, spinning the bō into a blurring series of impressive moves.

Bolin said nothing but threw his body into several rapid aerials while working the broadsword in sweeping, slicing, jabbing motions as he soared through the air. The moment he landed, the brothers went into fighting stances, facing Tano.

Without smiling, without acknowledging the acrobatics and flashy weapons manipulation of the brothers, Tano slowly drew his sword from the black-lacquered scabbard and smoothly dropped into the Suwari Migi Gedan stance. The toes of his left foot remained pressed into the wood as he dropped his left knee to the floor. He placed his right foot out and forward, giving him balance as the sword, both hands on the Tsuka, or hilt, was lowered to waist, the blade leveled horizontally at the ready. The three men stood like statues for what seemed to be an eternity.

Bohai moved first, spinning his bō and striking out, the wooden staff intercepted by the flat of Tano's sword as it rose up to meet the attack in what seemed like slow, fluid movement. Bolin launched forward, jabbing the Chinese broadsword into the center mass of Tano's Gi, but the strike had easily been swiped aside as Tano quickly raised to his feet, his katana spinning and slashing out in rapid attacks, moving from one brother to the other, the flash of metal like lightning. Tano fought his way to the weapons rack, retrieved a second katana, and flung the scabbard at the two men. Now with two swords, Tano moved to meet them. Each katana appeared to have individual strategies as they countered the brother's attack. As one brother continued to strike with sword, the other attempted to manipulate a Katana from Tano's hand with the staff.

Within seconds, the brothers soon found themselves on the defense. With flying leaps, Bolin's sword flashed and slashed to meet every equally fast slash and jab of Tano's Niten Ichi, or two-sword advance. The bō struck true into Tano's side, forcing and unbidden grunt from his lungs and a moment of lost concentration. Without hesitation, Bolin moved in for a lethal jab to the chest, but met, instead, the flat side of Tano's blade, slapping him hard across the face as a mother would slap her child for disrespect. Bolin ceased his attack and dropped to his knees in submission, acknowledging that in a real fight, half of his head would be lying on the floor next to his body. He watched with intense interest as his brother unleashed a torrent of spinning bō attacks, each one deftly striking areas of Tano's forearm and hand, trying desperately to force Tano to drop a sword. Tano did, but just as Bohai moved in for the killing strike, Tano's second katana came up and cut the bō in two. In another ghostly smooth move across the dojo floor, Tano slid up against Bohai, his blade pressed up against the younger man's throat, drawing just a drop or two of blood.

"I'm getting too old for this," Tano said, and backed up, bowing deeply to his opponents. Bolin stood, walked over to his brother, and both bowed to Tano in reverence.

"He's like a seasoned Italian wine," Bohai said, smiling and licking the droplet of blood off his fingertip

"Yes, he's getting better with age," replied Bolin, and both men bowed again.

"We have work to do," Tano said. "But shower first. I don't want to smell you two."

09
GHOSTS

R obert Kore pulled his Audi into the hangar bay, parking right next to the sleek X-47A Pegasus drone. He gazed into the rearview mirror; bloodshot eyes stared back at him. "God you look terrible," he murmured. He had slept over fourteen hours and felt as if he hadn't slept a wink. Dreams of screwing Laina on his desk, who turned into Maria, skirt up on the floor of the computer room, and other nonsensical computer shit filled his brain and made his head throb. He felt certain that if he ate another round of migraine pills, he would end up being rushed to the hospital with a bleeding ulcer. *That still might happen,* he thought.

He glanced down at his Rolex, barely comprehending how being an hour-and-a-half behind schedule had crept up on him this morning. His alarm went off on time, and he hadn't bothered to shave. He groaned at the terrible feeling throbbing through his entire body and looked back at his car, considering getting back in and driving home. He shook his head slowly; he shouldn't have been behind the wheel at all this morning. He had barely enough energy to pull on a pair of pressed slacks and polo from the closet. Tying his shoes, however, turned out to be a challenge that almost whipped his ass.

He walked drunkenly past the Unmanned Aerial Vehicle and reached up, running his hands down the smooth stealth material covering the UAV's fuselage. Once to his private elevator, he stumbled through the door and almost fell into the back wall but managed to lean against it for support. As the door opened, he spotted his receptionist, Mrs. Bartlett, who looked to her left and smiled at him.

"Good morning, Mr. Kore," she said. Robert staggered forward. Her smile faded as she stood up. "Sir, are you alright?" She rushed from behind her desk to lend Robert a sturdy shoulder.

Just before she reached him, his body shuddered violently, and he gasped. For a moment, he saw himself walking towards the reception desk from the main elevator. The image looked like real-time television, with a few bursts of static to confirm he wasn't looking at his twin. He shook the image from his head.

"Mr. Kore, how can I help? You need to sit. Let me call the medics."

"No medic." Even to his own ears, his voice sounded slow and slurred, but he accepted her guidance to one of the plush chairs in the lobby and plopped down. "Thank you," he said, as graciously as his impaired speech would allow. "I'm obviously not feeling well, but I'll be okay in a minute. Can you please bring me some coffee?"

"Yes sir, right away."

As the woman scurried from the room, Robert reflected on what he had just seen. The image of himself walking toward the reception desk appeared too vivid to be a hallucination. It felt more like a memory. But as he pressed his mind to remember, a searing jolt of pain shot through his head. He cried out in a tiny yelp.

Mrs. Bartlett came from around the corner with a fresh cup of coffee in her hand and two Excedrin. "Here, sir, this will help. You look like you're having a migraine."

If you only knew, he thought. He took the pills and ate them anyway. Chewing the tablets, his face screwed up into a disgusted mask as the battery acid slammed into his taste bud sensors. He sipped at the coffee. "Thank you."

"Shall I ask your guest to leave?"

Robert's bloodshot eyes glared at the woman over the dark frames of his Oakley sunglasses. "Guest?"

"Yes, sir. Mr. Tano. He arrived about an hour ago. You had him on your calendar for a visit at eight and a note for me to let him wait in your office."

Robert's stomach clenched. He felt out of it, but he would never space-out on a visit from Tano. "A handwritten note?" he asked.

"No sir, a mail message in my inbox. Showed up about 7:30 this morning from your email account."

Robert nodded. *Fucker hacked my email.* He knew The Benefactors had passive access to all of his servers, but this still felt like a low blow. Especially since he hadn't seen Tano in years. Not since the SCIF project for the Department of Defense. He hadn't received a visit, a birthday card, or a *fuck you asshole* phone call in over six years. He knew Tano ranked as the voice for the Hōn Benefactors and wondered if the big man still looked as menacing as he had six years ago.

"I seem to have forgotten. No, I'll go in now." He stood up, rolled his shoulders back, and collected his briefcase. "How do I look?"

"Like shit, sir." She stood up, walked around the desk, and straightened his collar. "Seriously, Mr. Kore. You look like someone beat the crap out of you. I don't smell alcohol."

"Careful, Ms. Bartlett. I get the picture."

The woman scowled, turned on her heal, and moved back around her desk. "Good luck, sir."

Robert nodded and, feeling like he might die at any moment, concentrated on putting one foot in front of the other as he proceeded down the corridor to his office. Once in front of his door, he pulled out his card-key, and just as he moved to slide it across the scanner, another bolt of pain and the image of a second hand extending from his body, swiping the card several times, filled his vision. He placed a hand on the wall, waited for the pain to subside, and slowly ran the card against the scanner. As his office entry security protocols were already overwritten by Ms. Bartlett, the retinal scanner failed to activate, but the door lock clicked open.

Robert stepped inside to find Tano's back greeting him. The tall man stood facing the slanted observation windows, looking down at the plane in the hangar bay below.

"It is one sexy looking aircraft, no, Robert?" Tano asked.

Robert crept up beside the man and gazed down into the hangar bay. "Yes, sir. She's a beauty."

"I find it interesting that you Americans always refer to your airplanes, ships, and cars as 'she'," he said, glancing sideways at Robert. Tano did a double take. "Are you not well, Robert?"

Robert glanced back and smiled. "I've seen better days. I'm not sure what's wrong with me." He took a step toward his desk and added, "Do you mind?"

Tano glanced at the large, leather executive chair. "Not at all. You look like you need to sit. Should I call Ms. Bartlett for assistance?" he asked, a concerned and somewhat puzzled look on his face. Robert couldn't tell if the man really cared or put on a good act. He plopped down in the chair, steadied himself against the desktop, and leaned back.

"So, Tano. What brings you here?" Robert asked, pulling off his Oakley's and tossing them on the desk. He pressed the button on the underside of the desktop and shuddered again, pain ripping through him. He had performed this process of pressing the monitor lift button so many times before, the action had become part of his subconscious routine—like driving a car. But as the desktop dropped down and in, he saw it again. There was a clear, but somewhat translucent image of the large curved LCD computer screen rising out of the desk just before the actual monitor followed.

"Robert, you have me concerned. Let me call for assistance."

Tano reached for the desk phone. Robert slapped his hand down onto it first and glared at the man.

"No. I don't need help. I appreciate your concern, but what I need is to know why you're here."

"I'm hurt, Robert. Is that a way to treat an old friend?"

Robert knew without a doubt that Tano understood his question to be rhetorical. He worked hard to choke down what he really wanted to say to the man, something along the lines of get the fuck out, perhaps.

"Well, since you are apparently well enough for business, I'm here to find out how our project is forming up." Tano's smile, toothy as it was, didn't reach his eyes.

Robert conceded that following up on the project was fair enough. But he wasn't stupid, either. He had an innate understanding that The Benefactors had a ton of research and development money invested, and a billion-dollar defense contract hanging in the balance. The big prize, of course, was the inside intelligence they would have access to once the DOD signed on the dotted line. Built in spyware, paid for by the US Government. He eyeballed Tano. The man's smile reminded Robert of the messenger at Sauron's gate from the Lord of the Rings movie. Giant teeth on an elongated face that looked awkward with the blonde, spiked hair and tall muscular frame—about the only thing that impressed Robert about the man. Robert opened his mouth to answer but was cut off.

"And about the girl. Laina Main."

Now *that* caught him off guard. Robert sat speechless and hoped his jaw hadn't dropped to his chest. After a moment, he sat up in his chair and leaned toward Tano. "What are you getting at?"

Tano leaned in too. "Are you saying that you haven't been sleeping with a woman, who stands about five feet tall, muscular and fit, exotic looks, who goes by the name Laina Main?"

"No, of course I know her. She's a friend…"

"I'd say she is a bit more than that…"

"Hey now, you just hold it right there. What does my private life have to do with you? Or The Benefactors?"

Robert saw the muscles in Tano's cheeks undulate as the bigger man ground his teeth in his now closed, unsmiling mouth. "When it comes to the investment we have, there is nothing private about your life, Robert."

"Look, she's no threat…"

"Really, what do you know about her?"

"Enough. I mean, I met her at our CrossFit Box a couple of months back, we hit it off, that's all." Tano sat back in his chair and raised an eyebrow. "Look, Tano, she's no threat. I had Charles run a full background on her. I follow the same security protocols you put in place almost fifteen years ago. I didn't fuck this up. She's nobody. Just a piece of ass."

"Really. And where is she now?"

"She left a voice message that she had to leave for Reno to assist her father with something." The look on Tano's face made it clear that he was holding something back. "Look, she means nothing. Why don't you tell me what happened so I can help answer your questions?"

Tano leaned back and smiled again. "How did the simulation go yesterday?"

Robert raised an eyebrow. "Simulation? We didn't run a simulation yesterday. We've only run diagnostics. We plan to run the full package by Friday. That will give us a week out to crosscheck everything again."

Now Tano looked confused, and Robert saw the man was calculating something. "Your configuration manager used her code to activate KAGI-6 yesterday, at around nine in the morning." He leaned closer. "A full run of the system was performed. You two are on camera entering the computer room together and exiting at around ten-forty-five."

Robert couldn't hide the stunned look on his face. He remembered speaking to Maria, the configuration manager about it, then locking the door and fucking her on the floor of his office, but the computer room? He tried to remember if he had missed anything when that pain slammed into him once more, brutal to the point he cried out. Tano leaped from his seat and picked up the phone.

"Ms. Bartlett, would you be so kind as to call Maria Ricardi to Robert's office." He hung up the phone.

"What is happening with you, Robert? I need to know."

"I'm not sure. I'd tell you if I did. Every time I try to think about yesterday…"

"What about yesterday?" Tano pressed.

"Well, Laina said I left for work and returned home for an early lunch, and I had no recollection of going to work. Maria said something to me about our meeting that morning, but my head pounded so bad, like it is now, that I really don't remember what she said, either."

Tano stood up, walked to the buffet, and opened the small refrigerator hidden therein. He removed a bottle of Powerade, cracked the top, and set it on the edge of Robert's deck, deftly pushing it toward him.

"I don't have a hangover," Robert said.

"How do you know?" Tano replied.

Robert raised an eyebrow, nodded, and took the drink, downing it in several gulps. A soft, quiet knock came from the officer door. Tano walked over and opened it to a gasping Maria Ricardi, obviously startled at being greeted by someone other than Robert.

"Come in, Mrs. Ricardi," Tano said. "We've been expecting you."

TANO LISTENED WITH UNDIVIDED ATTENTION TO MARIA'S accounting of yesterday morning. She, too, had no recollection of running a simulation and needed a little prodding in order to admit she and Robert had sex. Now, all three of them stood at the access console in the computer room.

"Run a full diagnostic, test all functions, run the same simulator that was run yesterday."

Maria sat at the console as Robert watched. Suddenly, Robert staggered backwards into the wall. Tano rushed to him and kept him upright but said nothing. "Tell me, Robert. What it is?"

Robert hesitated, rubbing at his temples. "I just…just had a vision. It felt so real. I saw Maria and I, well…"

Tano grit his teeth, "This is no time for modesty, Robert. Out with it." Tano felt Maria's eyes shift toward him. "Don't stop working, Ms. Ricardi. I need that simulation run. Now."

"Well, I just saw Maria and I doing it on the floor. Here. Right there." He pointed just down and to the left of where Maria now sat. Maria turned to look, and simultaneously Robert and Maria yelped out in pain, both grabbing for their heads at the same time. Tano stood back and watched in utter confusion.

What in the hell is going on?

Tears flowed down Maria's face.

Robert started, "Maria, I'm sorry, I don't remember…"

"Hurting me? Raping me?" Maria said, then slapped her hand over her mouth. "I…I'm sorry. I'm not sure. It's like a flash. A vision or something. But I have no real memory of that happening." Her eyes filled with tears, and she looked at Robert. "I'm sorry, Robert, I shouldn't have made an accusation like that."

Tano looked between the two of them, stunned.

"Keep working, Ms. Ricardi," he said, then added, "With your permission, I'm going to call my physician. I'd like to run blood tests on you both." Robert and Maria looked at one another, then at Tano. "Don't try to remember anything. Think only about the task at hand, about running this simulation, and about finding any anomalies. Robert, you take the other console and do the same. Stay focused on what you are doing. Do not think about the past. I want to run a full drug panel on you."

"You think we're taking drugs?" Maria asked.

"Not at all, but I fear you may have *been* drugged. Loss of memory, pain, visions."

Robert stared at the man a long time. "You may be right," he conceded.

Maria glanced at Tano, then Robert, and nodded. Robert pulled up a chair to the mainframe, lowered a keyboard from a side kiosk, and within minutes, both geniuses were clacking away, and neither seemed to be suffering from whatever post-traumatic stress events he had witnessed.

That's what this is, Tano thought. *PTSD.*

'10

ONE UP

"**N**ǐ hǎo?" *Hello?*

"Bolin. Speak bloody English when you are working with me, understand?" Tano said, heat in his voice.

"Yes, sir."

"I need you to access the DVR recordings from yesterday. Run the time to around 11:30 in the morning. You may be viewing images of Kore screwing his little gym princess. What I need you to do is run it back to when Kore arrives. Watch it in real time from the moment he parks his car. Then call me back once you reach the point where he starts screwing the girl. Understand?"

"Dāngrán shì, uh, I mean, yes. Of course."

Tano cursed himself as he called over the Sync system to dial up Bolin's brother, Bohai, who should have been set up on surveillance at Main's Reno home by now. The signal rang busy. He would have to use the sat-phone. He was only fifteen minutes out from his house, so he would wait until he arrived to call. Tano gripped the wheel. After hearing Mrs. Ricardi's recollection of yesterday's events, he felt certain the Main girl was the center of some strange conspiracy, although nothing had yet indicated any involvement on her part.

The simulation ran flawlessly, if not a bit faster than expected. The configuration manager vowed to run another diagnostic on the system to find out why yesterday's run had lagged behind. But there were no breaches in data. There were no changes to the programming. The back-door codes were still in place, thirty-two random number and letter sequences that only a mad genius like Kore could remember. Tano had the only other copy. So why the odd behavior? The pain Kore and Ricardi experienced reminded Tano of some kind of punishment, the kind he had received at monastery for allowing his mind to become sidetracked. None of this made sense. But it would make sense. And Ms. Main would answer his questions.

Tano pulled into the garage, rapidly punched in the alarm's key-code, and rushed upstairs. Bolin stood at a military parade rest, the video on the screen cued up to Core entering the bedroom. Tano looked into Bolin's eyes, who nodded, then turned sideways to watch as Tano took a seat.

Tano watched the camera for just one minute and gasped. "How could I have missed this?"

Bolin leaned in. "I'm not sure what you missed, sir."

"Look." He replayed the video and pointed to the screen where Kore pulled what appeared to be an identical suit from the closet, mounted it on the valet, and after stripping down naked, stuffed the clothes he had worn into a bag. Then he hid it under the bed. "That".

"I don't understand," Bolin said, a genuine look of confusion etched on his face.

Tano continued to watch as Robert mounted the girl, spread her seemingly limp legs apart, and began thrusting. Once he touched the girls face, it was like she had risen from the dead, eagerly meeting each thrust with equal abandon. She rolled over and got onto her knees. Tano shut the DVR off. Bolin sighed.

"That is one wild woman," Bolin said.

"Yes, but did you see?"

"I only saw her waking up to his advances. Did I miss something?"

"Yes, you did," Tano said. "And so did I." He picked up the satellite phone and dialed.

"Shì de xiānshēng?" *Yes, sir.*

82

"Give me an update."

"Nothing to see here. I'm up on a ridge, using a telescope. The jeep hasn't moved."

"If she moves, call me, and follow. But not too close. Just keep her in sight until we get there."

"You're coming here?"

"Yes. I have questions for Miss Main."

JESSIE FINISHED A THIRTY-MINUTE SANDBAG ROUTINE AND, covered in sweat, vaulted the stairs to refill her water bottle. Steve Walters sat at his computer. "Any word?" she called out from the kitchen.

"Nothing yet. They still have no ID on the big guy, but he did leave the house this morning. Eyes on the house said he had visitors. On motorcycles. Both bikes are there, but there were comings and goings last night they couldn't keep up with."

Jessie tipped the bottle back and took a long draw of cold water. She snatched a small camel backpack off the kitchen chair, unscrewed the cap, and loaded the bladder with ice. She thought about the strange drone-guy having visitors and still didn't feel her normally keen suspicious-meter go off.

"I'm going for a run."

"Keep your phone on, and don't get too far out of Eric's Range."

"Right, no problem."

BOLIN WATCHED AS THE WOMAN JOGGED OUT ONTO THE FRONT porch and, without stretching at all, vaulted down the steps and sprinted down the driveway and out onto the street at a very fast paced run. He could see through the telescope that she had a small backpack and wore very, very little in the form of cloth-ing. Her small sports bra and even smaller skintight shorts left nothing to the imagination. She was extremely fit, muscular, and seemed to be on a mission. He raised an eyebrow as she ran out of sight. At first, he intended to follow, but then he changed his mind. She would be back. If the pack had water, she didn't have enough to make it to town, ten miles away, and the pack could hold very little else. He would wait. He would...

A flash of light caught the corner of his vision from the same hill he was on, but further away from the direction in which the girl ran. He checked the mesh on the end of his own lens, placed there in order to keep it from doing what he had just witnessed. Slowly, he turned the barrel of the telescope to the left and pointed it in the general direction of where he saw the flash. Nothing. No movement. Bolin had followed enough people through the streets of Hong Kong and into the urban areas of surrounding villages and watched enough video's on YouTube to know that if a sniper allowed that kind of flash in a battle zone, he'd be dead. Bolin wasn't a sniper, but he knew enough. He fixed his eyes into the distance and waited.

An hour went by and movement caught his vision to the right, down the hill. Moving slowly, he glanced over. It was the girl. She had retuned, running at an all-out sprint to the front drive of the house. He spun the telescope in her direction and focused on her as she walked around in circles, her arms over her head, breathing heavily. He could see her chiseled abdom-inal muscles even from this distance and decided they looked a little too masculine for his liking. Until she poured the remaining water from the pack over her head. Yes. That was sexy. She went inside. Show over.

Another eight hours clicked away. Bolin sat still as stone. Without taking his eyes off the target, he meditated throughout the setting of the sun, becoming one with nature and finding the all elusive nothingness that turned the hours into minutes.

In the absolute darkness of his hidden spot, he picked up the thermal spotting scope provided to him by Tano. He scanned the thickly wooded forest around him and caught only the image of some small creature curled up under a nearby bush. Bolin returned his gaze to the house but then froze. Once more, he turned and scanned the area. There was nothing. Bolin wasn't a highly trained ninja or military operative, but he had run surveillance enough to know when he was being watched. With what time he had left, he slowly, methodically worked his way down the far side of the hill, away from area where he had seen the earlier glint of light. By the time the sun crested the eastern horizon, he had reached his vehicle.

ERIC CREPT INTO THE SPACE ONCE OCCUPIED BY THE UNKNOWN observer. The spot would have been missed by anyone else, but Eric had caught the movement hours before, and once the sun had set, he'd spent the last several hours slow-crawling through the underbrush the half-mile to where he thought someone might be set up. He had been right. Right at sunrise, he'd decided to follow the track downhill. His target had spooked and jumped ship. He remained in position for another hour, controlling his breathing, listening intently for any sign the other might still be there. Slowly, he sat up. He grabbed his weapon, laid the rifle across his lap, retrieved his cellphone, and dialed. Then he froze as the cold steel of a long-bladed weapon gently rested on the side of his neck, the tip moving just to within his line of vision. It was a Japanese katana.

"Do not turn around. You can warn them, and die here, or you can simply say you are coming down and take your chances. Put the phone on speaker. I know the man in that house is named Steve. No games."

The voice behind Eric sounded Asian.

"Hey, Steve. It's me."

"How you holding up?" the voice on the other line asked.

"Fine, no problems. I'm coming down. See you in a bit."

"Okay. I copy."

Eric pressed the end button. "Good enough?"

"Keep your left hand up where my blade can easily reach it. With your right hand, pull the gun from your lap by the butt-stock. Slowly, or the last thing you will see is my face as your head lands next to your body. Understand?"

"Yes." Eric complied, slid the gun off, and tossed it back behind him. Another man moved in from the right and collected the rifle. *Two of them? Really?* If these guys had the ability to sneak up on *him,* there was no way he would attempt to defend. He had no choice but to go along with whatever the man had in store for him, and lucky he wasn't already dead.

"Good. You may stand up. Nice and slow."

A movement to his right caught his attention as he placed his hands on the ground for balance in order to get his feet under him. He glanced over and saw an Asian man smiling at him. Then the voice sounded from behind him. "You will follow him, and you do not need to look behind you. We will hike down." Eric nodded, cursing himself.

"You know, no matter what happens or what you do to me, I just want to tell you how impressed I am. I have been told I'm one of the best snipers in the world, and here you got me, dead to rights. What gave me away?"

The man in front of him, wearing what Eric might describe as black pajamas, the sort of clothing worn by the Vietcong back in the 70's, started out down a path to his left.

"The glint of your optic, yesterday. My brother caught it from the corner of his eye and knew enough to know if he moved, you'd probably kill him. So, he called me."

"Well, ain't that just shitty luck," Eric said.

"Do not get so close to him. You close the gap, I hamstring you. Understood?"

"Copy that," Eric said.

FRESH OUT OF THE SHOWER, WEARING ONLY A BATH TOWEL, JESSIE stood in the kitchen mixing up a protein smoothie when the phone rang. She glanced up when he waved at her to shut off the blender while he answered it. She watched as Steve froze in his footsteps, then exploded into action, rushing around the house's interior, closing shutters and punching a code into the alarm panel at the front door. He then hurried into the office and came out a few seconds later with a loaded M4 carbine.

"What's going on?" Jessie asked, holding the bath towel in place. "What's wrong?"

"Eric called," he said. "Didn't use the check in code. Said he was on his way down."

"Shit." Jessie grabbed her drink on her way to the bedroom. Steve's phone rang again. Jessie stopped at the door and spun around. Steve looked at the caller ID and mouthed the word 'Eric'. He put the phone on speaker and answered.

"Hello."

"Obviously, you know we have your friend." Steve opened his mouth to speak, but the caller cut him off. "Say nothing. We watched you close your blinds, and we see the alarm has been activated. We are monitoring electronic signals coming from your house. You will stand by for further instructions. Make a call or jump on the computer, we will know it, and your friend will die. Do nothing until we call you back." The caller hung up.

Steve shook his head. "They have Eric."

"Call Jon. I'll get ready," Jessie said.

"The guy on the phone had a kind of accent. European or something. He said they are monitoring electronic signals from

87

the house. I wouldn't risk it. Right now, we'll have to play along."

"Wait. We have ethernet," Jessie said. "Unless they got here before us and bugged this house, they can't tap into hardwire connections." She moved to the office and wiggled the mouse to wake the computer up.

"I wouldn't chance it," Steve said. "They could have hacked the computer externally and installed spyware. I agree it's unlikely. You've only been here a day. We guessed you might be tracked, but I can't believe they could shut us down so quickly. Eric's life isn't worth the risk."

Jessie nodded. "I'll get dressed and ready," she said. "And then we wait."

11

QUESTIONS

Two hours later, Steve's phone rang again. "Hello?"

"Let me speak to the woman, Miss Main," the voice said. Steve nodded and handed the phone to Jessie.

"Yes?"

"You will meet us at the crossroads in twenty minutes. You will travel on foot, which means you're going to have to run. Should anyone be in attendance, should your..." the voice paused for effect, "*father* attempt to contact anyone from that house, your friend will lose his head. If Mr. Main, creative names you have, by the way, attempts to leave that house, he will be shot before he gets to a vehicle. Is that understood."

"Yes, but that's about three miles away. I..."

"If you are late as much as one second, you will arrive to find the head of your friend in a basket, waiting for you in the center of the crossing."

"How do I know he's still alive?"

A short pause, then, "Laina, fuck these guys, don't come. Stick with..." A thud, then a grunt in the background, followed by silence. Then the male voice continued.

"We've seen you run, Miss Main. You may have to elevate your performance to a new, personal best. If you carry water, it must be in a clear plastic bottle. One bottle only. You can ditch the empty one along the way. If you carry anything else, a watch, a camelback, anything like that, then you will be shot right there on the road and your friend will die. Then we'll burn your house to the ground with your father still in it. We are ready to strike, Miss Main. Don't toy with us.

"Anything else?" Jessie asked, stripping off her jeans as she spoke.

"Yes. You will wear only a sports bra, running shorts, and your running shoes. Clothing not dissimilar to your run last evening. The less material, the less you can hide. I understand you are quite the sight to behold."

"But you have to give me…"

"Your time begins…now." The voice hung up.

"Fuck!" Jessie vaulted to her feet, peeling off her t-shirt and bra in one fluid move. She dumped her bag onto the bed, picked her gym clothes, and tried not to panic.

"What? What are you doing?" Steve asked.

"I've got to run to the crossroads."

"Run? You mean, like run? On foot? To the crossroads? That's three miles away!"

"I know." She pulled on a pair of lycra lifting shorts, no panties, and a multicolored sports bra before getting into her Asics running shoes.

"He wants you to wear that?"

"Yes, nothing to hide. I'll activate my tracker once I'm far enough from the house." *Two minutes gone.* "Fuck! Eighteen minutes, gotta go!" She ran into the kitchen, pulled out two bottles of water, and headed out the front door at an all-out sprint.

Within a few minutes of running, a stitch of pain struck in her left side, almost doubling her over. She had no idea of the elapsed time as she dared not wear her fit-bit. "Oh God. Eric," she said, and picked up her pace. The harder she pushed the faster time seemed to slip by. She had no idea how fast she might be running, other than running at full speed. She imagined the finish line in sight, and the little generator that powered her slip-stream ability cranked up to full throttle, giving her even more energy to maintain the blistering pace. She concentrated on that. On the power coursing through her. She found a new use for it.

Electrical performance enhancement, she thought.

Her tactic worked. She lost track of time, and soon the crossroads came into view. She tossed the empty water bottle and let loose with everything she had. Power flowed through her at full force, more juice than she could ever remember experiencing.

It has to be the fear, she thought. Something had gone terribly wrong with their planning, or Eric and Steve wouldn't be in danger. She exploded into the center of the intersection like she had just won an Olympic medal, dropped to her knees, and vomited up the water.

She looked around. No one there. She didn't see a basket in the crossroads. She grunted and walked around in circles, arms over her head, doing her best to breathe deeply to slow down her heart rate.

"Holy shit," she gasped. "I feel like a low-yield nuke, ready to detonate." She looked around at the expansive fields on each side and toward the mountain range behind her, wondering if this might not be a trap. That they might not have lured her out of the house, maybe to get to Steve, not her. Suddenly, she remembered. The tracker. She felt around the inside of her forearm until she located the small power nodule. She went to push it, to snap the capsule that would close the connection to the hydrogen-ion battery, but she paused. The man said they were tracking signals. She had to take this as gospel. She pulled her fingers back. She flexed her forearms and decided to reassess once the men arrived.

If they arrive, she thought.

She put two fingers to her carotid artery and called out her best ten count. Her heart rate had already lowered by degrees and now hovered around 115 beats per minute and falling.

Again, she thought, *thank you CrossFit.*

She caught sight of movement from the west-bound cross-road. She saw a dust cloud forming up behind a vehicle traveling at a high rate of speed. She took deep breaths, doing the best she could to calm her nerves and slow that little generator, lest she spark off and get killed. Nothing would stop her now. Except maybe a long-distance bullet, and her gut said that wasn't going to happen.

A small black Mitsubishi SUV pulled up within twenty feet of Jessie. The windows were tinted so dark she couldn't see in. After a moment, two men, both looking like Chinese actors from a Bruce Lee movie, climbed out of the vehicle. They were both Asian, handsome model-types, and wore matching motorcycle jackets. At first glance, she thought the men might be gay. Or brothers. Then it clicked.

Twins.

"Spread your legs out and raise your hands out to the sides, at an angle, like this," one twin said, demonstrating. Jessie did so.

"Can I have some water?" As the man giving her instructions approached her, the other twin hung back, eyeballing her scantily clad, sweaty body.

"Turn around," the second man said. "Slowly."

Jessie extended her arms to her side and shuffled her feet as she spun around, spread eagle until she faced them again. Both men's eyes rose to meet hers, so she smiled. The first twin, now standing about four feet from her, crouched down and eyeballed her crotch and breasts, apparently looking for a weapon hidden in the thin fabric.

"Scan for wire," the second man said and tossed a small bag to the first. He deftly snatched it out of the air and removed what Jessie thought might be an RF signal detector. He turned it on and approached her. He scanned every inch of her body. "No signals," he said.

"Check her. Keep your arms out, do not look at him."

Jessie straightened her head, then felt fingers touch her back, working their way just under the edge of the fabric, thumb and forefinger rubbing for a wire. The man's hands worked deftly around and under Jessie's breasts. Then they slid down her back to her shorts and followed the same path around the waistband and leg seams right up into her crotch. The man paused and rubbed. She didn't move, say anything, or give the man any joy by reacting in any way.

Thank God I didn't activate the beacon.

"She's sweaty, but no wire," the first man said and opened the rear car door. "Come."

Jessie bent forward and looked into the back seat. Another man inside sat in the spacious, limo-style interior, pointing a pistol at her. The second twin reached into the back seat and snatched a towel from inside and tossed it to Jessie. She took it and toweled off, draping the cloth around her neck.

"Get in." She paused before climbing into the backseat. "Sit next to him..." twin one said.

"He won't bite," the second said, "but he may shoot you if you don't behave." She paused. The gunman smiled. "Go on, get in." The twin behind her pushed gently on her back. She climbed in and put as many inches as possible between her and the gunman.

"If you move too suddenly, or if the driver hits an unexpected pothole, the man sitting next to you will shoot you. Do you understand?"

"Yes." Once the car started rolling, the driver did a U-turn in the road and headed back up the road they came. "You are identical twins," she said.

"Shì," the men said in unison.

"May I have some water now?"

The twins looked at each other, then one of them reached into a cooler, built into the console between Jessie and the man holding the pistol. He removed an ice-cold bottle of water and handed it to Jessie. She glared at it but didn't take it. As if understanding Jessie's hesitation, the twin cracked open the top, took a long swig of the water, swished it in his mouth, and swallowed. He grinned and handed the bottle to Jessie. She took it and downed it.

"Another, please."

The twin shrugged and thrust his closed fist to within an inch of her face. When she flinched at the sudden strike, a small smile rose on the edge of his mouth as his index finger came up.

"One more," he said and handed her another. Jessie nodded, drank half the bottle, and held onto the rest.

After about ten minutes of driving, she noticed the interior windows weren't tinted. They were blacked out. She had no idea where they were taking her. Despite the air conditioner being set to just above freezing, her body's core temperature remained high, although, the sweat had finally stopped seeping from her pores. She opened the bottle, used her forearms to squeeze her breasts together, and poured a little down her neck. Water her cleavage couldn't hold ran down her paved abdominals and soaked into her shorts, making the fabric appear almost transparent. She planted her feet a little wider and opened her legs a little more.

"Ahh," she said, "that feels better." She glanced down at her severely erect nipples, clearly visible through the sheer, wet fabric and then glanced at the three men. As much as the twins tried to avert their eyes, they could not. The man with the gun looked to be about to have an accident in his slacks as he squirmed in his seat. She poured some of the water on the towel and dabbed at her face. Jessie prepared to pounce on the first opportunity, understanding that her attention needed to be focused on the less disciplined gunman. His eye-line moved from her breasts, up her sweaty neck, and ended at Jessie's smiling face. She winked at him. He started to smile until one of the twins kicked him in the shin.

"Qiāo diào tā, báichī." *Knock it off, idiot.*

Jessie gasped, grateful that the kick hadn't cause the idiot to pull the trigger. The twins were too sharp. She wouldn't be able to take any of the men right now. She refocused on how to get Eric out of his jam. She would continue her little tease with the intent of being just enough of a distraction to create an opportunity to attack. Convinced these people intended to kill her, she knew they wouldn't have gone through all this trouble unless they planned to interrogate her.

Time is my ally.

Now, she had to figure out a way to make the most of it. She used the towel again, wiping her body down as slow and sensuously as she could, and in the process, she pressed down into the tissue of her forearm, activating the tracking beacon.

Within a short time, the driver, whom Jessie could not see through the dark tinted window separating the front of the cab from the back, turned off the main road onto what felt like a packed road surface, probably gravel. They drove for another ten minutes or so, then turned again, this time onto what Jessie thought for sure had to be an animal trail.

"Be careful with that gun," she said.

"Shǒuzhǐ tuō xià bānjī, báichī," one of the twins translated into what she suspected was traditional Chinese. Something about 'careful, idiot'. She didn't know many words but didn't want to tip her hand that she knew a little. The guy called 'idiot' took his finger out of the trigger guard. Jessie looked at the twins, smiled, and nodded.

Within a few more minutes, the car bounced to a stop, and everyone got out. They motioned Jessie out and pointed to a tree for her to stand by.

"Aren't you worried I will run?"

"Interesting question," first twin said.

"But one we have discussed between us," said twin two.

"Only an amateur, a non-skilled innocent would run." They looked to one another and back at Jessie, and said in unison, "You're no amateur."

Jessie couldn't argue that point.

They led her to the doorway of a well built, but older cabin, nestled in the trees. Jessie listened for any sounds of civilization and thought she heard the sound of running water coming from somewhere beyond the cabin. The driver of the car, an average looking Asian man, walked to the cabin, up the steps, and onto the porch. He held the door open.

First twin spoke, "Please, Miss Main. After you."

Jessie nodded, took a deep breath, and headed up the stairs. She hesitated a moment before entering the darkened cabin. She took a couple hesitant steps and froze. In a dark corner of the room, bathed in the light of one harsh lamp sat Eric. Her heart lurched. They had him duct-taped to a chair, coagulated blood all around his nose and mouth. His right eye was blackened and swollen closed; his left eye not that much better. A creepy Latino looking male sat on the edge of the table, a few edged instruments and other devices of torture laid out beside him. Jessie measured him up to stand around six foot two, probably weighing in around two-eighty or more. Despite the thick layer of body and belly fat, Jessie made note of the rippling muscles that lay beneath. The man sneered at her while picking at his fingernails with what looked like a WWII British dagger. It had an elongated, double sided blade that tapered down to a needle-sharp point.

"What a wasteful use of such a nice knife," Jessie said. The big man smiled.

"They haven't even asked me any questions," Eric choked out, and as quick as a snake-strike, the big Mexican slapped Eric hard across the face. Jessie said nothing but recoiled at the shock of it as a tremor of fear and anger pulsed through her.

Another man stepped forward out of one of the rooms.

Jessie's heart rate shot up. She had seen photos of this guy as he had searched Robert's neighborhood for the drone, but she'd had no idea he was this big. A giant of a man, she guessed him to be at least six-foot-six or more. His fancy khaki-colored suit did a poor job of hiding his muscular and fit frame. The man's face was long, his smile broad and toothy. Even in the darkened room, his hair looked so blonde it appeared white, cut short into standing spikes. The man's voice was not low like she might have expected from a man this big. His tone was higher, surprisingly melodious.

"Good evening, Miss Main," the man said. "My name is Tano."

12

TURNABOUT

Jessie tried to place the accent and could only guess that because of his light complexion, blonde hair, and ice-blue eyes, he had to be Norwegian or the like.

"Please, Miss Main, if that's your real name. Sit." Tano motioned an open hand to a wooden chair bolted to the floor about six feet in front of Eric. Jessie moved to it but did not sit.

"We didn't do anything, mister. Let us go," Eric said.

The big Mexican stood up, marched toward Eric, and launched a brutal punch to his ribs. Jessie jumped at the sound of bone cracking. The Mexican then pulled a ball-gag from his pants pocket, shoved it into Eric's mouth, and tightened the rubber straps around the sides and back of Eric's head. He eyeballed his handiwork, checked the tightness of the gag, and then walked back to the table where he casually returned to picking his fingernails with the pointy knife.

"Do that again, and I swear I'll shove that knife right up your fat piggy nose," she said.

Calm enveloped her. The room had just enough ambient light to hide any tiny sparks that might escape her body. She knew if they witnessed *that* little trick, she'd be toast. The Mexican eyed her body up and down and licked his lips. The noise coming from his throat sounded more like a lion's chuff than a laugh, but the man jabbed the knife into the tabletop, stood up, and walked to Eric, slugging him hard across the face. He looked sideways at Jessie, smiled, then started toward his table.

Jessie stepped in front of him, arms to her side, fists clenched. "Let's go big boy."

The big Mexican lurched forward. Jessie coiled up to strike.

"Wait."

Both combatants stopped cold. Jessie's head tilted slightly to the side, keeping the fat guy in her peripheral vision while splitting her attention to Tano, who stood there with a big, Cheshire Cat grin on his face. "There will only be violence when I approve it," he said, and then added, "Sit, Miss Main."

"I will not sit. What do you want with me? What do you want with him?" She shot a quick glance at Eric, who's look said enough.

Don't do this.

"For one so small, a college bartender, with a GPA of 4.2, the body of an Olympian goddess, a short goddess, but goddess nonetheless, you demonstrate a level of confidence and tenacity I find equally refreshing and concerning." The twins moved to each side of Jessie and waved off the Mexican. They positioned themselves in such a way as to force Jessie to deal with one before dealing with the other but stayed in her peripheral vision to add a level of sport to the encounter.

"That man is easily double your weight, maybe more. You took a fighting stance I have seen before. A karate stance, and that alone is enough of a red flag for me. To see a tiny woman like you attempt to even the odds with the likes of Gerardo confirms my suspicions that there is more to you than just, how did Robert put it, a piece of side ass."

"That's a bunch of shit," the offended Mexican said. "I'll crush her."

"Perhaps," Tano said, "but not if I put a bullet in your feeble brain first. If you'd like to test that theory, interrupt me again."

Gerardo backed up, looking dejected, and leaned his rearend onto the table once more. He opened his mouth to speak until Tano's head snapped toward him, one eyebrow rising. Gerardo nodded.

"Now, where were we? Oh yes. You." He glanced down at Eric and smiled. "Who is this man to you?"

"He's my boyfriend." Jessie felt her heart lurch at the words. The truth hurt.

"Why would he be running sniper overwatch on your house?"

"A what-watch?" Jessie said, looking incredulous. "He was supposed to be hunting. Besides, I can take care of myself."

"That remains to be seen," Tano said, smiling. "What is your connection to Robert Kore?"

Eric's head shot up, a questioning look in his eyes.

"Robert? My friend Robert? We just work out together. We…"

"Liar." Tano glared at her. He marched straight to Eric's side, drew out an FN-45 Pistol, and twisted a silencer can onto the end of the threaded barrel. Jessie thought the large framed gun looked tiny in the man's huge hands. She decided not to voice that observation. "One last time. Try me," Tano said, and whipped the gun's silencer up, pressing it right up against Eric's head. A tear rolled down Jessie's cheek as Eric's head swiveled to look at the silencer. He slowly turned his eyes back to Jessie, and then, almost imperceptibly, shook his head from side to side.

Don't do it.

Jessie didn't flinch as she watched Tano's index finger slide off the frame and onto the trigger. Jessie felt the little generator crank up to full power, flooding her body with so much energy, she stumbled slightly. Tano saw her falter and smiled. Jessie could only guess the man mistook her powering up for being weak at the sight her boyfriend's life as it flashed before her eyes. Tano's smile faded as his finger slowly squeezed the trigger back, right to the wall, or breaking point.

"We're lovers," she blurted out, "We met at the gym. Eric didn't know about him until…"

"Liar!" Tano bellowed, but released the tension on the trigger, unscrewed the silencer, and leaned down to place his lips against Eric's bloody ear. "I'm certain you have a sexual relationship with her. But she's more, isn't she?" Eric didn't move. Tano continued. "Did you know she sprinted for three miles to make the meeting point?"

Eric made no sound. No acknowledgement, but his eyes did roll up to meet Jessie's.

"That's proof that you are more than just lovers. I'm thinking co-workers." Tano stood up and shoved the pistol back into the shoulder holster hidden beneath his jacket.

"Now, Gerardo, tape Miss Main to the chair. It's time to get the truth." Jessie looked at Tano incredulously. "Oh, I would have shot him, but I certainly don't want to shoot anyone. Especially in the head. Too bloody messy. Gerardo, do it."

The big Mexican smiled, stuck the stiletto in the tabletop, and hunched slightly at the shoulders. With his hands splayed out and forward, like some kind of Lucha Libre' masked wrestler, he moved forward. Jessie waited until the last moment, slid beneath his reaching arms, and got behind the man. She kicked toward his knee to knock it in from the side, but the bridge of her foot hit solid bone and muscle. The big man turned toward her, laughing. Jessie glanced at the twins who stood watching with interest. Tano stood at the farthest angle away, the FN pistol nestled in the crook of his folded arms. Gerardo stalked forward, eyeing Jessie's body with each, purposeful step. Jessie backed up until her lower back struck the edge of the table.

As Gerardo lurched forward, Jessie snatched the stiletto blade from the table, sprang forward, and then up into the man's arms. Wrapping one hand around the back of his head, she rammed the blade straight up and into his nostrils. Gerardo's body shot upright and swayed. Jessie let go, landed nimbly on her feet, and sent a flying front snap kick up to the handle of the blade, driving it to the hilt in the Mexican's skull. Gerardo's body swayed slowly, like some great piece of timber deep in the forest. His dead body fell backwards, landing on the wooden floor with a bouncing thud.

The sound of slow, purposeful clapping snagged Jessie's attention. She glanced up at Tano as the twins took on fighting stances. "Most Impressive, Miss Main. It took a college bar girl less than a minute to dispatch one of my most skilled interrogators."

Jessie moved into the karate 'horse-stance' and motioned with her forward hand for the twins to come.

"Well, if that was one of your best, then these two will take just a minute longer."

Tano chuckled. "Obviously, you are an operator of some kind." He looked toward the twins. "I have more pressing business ahead of me this afternoon." Tano glanced at one of the twins. "Do what you want, then kill her." Tano glanced at Eric. "Make him watch. Then kill him, too. Get me a good set of fingerprints from the girl. And him, too, I suppose."

"How are we supposed to do that?" Twin one asked, stalking around Jessie, sizing up his opponent.

Tano looked from Jessie to Eric and back. "Cut off their hands. While they're alive, if you can. They are too well trained to talk, and I don't have time for these games. We've wasted too much time already. I will drive separately. You two take care of business, burn the cabin, and use the other truck to get back."

With that, Tano turned and walked out the door.

Jessie didn't take her eyes off the two men. "So, your boss is some kind of big guy," she said, turning and measuring the striking distance as the two men circled her, closing in.

The first one said, "He's not our boss. He's our… "

"Bosses head man," the second one finished, reaching out and collecting a filet knife from the Mexican's tool kit.

"Why don't you give it up?" Jessie said. "No reason to die today."

The twins chuckled in identical cadence. "Not for us. No," the first one said, following his brother and picking up two identical skinning blades.

"But there is for *you*," number two followed up.

"Really? You're not even going to give a girl a fighting chance?" Jessie said, really *not* wanting to be sliced up by the edged weapons. "Ugly there deserved it. You know it."

The brothers circled back around again, glanced at each other, then shrugged and said in unison, "Sounds fair to me." The first twin tossed the filet knife into a dark corner of the room. The second brother completed a spinning jump in the air and rammed his two blades into the Mexican's wooden table. And then they danced.

Jessie spun around, crouching and moving into a kung-fu position, lotus, which caught the twins off guard. "You know kung-fu?" twin one asked.

"Let's find out," Jessie said. Taking two steps forward, she leapt off the ground, pulling her hand and legs around her spinning body and kicked out, mid-air, toward one's face. She landed on one foot, spun, and leapt again and again as the twin only just deflected her kicks. Two moved in, taking dragon stance and sending his own kick forward just as Jessie jumped a third time. The kick found its mark, knocking her from the air onto her back. Jessie set her hands backwards over her shoulders, arched her back, and sprang up off the ground, delivering a shocking punch right into the chest of twin two, sending him reeling backwards. Snatching a pair of long polished metal rods off the table, she spun them Escrima style, expertly maneuvering through a series of aerial attacks, driving off her target.

All three fighters spun around, danced, and deflected until

they suddenly stopped in their chosen stances to catch their breath.

"You said no weapons," twin one said.

"If you ain't cheating', you ain't trying." Jessie sprang forward, spinning and striking out as the two bothers used what blocks they could to fend off Jessie's blows.

The rod struck true on the forearm of twin one, breaking the large forearm radius bone with a sickening snap just as twin two moved into her body space and in one swift strike knocked one rod from Jessie's hand. She moved to a spinning backhand with the second rod when the twin spun into the attack and wrenched the rod from her hand. He reared back to strike her at the moment Jessie reached up and clawed the side of his face.

The twin dropped the rod and screamed as her nails sunk into his skin. He then delivered a dynamic punch to Jessies sternum, knocking her backwards onto the wood floor. Jessie lay on her back. Not moving. Eric screamed through his gag. The twin marched up and sent a vicious kick into Jessie's ribs. She did not move. The twin, his face bleeding from Jessie's nails, walked over to the aid of his brother and did what he could to set the arm.

"It's broken," he said.

"No shit, Sherlock. What about the girl?" the first twin said.

Two's head snapped to the side to look at her. He stood up, walked over to Jessie's still body, kicked at it once more, then cautiously leaned down to take a pulse. "She's dead. Doesn't matter. Tano only wanted her fingerprints anyway, right?" The broken-armed brother nodded. "I'll take care of that, and this one," two said. "Let's get you into the truck."

Jessie watched from cracked lids as two led his brother out the door, down the stairs, and sat him in the pickup truck's passenger seat. He reached for something, placing it on his face. Sunglasses, maybe? Then she heard him say, "I'll be right back," and he turned toward the cabin, his hands balled into fists.

AT LEAST TWENTY MINUTES HAD GONE BY WHILE BOLIN SAT IN the car, holding his broken arm and cursing himself for letting that tiny woman get the better of him. He didn't think her training to be that exceptional. Her form looked good, but she had not fought at a Master's level. What she lacked in skill, she made up for in strength and aggression. He shook his head in disgust and had to admit it: he underestimated her. He reached over and turned the air-conditioning up to high and was just about ready to exit the vehicle when two loud gunshots rang out. A minute later, his brother Bohai came out and held up a blood smeared plastic bag that clearly held two hands. Bolin shivered at the sight. Bohai got in behind the driver seat, slammed the door, and turned his bloody face toward his brother. He smiled and tossed the bag in Bolin's lap.

"Húndàn," Bolin said, carefully tossing the bloody sack into the backseat.

"Me? An asshole?" Bohai laughed. "Since when are you squeamish?"

Bolin looked sideways at his brother. "Call Tano. Let him know we're on our way back."

Bohai opened the center console, retrieved the satellite phone that was still on, plugged it into a power outlet, and faced the dial pad. He rubbed at his temples and groaned in pain.

"What's wrong?" Bolin asked.

"That bitch really dug into my face, pain is just setting in. I hope it doesn't leave a scar?"

"I do. Then they won't get us confused anymore." Bohai cocked his head sideways at his brother, searching his face for sarcasm, but he saw only the grimace of pain as Bolin cradled his arm. "I'm kidding. Just call."

Bohai dialed the number to Tano's cell and put the phone on speaker.

"Update." Tano's voice was cold. To the point.

"We are on our way back."

"You have what I asked for?"

"Shì. Dāngrán." *Yes, of course.*

"Is everything…"

An explosion from the cabin rocked the truck. The twins ducked then looked back at the flames engulfing the cabin. Then they pointed at each other asking the silent question, *did you do that?* Both twins shook their heads. They both mouthed the name Tano and realized at the same time that the man had planted an incendiary device in the cabin, set to go off whether or not the twins were still in there. Bolin mouthed the word asshole in English. Bohai nodded.

"I can hear it," Tano said. "Get back as soon as possible."

"Shì de xiānshēng." *Yes, sir.* Bohai hung up. "I didn't want to tell him we are injured."

"Good idea," Bolin said, "especially since the húndàn tried to kill us."

"We need to get you fixed up. Let's find a hospital."

Bolin frowned and pushed his brother in the arm with his free hand. "Are you an idiot? You know better than that. No hospitals. Ever. Besides, I can make it to the house."

Bohai looked at his brother. "It's a four-hour drive to the house. It's going to get worse."

"I'll make it. I'll meditate until we get there. Just don't hit any potholes."

13

INTO THE UNKNOWN

TEN MINUTES EARLIER...

E ric's eyes fixed on Jessie's lifeless body lying on the floor. He struggled with his bonds the moment the two men walked out the door. Eric wasn't sure. One man had received a broken arm, the other—the one who had sneaked up on him on the hillside—had deep scratches in his face. Eric thought Jessie had fought smart, just going for it and not pussy-footing around with the twins, but after that vicious kick, he still wasn't sure. He glanced down at dead Mexican, Gerardo, the hilt of the battle dagger wedged in the big Mexican's nostrils just as Jessie had promised. Then he reassessed his own predicament, looking around as best he could. He stopped moving when he saw it. The smooth, carved groove in the wood floor about two feet in front of him.

Shit.

The groove brought forth a memory from when he had worked drug interdiction with the DEA in the past, where the team found dead informants taped to chairs just like this. Within that slot in the floor, a mirror would be placed, and victims—men, and sometimes women—would be forced to watch as the inquisitor carved off the skin of their faces while they tried to scream past the ball gag.

Eric shuddered as a memory flashed in his mind's eye of the

109

next step, when the victim's balls and penis were cut off, shoved down their own throats for them to choke on while they bled to death. Eric knew with certainty that this had been Gerardo's plan.

The door pushed open, and in walked the Asian man with the fresh scratch marks on his face. Eric froze as the man stomped over to the Mexican's tool bench and wrenched the two skinning knives free from the tabletop. The man spun on Eric and tore off the sunglasses. Now he was sure.

Eric let out the breath he held and would have said, "What took you so long," except the ball gag in his mouth kept him from speaking.

Jessie stepped up and slid the blade between Eric's temple and the gag's rubber strap. A quick pull, and Eric was free.

"Are you fucking craz…" he started to say, but the guy's lips were suddenly pressed against his mouth.

Jessie pulled away, smiling at Eric and examining his bruised face with her glowing red eyes. "Glad to see you too, honey," she said in a thick accent.

"Don't do that!" Eric said, spitting like a cat gagging on a furball. "That freaks me the fuck out." He shivered at how much it grated on him hearing Jessie speaking to him with someone else's voice. But right now, he'd take what he could get. She sliced away at the tape. "What's the plan?"

"I heard water," Jessie said. "Maybe a stream or something around the back. Sounds like it's running in the direction of the road. Head out to the stream." She handed him the skinning knives. "They could have someone watching the place. I mean, they've obviously been counter surveilling us from the get-go."

"Yeah," Eric groaned, standing up. He quickly scanned the other rooms and came out of one wearing a fresh, plain grey t-shirt, covering the bruises on his body. He eyeballed Jessie's host body head to toe, then turned away. "The one you're in got the drop on me, somehow. I slipped up."

"Well, they know now I'm more than just a distraction for Kore," she said.

Eric glanced at her and saw she was looking at him, searching for that overt sign of jealousy. Eric felt it, alright, and he didn't like it. Not one bit. He knew what Jessie had to do, and he knew that Jessie, even without her unique ability, was probably one of the best field operators he had ever seen. Regardless, he had forced himself to accept the Mata-Hari aspect of her techniques. It was hard not to walk on eggshells when the subject of having to share her came up. He shook off the stupid feeling and rifled through kitchen cabinets until he found a box of Ziplock bags and a meat cleaver from the wood table.

He walked over to the Mexican, knelt down beside him, and with one ferocious swing, lopped off a hand at the wrist. He did the same with the other hand, turned one of the large Ziplock bags inside out, and picked up the hand. He squeezed some blood from the wrist into the bag and zipped it shut. He did the same with the other hand, then did his best to stuff the two bags into a third, holding it up.

"Think they'll notice it's not your hands?" he asked.

"Not until it's too late, if I have anything to do with it," she said.

"What are you going to do?"

"Get closer. See what more I can find out about who this guy is. He's obviously the main contact pulling Kore's strings."

"You're treading on dangerous ground, Jessie."

"Yes, I know. I activated the GPS tracker in my forearm. Just get as far from the cabin as you can and hunker down with my body until someone comes for you. Then get to Palo Alto. I'm sure that's where we're heading. I'll send a signal, somehow, someway, as soon as I can."

"Did you have to kick your body so hard?" Eric asked, kneeling down to inspect Jessie's entranced body. "I hope you didn't break a rib."

"I pulled that kick," Jessie said. "At least, I think I did. I didn't hear any bones break, and I didn't feel any residual neural signal that I might have gone too far."

Eric rolled his eyes. "Yeah, whatever the fuck you just said." He examined and felt along Jessie's barely responsive body for any breaks. "I think you're okay."

"I think you're okay too, dear," Jessie said.

Eric hoisted Jessie's body off the ground like a mariner's sea-bag full of sand and made eye contact with the Asian. He could almost see Jessie smiling at him through the stranger's face as she donned her sunglasses, turned on her heel, and walked out the door, holding that bag of bloody hands like it was just another Monday.

JON DALY SAT IN THE PILOT SEAT OF HIS 1943 B-25J MITCHELL warbird and flipped the first starter switch, while his co-pilot and wife, Krys Johanseen completed the preflight checklist and lifted the left red-knobbed starter handle. The first engine cranked right up. A few more switches, a firm lift of the right red starter knob, and the second one sputtered before roaring to life. Both engines synced up. Jon looked out the window at his former US NAVY Brown-shirt who had spent years as an aircraft carrier flight-deck "plane-captain" on the USS Carl Vinson. The man saluted. Jon returned it and taxied down the runway.

Once airborne and stable, Jon banked the old plane left, reached up, and pressed the side of his headset. "You got the nav's," he said.

"Roger. I'm going to check for the tracking signal," Krys said. Jon nodded, then slipped off to his own thoughts in the noisy cockpit. Krys reached over and squeezed his arm. "We'll find her." Jon nodded again but hated the gut-wrenching feeling tearing through him. Jessie taken hostage.

He could have, probably should have, hitched the ride on the company's AC-130 and been part of the recovery team. Six men, two women, and two K-9 handlers and their dogs—his very best combat operators dispatched to Reno to hopefully rescue Eric and Jessie. He'd set that wheel in motion the moment Steve Walters hadn't checked in or answered his encrypted cellphone, or any emails. Jessie hadn't answered either. Neither had Eric, which solidified confirmation of a problem.

He let out a long, slow breath. *No,* he thought. *This was the right choice.*

He chose not to ride with the team because, first and foremost, they were going Airborne. Dropping in over the Oxbow Wilderness area at night, wearing Night Vision Goggles, or NVG's, and armed to the teeth. Two would also be jumping with their dogs. It wasn't that he didn't love to parachute in, or be part of the OP, but he always seemed to get so deep into the operational aspect of team missions, he sometimes ended up taking over.

Well, most of the time.

Chip Rasher, his more than capable former Army Intel Major, Airborne and Ranger certified, deserved to take the lead on this mission without Jon's interference. Trust meant everything. His taking the lead, and the team going on OP without him, would instill a hearty dose of confidence, in them *and* in him.

Besides, driving the old warbird gave Jon time to think and time to release some of the tension that had shot through him the moment the news of Jessie and Steve's silence had reached his ears. As age crept up on him, he found stresses like this affected him more than it had twenty years ago.

No shit. Besides, he thought, trying to convince himself, *I'll be needed later.*

The team would be over target soon. They would secure the safehouse and no doubt uncover anyone who might be performing surveillance on the house. It would take them several hours to sweep, but these former soldiers and airmen were the best of the best. Even the dogs had been veterans of the Iraq War. If danger existed, they would eliminate it without hesitation and with extreme prejudice.

Jon glanced over at Krys, her face pressed up against a custom eye port that jutted out from the instrument panel, over the secondary steering wheel. The oblong shroud could be retracted to take up as little space as possible. Some of the old instruments, mostly redundant, had to be removed. They were stored, in case Jon ever decided to sell the plane, but he doubted it. The new instrument, similar to what the bombardier/navigators on US Navy A6-intruders used, had been custom built to give real time information of any Crue member's personal safety beacon from anywhere in the world. The sensor had a direct link to several Crue Intellis satellites, which doubled as communication satellites for civilian cellular and satellite phone services.

"I have her signal, Jon. And Eric's. Home base has it, too. They are together up near the Hunter Creek Trail head. It's heavily wooded there. Glad the team brought the dogs."

Jon nodded. He calculated the B-25's flight to be ten hours long and felt confident in the mechanical aptitude of the airplane and its ground crew. "We'll be stopping in at Renner Field, Goodland, Kansas for fuel, to stretch our legs, and then get straight back at it for Reno."

"With the spare fuel cells in the bomb-bay, we could make it straight through."

"Yes, I know, but I don't want to be cramped up for ten hours straight."

"Going to let me fly a little?"

"Sure. Of course," Jon said, glancing around at the inside of the cockpit, looking to the old warbird for reassurance. Krys had flown it before, she'd be fine. "I'll take a little nap."

A nudge on Jon's knee pulled him out of a weird dream. His eyes fluttered open to the darkening horizon. "We're on approach to Renner Field," she said, handing him a thermos of coffee.

He nodded. "Wanna bring her in?" He had taught Krys to fly the old warbird, and she took an even greater interest in flying the inherently more complicated AC-130, as well.

She turned to him and smiled. "No. That's why I woke you up. I need you to land. I'm sorting through message traffic."

"What you got?"

"Chip let us know he's called off the air-drop for now. He's sending a squad of two to pull Jessie and Eric out of the muck. The local police and fire department responded to a house fire, or explosion, or something like that about a mile from where Eric and Jessie's signals are sitting tight. With all that attention, Chip thought it best to land it, go in, and get the package before heading back to Spooky."

Jon nodded. "Good thinking on his part. What's his ETA?"

"They've landed, rolled out one of two Yukon's, and are bringing Pancho with them to find Eric. We've had to reach out to DOD to get with Reno Fire and PD to keep their mouths shut and keep the explosion under wraps."

"Why?"

"They found a body in the house, or cabin, that burned to the ground. It has no hands."

"No...hands?" Jon repeated. He frowned and slipped back into thought.

"Yeah, although burned to a crisp. I talked to the Detective Captain at Reno, and he says it looks like the hands were cut off at the wrist. Said the guy was about six-foot-two."

A wave of fear zipped through Jon. Steve, he thought.

"We haven't made contact with Steve yet?" he asked.

"No. No way of knowing if it's him or not. But Chip thought it best to get Jessie and Eric first."

"Roger that. I'd have done the same thing." Jon moved his body, extending his legs out a bit, and gripped the yoke. "Let's bring it in. We'll get more information once we land."

Eric checked the tiny map on his Garmin Tactix Charlie GPS watch. After leaving the house, he made the decision to hold tight a few hours, then work his way northeast along Hunter Creek, where he knew he would eventually run into the Hunter Creek Trailhead. Now was the time to move. The dead weight of Jessie's tiny, one hundred twenty-pound frame didn't help him move any faster. If lucky, he might make it before dark. Movement caught the corner of his non-swollen eye, his sixth sense screaming at high-alert that someone, or something, watched him from the tree line. The bushes moved again from the direction Eric and just come—the cabin. Had he been followed? Why not take him and Jessie out sooner, then?

He slowly lowered Jessie's body to the ground, and as he reached for the skinning knives in his vest, a large dog bolted toward him from the brush. Yipping with excitement, K-9 Pancho rushed forward, leapt into Eric's arms, and licked eagerly at his face.

"Pancho!" he said, hugging the animal. "What a pleasant surprise!" He gently set the dog down. Pancho refocused and cautiously approached Jessie, whimpering as he sniffed at her body. Pancho's handler, former Army M.P. Nicky Coates, exited the woods followed closely by Chip Rasher. The two strode up to Eric.

"Damn, Gunny," Chip said, "you lose another fight?"

"Yeah, I'm getting old," Gunny said.

"How's Jess?" Chip asked. All three men looked to Jessie's

scantily clad body as Pancho snuggled close to her, resting his head across her chest.

"She's fine. Saved my ass. She's holed up in some young kung-fu Chinaman now. Embedded with the enemy."

"Sounds like Jessie to me," Chip said. Eric saw that his pal's face looked concerned, despite the casual comment.

Coates removed a med-kit from the backpack and stood up to clean Eric's wounds. "Not that it would make you any prettier," she said. "Just need to clean these up, seal that cut over the eye to prevent infection."

Eric nodded. He looked over at Jessie and Pancho and said, "Lucky dog."

14

TWINS

"Where are you going?" Bolin, Jessie's new brother, asked. She glanced over at him, smiled, then returned her attention to the road ahead.

"To the girl's Jeep," she said.

"Why?"

"I saw a bag in the back. We might learn more about her."

Bolin turned his gaze away. "It's a good idea, but we're losing time."

"It's a great idea, and what's twenty minutes?"

"What about the man in the house?"

"The girl's fake father? He's probably hiding in his closet. All that bullshit Tano laid on him about attacking the house and all." Jessie had pressed hard into her host's mind the moment she took him, feeling confident with the information extracted so far.

"If he's anything like that girl, he's going to be ready for someone to show up."

"I'll take my chances," Jessie replied, hoping like hell Steve didn't shoot her. Then she thought of something. "Did Tano call the house from the sat-phone?"

"I think so, I'm not sure. Do you remember the number?"

"Why would I remember?" Jessie said, hoping her lie didn't shine through.

"Are you kidding?" The brother sat up straight in the seat. "All that research you did on the house?"

There's another little morsel of information I hadn't expected. "I only remember the area code was 775."

Bolin reached for the console and tried to manipulate the button to open it. He groaned, released it, and hung onto his arm instead. "Shit that hurts. Fucking bitch."

"I'll do it," Jessie said, using her free hand to retrieve the phone. "Show me your arm."

Bolin pulled up the baggy sleeve. The forearm had swollen, skin so red it looked to be pulsing with anger. "That looks as bad as I'm sure it feels. We need to get you some ice."

"Yeah, well, you're driving the wrong way for that, too."

Jessie huffed, glanced down at the sat-phone and activated the dial pad. She scrolled through the numbers and found it. "Ah, this must be it," she said, and dialed. Steve answered on the first ring.

"Mr. Main," Jessie said, "the girl, J…" she almost said Jessie, "your daughter is safe. We are taking her to an alternate location and have been instructed to retrieve her bag. We will be arriving in two minutes. Put her green pack in the back of the jeep, along with a cooler containing bottled water, plenty of ice, and Ziplock bags."

"What? Why would you want…"

"Do what we say, Mr. Main, if you do not want any harm to come to your daughter. Walker out of the house slowly, arms to side. Do not try anything funny or our sniper will shoot before you touch your waistband. Understand?"

The line was quite for several moments. Any normal person would be begging for the kidnappers not to hurt their daughter. Jessie hoped this to be a strange enough request, he would comply, but play along. Steve didn't disappoint.

"I'll do whatever you want. Please. Please don't hurt my little girl. I'm begging you, I'll…"

"Put the bag in the Jeep, now, Mr. Main. You have one-and-a-half minutes." Jessie hung up the phone.

"What do you think you'll find in a woman's bag? Other than underwear and tampons?"

"Did you see how fit she was? She seems pretty tacti-cool to me," Jessie said. The brother nodded. "I'm betting there is ibuprofen, maybe other pain killers, wraps, things an athlete needs to perform through pain. Perhaps her real identification." Bolin said nothing, then nodded his head.

Jessie stopped the truck and pointed toward the house about twenty yards down the road. Steve had exited with a smaller Yeti cooler in one hand and her bag in the other. He dropped it in the back seat, looked around, and headed back into the house. "That was easy," she said.

"Too easy. Search the bag with the scanner," Bolin said.

Jessie pulled the truck up to the Jeep. Bolin lowered the passenger window and leveled a pistol at the house. She rifled through the center console again and found a hand-held scanner similar to the one used on her earlier. She held it up, smiled, and exited. She snagged the cooler and duffle, and glancing back toward the truck, she also collected her go-bag, which she always left stuffed under the back seat.

She quickly moved to the truck's driver side back door, opened it, and tossed the items inside. Seeing the plastic bag full of bloody Mexican hands, she opened the cooler and removed the box of Ziplock bags. Steve had wisely selected the largest bags. She quickly filled two with ice, tossing them up front to the brother. She then pulled out two bottles of water, searched through her go-bag, and removed the small tube of Tramadol, a mild painkiller, and tossed that up into Bolin's lap as well.

As the brother worked to remove the top of the pill bottle, she removed her Glock 43 pocket pistol from the go-bag and stuffed it into her waistband.

That's better, she thought.

As she moved to close the car door, she remembered something else. Glancing back and forth between Bolin and the bag, she rifled through the contents until she found the small, white contact case. Although made to match Robert Kore's eyes, she hoped they would fit her host's eyes well enough.

She climbed back into the driver seat and saw that Bolin had put on his own matching sunglasses. He'd already tucked the icepacks into the sleeve of his black shirt. He leaned against the truck's door panel. Good. The painkillers would kick in any minute. She dropped the shifter into drive, took one last deep breath, and sped off toward Palo Alto.

———

WITHIN MINUTES AFTER RECEIVING THE CALL, STEVE WALTERS prepared to leave the safehouse. The Chinese man spoke in broken English, but he had no doubt the man had said 'walker out slowly', which anyone could have mistaken, except that Jessie's operator nickname happened to be 'Walker'. He donned a set of heavy battle armor, made up of thick, ceramic plates that could repel an armor piercing round––one round only. Steve thought that if the sniper had serious skills and decided to take a head shot on a moving target, well, then he'd have nothing left to worry about, would he?

He also assumed these guys might be monitoring calls from the house and even considered that Kore and his pals might have the tech to crack encrypted sat-phone signals. But that would take equipment. Resources.

Yeah, he thought. *Kore had resources all right.*

Steve set the remote triggers to activate the house's elaborate camera system, crossed himself, and did the old one, two, three before sprinting from the front door. He dove behind Jessie's Jeep, kept as low as possible, and climbed into the driver seat. Once started, he hunched over, put the manual shift into reverse, and gunned it backwards out of the driveway. There were no shots. As he slammed the shifter into gear, he gunned it again, the rear tires spitting gravel as he headed away from the mountain towards Reno. Fifteen minutes later, he pulled over, stripped off the hot, heavy armor, and looked overhead for drones. Pulling his Leatherman tool from his belt holster, he moved to the back of the open top jeep, located the half-dollar-sized GPS tracker, and pried it loose. He opened a toolbox mounted to the inside wall of the cargo area, found a hammer, then smashed the little disk to bits.

"Track that, mother fuckers," he said, then continued to drive northeast. He pulled his sat-phone out of his pack and dialed.

"Steve, thank god you're alive. Where are you?" It was Krys.

"I'm fine. We're made, but I'm guessing you know that already. I'm halfway to Reno. Bailed out of the house after... well, I'll tell you about when I see you. I hear background noise. You and Jon in the B-25?"

"Yes, we are."

"Any word from Jessie?"

"Well, according to team report, she's slipped into one of the bad guys. We have her body. We have Eric, too."

"Thank God. I suspected as much but wasn't positive. I'm about thirty minutes away from Reno. Where do you want me?"

"The Reno airport. Spooky is there. We'll be there within the hour to debrief with the team."

LESS THAN AN HOUR LATER, STEVE TRUDGED UP THE CARGO RAMP of the company's AC130 gunship as the rest of the team worked on strapping down the Yukon's, dogs, and equipment. As he moved toward the jump seats mounted to the left bulkhead ahead of him, he stopped short and gasped.

"What the hell?"

Strapped down to the deck rails in front of the forwardmost Yukon sat what could only be described as a cross between an Egyptian sarcophagus and a cruise missile. The entire unit couldn't have been more than eight feet long and tapered to a somewhat flat point at what he guessed was the foot-end. The whole thing looked like some kind of wedge. The opposite end was at least as wide as an NFL lineman's shoulders, and light glowed from what appeared to be a thick glass window cut into the top.

At first, he thought the wedge to be constructed from stain-less-steel, but after running his hands along the smooth, almost slick surface, he guessed it was probably some carbon-fiber composite material, like what he had seen on an F-117 Nighthawk on display at an air museum. He leaned over to peak through the window and gasped.

Jessie.

At the sight of Jessie's eyes bouncing around behind her lids, and from the weird, multi-colored wire harness that looked to have grown from the top of her head, a memory triggered concerning a conversation about a project Jessie, David West, and some big hitters from MIT were working on to enhance her abilities. That had been a few years ago, and he had heard nothing since.

His eyes followed the pony-tail of thin, multi-colored glowing wires coming from Jessie's head harness to where they culminated into some kind of port affixed to the inner wall of the capsule.

Well, I'm guessing it's a capsule, he thought.

Someone had cleaned her up from the ordeal in the woods and dressed her small but densely muscled body into a skin-tight silver bodysuit. Steve's heart thudded in his chest. The last time he had seen Jessie was when she had left to save Eric. She was more to him than a role-play daughter, and it pained him to know he had almost lost her. But she lay here, now, safe. At least physically. He shook off his dark thoughts and leaned in once more to look at her. He noticed more wires embedded into the fabric of her bodysuit. They looked to be attached to contact pads positioned around her torso.

"Those have to be to monitor vitals," he whispered.

He jumped a little when the padding Jessie's body lay in started to undulate on her shoulders, then he understood. The bed had a built-in massage therapy apparatus, like one of this shiatsu chairs one could sit in at the mall for a buck. He still thought he would go bat-shit crazy being stuffed into such a small contraption. Finally, he noticed the racing harness strapping her in.

He stood up and studied the design of the container. It had the curves of a retro-1930's Hollywood spacecraft. He leaned forward and found logos for both Lockheed/Martin and MIT affixed to the lower area where Jessie's head lay, obviously a joint effort. He dragged his fingers against covered slots that ran horizontally along the bottom edge, with others on top and at the foot of the tapered chamber. There were also six long thin fins affixed to what he guessed was the lid, traveling the length of the chamber from nose to tail. Curious, he reached out to touch one.

"No touchy," came a young voice behind him.

Steven turned to find a young girl who couldn't have been more than fourteen years old standing in front of Krys and Jon, a scornful look on her face. The adults grinned at him.

"Those fins are powered antennae," the girl said, pushing her way into the space between Steve and the device. She pulled out a thin, microfiber cloth, wrapped it around one of the fins—the one Steve was touching—and methodically wiped down its length. "It expands Jessie's ability to maintain control of her host with less drag time created during long-distance missions."

"So, this is it. The amplifier she told me about?" The girl said nothing, her attention riveted to the chamber like some proud mother focused on her newborn child. Steve continued. "I'm still not really sure how she even does what she does, so I'm at a loss as to how this," he reached out again to touch the chamber's surface, resulting in a quick, but not too hard hand-slap. "…can help her."

"We call it the Star-cophagus," the girl said, her tone matter of fact. "Did you know she experiences a time-lag from when she issues a mental command to when her host's body responds?" the girl asked.

"Sort of. I remember she had said something about a lag, but I also remember she said it was only a couple seconds."

"That's right. And doing what she does, a couple of seconds delay in making a decision could result in death." The girl turned toward him, a serious look on her face. "Or worse."

Steve knew exactly what the girl meant, and she was right. For Jessie, getting caught would be the worst possible outcome, and this mission had already brought that reality much, much too close to home.

"Point taken." Steve watched as the girl walked to the viewing window and peered at Jessie just before running her own hand along the side of the sleek surface, finding several indentations he hadn't noticed, and punching in some code sequence with her fingertips. A moment later, a panel slid open, revealing a keyboard and display screen.

"I'm going to run a diagnostic," she said.

Krys walked over to Steve and reached up with a finger to close his jaw. "Steve, I'd like you to meet Melanie Banks," she said, still grinning. "She's with the team who developed this amplifier. She's on loan from MIT's Defense Division."

"On… loan?" Steve put out his hand, and after a moment's hesitation, the girl shook it.

"I'm pleased to meet you, young lady," Steve said. "Obviously, I'm not one of the tech-guru's around here…"

"Obviously," the girl said, the smile on her face telling him she meant that light-heartedly. Steve's hand waved toward the Star-cophagus, "All of this is just freakin' amazing. I remember Jessie telling me something about it, but I had never actually seen it." He walked around the unit, his hands deep in his pants pockets. He found it hard to resist reaching out to touch the sleek surface again. "Seems a little claustrophobic to me."

"Well, I'm guessing it would be confining if one were wide-awake. She's in deep meditation right now and only somewhat aware that she's plugged in from this end. I'm sure she felt the effects immediately once we powered it up. This is the portable unit. Unlike the main unit back at Camp Summit, it has limited capabilities but more than enough juice for most missions," Melanie said.

Steve leaned in to look over the young girl's shoulder at the data screen she interacted with. "Now this I know. It's her vital signs, yes?"

"Some of it is, yes." She touched her finger to the touch-screen display. "There is also a brainwave monitor that measures her bio-electrical power output and stress levels." She swiped the screen, bringing up a different display. "This one controls life support, which she doesn't need right now. Fresh, oxygenated air is automatically being pumped in."

"Doesn't being strapped down in a big metal plane interfere with the signal?" Melanie looked up at him as if she were being challenged. "I'm serious. I just thought of it. Like a cellphone in a brick and steel structure, signal strength and all that."

The girl's demeanor relaxed. "You're smarter than you lead on, Mr. Waters," Melanie said, smiling, "The system is a kind of booster which sends the signal through similar fin antennae mounted to the skin of this airplane. That cable there is fiber-optic and connects the pod to the antenna on the fuselage."

Steve looked to where Melanie pointed, her index finger following the path of the thick, bright red cable. He nodded, impressed. "Good observation for an old guy."

"Hey now," he said. "I resemble that remark."

Jon and Krys chuckled behind him.

"You said there is another unit like this back at our home base?"

"Not like this," she said, turning her attention back to the displays. "The one at Camp Summit is much, much bigger. The size of a large office. Two offices. It has a big reclining chair, many more controls and monitors, and is directly connected to the operating system, whereas this one is just remotely connected. In the 'hot-seat', as we like to call it, Jessie can stream from anywhere in the world."

Steve turned to Jon. "I've never seen anything like that at headquarters."

"You never asked to see it," Jon said. "Maybe Melanie can give you the grand tour when we get home."

The girl shrugged but didn't look away from her monitors, continuing to tap furiously at the iPad.

"And you and your team created it? This?"

"It was a joint effort that some of my classmates and I have been part of for about five years now. David West came up with the idea, the initial designs. Dude's a freakin' genius. We got called in to help refine the design, develop the operating systems, and with your this new A.I. system coming on-board, well, we're going to be entering into a whole new world of remote viewing, ala Jessie Richter," Melanie said, unplugging the iPad and closing the access door to the monitors.

"Five years? You don't look more than twelve." Steve flinched at the girl as she glared up at him. "Thirteen? No disrespect, but this is all new to me."

"I'm fifteen, thank you very much. It took time to get vetted by the Pentagon, but our team is growing. Miles is the youngest.

He's twelve. He's back at Camp Summit. There are others involved, too, but ultimately, this is David West's brainchild, built at Lockheed Skunkworks.

Steve had no idea and turned his attention back to the unit in front of him. "Now that I really look at it, your 'Star-cophagus' looks kind of like a cruise missile."

Jon chuckled and finally stepped up. "It is. Sort of."

Steve looked at him, confused. "It's a cruise missile?"

Melanie shook her head and turned to look up into the faces of the men towering over her. "I'm heading to the flight deck to buckle in. Getting another flying lesson today. It was nice meeting you Mr. Walters."

"You too. And call me Steve," he said as she made her way to the cockpit. "How long has this been used? Why didn't we have it for this mission at the beginning?"

"Because it's the first time we've tried it in the field. It's been in testing phases for a couple of years."

"And it's working? No issues?"

"None so far as we can tell. Jessie will debrief us when this is over."

"And the cruise missile part?" Steve asked, pointing at the slots along the bottom edge of the device.

"Well, in an emergency, say, if this plane were to go down. We could drop her out a bomb bay or roll it right out the back. Short wings will pop out here," he pointed at the slots along the bottom edge, "and stabilizer fins will protrude form the back. It's got a built-in gyroscope and a cutting edge propulsion-assist system that will allow it to fly a pre-programmed path to the nearest US Military facility, broadcasting an emergency military identifier code the whole way."

"It's kind of small, does it have enough fuel?"

"Not a lot, but we hope enough. We will track the flight path and have folks ready if it runs out. Parachutes will deploy, and we'll pick it up. It's waterproof and has enough air for seventy-two hours because her metabolism is so slow while she's streaming, and we'll send the Navy or Coast Guard if it's over water."

"Wow, some safety feature." He held back sharing his thoughts about what that meant if a foreign entity ended up retrieving the pod.

"Let's hope it doesn't come to that," Jon said.

"What do you mean?"

"We haven't done any flight tests, yet. Not with a person in the pod, anyway."

Steve stood there stunned, until Eric Ramos walked up. The man held a big icepack to his ribs, and his face looked as if he'd lost a fight to a mountain gorilla.

"Holy shit, gunny," Steve said.

"Ah, just a couple of cracked ribs. I've been beat up worse," he said, gingerly lowering his frame into a free jump seat across from Jessie's sarcophagus.

"Now what do we do?" Steve asked. Jon leaned back against one of the flat gray Yukon's as Krys sat next to Eric, examining his face.

"We wait," Jon replied. "Eric advised they are headed back to KORE. It's where this all started. The big guy."

"He introduced himself as Tano," Eric said.

"Yes, Tano ordered Jessie and Eric's death, so for them, it's back to the task at hand," Jon said, locking eyes with his long-time friend. "For a little while, we thought the body they found in the cabin might be you."

Steve nodded, but said nothing. Chip Rasher filled him in on what the team had found at the burned-out cabin.

"Yeah, Jessie had other ideas about the killing us thing," Eric said, wincing as Krys poked at the swollen eye.

"They'll be scrubbing Kore's AI system to find anomalies," Krys said.

"I'm sure they've already done that, but we're a step ahead in that department," Jon said. "They won't find anything. That said, I'm sure that Jessie's existence has them totally confused."

"They know she's a combatant of some kind. There's no way around it after what she did in the cabin. Don't get me wrong, she had to do it. We were goners otherwise. That Hispanic guy? He was going to filet me and feed me my balls."

"Seriously?" Steve asked. Eric nodded.

"Do we know anything about these twins? These guys are experts," Eric said.

"Nothing. Yet. We have Mario working on it now. Running what photos the safe-house camera took of the one twin through facial recognition. If it can identify his features with the scratch marks down his face. There are still no hits on the big, blonde guy, Mr. Tano."

"I'm surprised Mario hasn't ID'd the big guy," Steve said. "That Tano guy has got to be deep." Steve thought about when Jon brought Mario Cabrisi into the fold of the Crue the day after the man had retired from the FBI. Mario maintained his friendships and still consulted for the Bureau. In exchange, the full spectrum of FBI resources was at the Crue's disposal. In this case, the FRS—Facial Recognition System. Although not *technically* legal to be used in all fifty states, the Bureau always seemed to hold up their hands in a *Who? Us?* fashion when some question as to the system being used for domestic purposes came up. Of course, the CIA used the system indiscriminately.

"Okay. It's about time to go. Krys, can you work on getting rid of the house?" Jon asked.

"Done. It's a DOD...well, *was* a DOD safehouse. I have notified them. They'll take care of it."

K-9 SamSam and his handler approached. "We're ready to raise the ramp and take off, folks. Please strap in."

Steve pet the dog, who nuzzled his leg as he buckled into the jump seat. "Did you guys find anything on the hillside?"

"Yes, sir. We did. After sweeping the area, SamSam hit on

both locations of overwatch and followed a scent down a deer trail. By that time K-9 Pancho had already located Jessie and Eric about twenty clicks away at an old cabin in the mountains."

"What happened there?" Steve asked, turning to Eric.

"I'll tell you all about it," Eric said, wincing again as Krys helped him with the safety harness. "As soon as we get airborne."

DEEPER

As she pulled into the driveway of the expansive house, Jessie couldn't believe that Tano's lair had always been less than a city block away from Robert's house. She glanced over at a sleeping Bolin and nudged his arm. "Hey Bàichī, we're here. Time to get that arm fixed." Slowly, the twin roused, looked around, and nodded.

Jessie bailed out of the driver seat, hurried around, and opened the passenger door. Bolin almost fell out of the door, the Tramadol having more of an effect that she thought it would. "How many of those did you take, brother?" She asked.

"A couple," he replied. "Three. Four, maybe." Jessie cursed in Chinese then threw her arm around Bolin and got him on his feet and helped him to the house. There were others she did not immediately know who met them at the door. She pressed hard, seeking deep into Bohai's mind, and had he not been raised speaking English, she might not have understood the names of the people who swarmed about them to assist.

"What happened?" This was the driver of Tano's vehicle. Jessie staggered as the name came forth from some deep memory chamber in Bohai's head. For some reason, when she went to speak, the man's name flowed off her tongue.

"Thank you, Peng," she said in fluent Mandarin, then switched to English. "Let's just say we underestimated the skill of our opponent."

"That girl? That little girl?"

Jessie turned to look at the man speaking—the man who'd

133

held the pistol in the SUV and almost shot her after Bolin kicked him for ogling her boobs. He stepped up to lend a hand. His name popped right into her mind. Richard Woo, or Ricky. He'd obviously overheard and couldn't contain his stupid grin.

"Did you see the muscles on that girl?" Ricky said. "Have you told Tano about this? He didn't say anything about you two getting injured."

"No." Bolin said, speaking up. "We didn't want to distract him. Besides, we won in the end."

"What a loss," Ricky said. "The things I could have done to her."

Jessie laughed and slapped her knee with overzealous intent. "You?"

With one word, Jessie crushed the man's ego, wiping the wistful smile from his face. Jessie reached out and patted him on the shoulder. "It is probably for the better, Ricky. It may not have turned out so good for you." Then she leaned in closer to whisper. "The big Mexican wanted her too, but she killed him in a matter of seconds. Stuffed a knife up his piggy fat nose." Bolin couldn't hold back the chuckle.

Ricky gasped. "That little, tiny hot girl killed Gerardo? Tano didn't tell me that, either."

"Well, he was there. Watched the whole thing," Bolin said. "Maybe he doesn't want you to know everything, did you ever think of that Bàichī?"

Ricky didn't take well to the twins teaming up on him, but he continued to assist Peng in escorting them to the kitchen. As they sat, a pretty Chinese woman, probably in her early twenties, came into the room. The girl headed immediately for Jessie and reached up to take off the shades. Jessie dodged her and saw hurt spring to the girl's face.

So Bohai has a girlfriend, she thought.

"We drove straight through. I've got to pee, and I need to

shower," Jessie snapped. "Call the doctor for Bolin. I'll be out shortly."

Dejected, the girl nodded, then assisted the other men with caring for Bolin. Jessie walked out of the kitchen and down the hall, immediately finding a small bedroom that she sensed Bohai might be using. It had a shared bathroom with a stand-up shower, and she walked through to the other room but only took one step in the doorway, looking around. Her host's senses, perhaps a thread of memory, confirmed this to be Bolin's room. She closed the door, returned to Bohai's room, and made for his dresser. She only lightly probed the drawers but found nothing other than clothes. She selected a pair of silk pants and shirt, went into the bathroom, and removed the small Glock 43 from her waistband, laying it on the sink. Slowly, she removed the sunglasses and glared at the reflection in the mirror.

"You are one damn lucky girl," she whispered, eyes glowing like hot embers in Bohai's head. She patted her pants pockets, retrieved her contact case, and quickly inserted the brown lenses. She leaned in, looking for light leaks around the edges, and hoped Robert's eye color would be close enough to her hosts. She threw her head back, squirted several drops of saline into each eye, and blinked rapidly as she stripped out of her clothes. She started the shower but stopped before getting in to examine Bohai's naked reflection. She ran her hand down the arm of his smooth, almost ecru-colored skin.

The man had muscle, but not the kind you get from lifting. This man's physique had been earned through combat. She wasn't impressed with his package. She stepped into the shower and hissed as the hot water ran over the claw mark's etched deeply into Bohai's face prior to hijacking his body. She stayed still, enduring the discomfort until the pain subsided. She left the long braid of hair tied up, managing to soap it up and squeezed it out as best she could. She lathered up a sponge and started to wash the body when the shower door pulled open.

Startled, Jessie wiped the water from her eyes. It was the girl, Mei-Lin. She stood there naked, her medium breasts and fair, milky skin setting off a wave of arousal too primal for Jessie to control. Both she and the woman looked down. So, Jessie thought, he's a grower. Mei-Lin noticed too, giggled, and stepped in. She pressed herself into Bohai's arms, not knowing it was Jessie who kissed her deeply.

"I've missed you," Mei-Lin said, looking up at Bohai's face with huge brown, oval eyes. She reached up to touch the scratch marks on Bohai's face.

"Mei-Lin," Jessie said, opening her mouth to question her, but Mei-Lin had already set to work, kissing her way down Bohai's chest until she ended up on her knees, taking his member into her mouth. Jessie didn't resist.

A quick twenty minutes later, Jessie had dressed and returned to the bathroom. Mei-Lin dressed as well, slid in behind Jessie, and wrapped her arms around Bohai's waist, watching as Jessie applied ointment to the scratches.

"I didn't know you carried a gun," she said.

Jessie stopped for only a heartbeat, glanced down at the pistol on the counter, and continued with her medicinal application.

"Normally, I do not. But it's small and handy. Good to have when you might need one." Mei-Lin nodded, smiled at their reflections, then left the room. Jessie headed out right behind Mei-Lin, with the intention of collecting her bags and the cooler. She paused at the kitchen door. The doctor had arrived, and everyone appeared to be focused on setting Bolin's arm. She moved off until a voice stopped her.

"Long shower."

Jessie froze, took a half-step back and met the eyes of the

twin brother. He grinned from ear to ear. Jessie smiled back and shrugged, hands up in defeat. "What can I say?"

"Where you going?" Bolin's face turned serious.

"To the truck. I want to snoop through the girl's bags, see what I can find." Bolin nodded, saying nothing more.

Five minutes later, she re-entered the kitchen and set her bag and the backpack on the center island and the cooler on the kitchen counter. Mei-Lin stood at the stove, brewing what smelled like tea, and reached for the cooler.

"Don't open that," Jessie snapped, a little more harshly than she intended. Something about Mei-Lin suggested the girl might be more of a result of this group's criminal enterprising, than part of it.

"Why? What's in it."

"A pair of hands," Jessie said, truthfully. "I'm not kidding. If you don't believe me, go ahead and look." Mei-Lin visibly shuddered, pulled her hand away, and went back to work on the tea. A moment later, the doctor, whose name Jessie couldn't pry from Bohai's mind, and the other men re-entered the kitchen.

"He's resting now and will be fine. It's a clean fracture but will still take a few weeks to heal as long as he doesn't injure it again. In the meantime, I have set his arm in a cast reinforced with a few bars of steel, in case he needs to fight. His request."

"I'm surprised he didn't ask you to put one on his other arm," Jessie said.

"He did. I polity declined. I only had a few pieces with me."

Everyone chuckled as the men bowed to each other in preparation for the doctor's departure. Tano's driver, Peng, handed the doctor a fairly thick envelope and ushered the man out the side door to his car. As the outside door closed, Tano entered the room. Jessie glanced at the man, then returned to the task of sorting through her clothes, acting like she was looking closely at the contents therein.

Tano walked over and stood beside her. "Find anything?"

"Nothing suspect," Jessie said, tossing Laina Main's wallet, a passport with stamps from visits to France and Italy, and the basic items one would find in a woman's bag. Tano picked up the passport, dropped it in his pocket, and flipped through the other identification.

"I already know this information," he said. "She's lying. A college kid with no history of professional training does not fight like that."

Jessie reached over and picked up the wallet. "Did you see her MMA card? From Las Vegas? She has been fighting for…" she opened the wallet and looked at the date, "about ten years. She fights like she kept up with it. Like she enjoyed it."

Tano shook his head. "I don't think so."

"Well," Jessie continued, "her forms were many. What I observed was most definitely mixed-martial arts. She had the heart of a tiger." Tano cocked his head to the side and glared at her.

"I'm surprised at your comment, Bohai, being the seasoned fighter that you are. You know full well that MMA doesn't typically use the Kung-fu lotus stance or teach weapons. She has expertise in handling knives."

"And Escrima-sticks. I think that's the form she used to break Bolin's arm."

"About that," Tano said, turning to look at Bohai. "Gerardo, I can understand, but you two? Her getting even a strike on the Great Sòng twins makes no sense. I should have stayed."

Jessie bowed. "I'm sorry to disappoint. There is no excuse. Even with how she handled Gerardo, we felt she would be no problem. We obviously underestimated her," she said.

"Hence why I am certain she was lying." Tano moved to the cooler and Jessie froze. Anyone would be able to tell that the two hands contained therein were the hands from one very large man. She held her breath. Tano opened the cooler and frowned as he glanced at the gruesome bag, but he did not touch it. He closed the lid and headed out the kitchen, stopping at the entryway. "Call someone to come and get that. Process them for prints and have them email me their findings."

"Shì de xiānshēng. Mǎshàng," Jessie said, bowing deeply. *Yes, sir. Right away.* The words flowed from her lips with confidence. When in a host, if she didn't think about it too hard, the correct words usually came easily from the host's mind, then off the tongue. Tano nodded and left the room but stopped again.

"Do more research on her. Track down that MMA card, and do a little more digging. I'm heading over to Kore's.

"Shì de xiānshēng," Jessie said, bowing once more. She repacked her bag and felt her pants pockets for the item she had pocketed a minute before Tano walked in. The single most important thing Steve had known to add to her bag: the data transfer module she had used to copy the A.I. program from the server. Jessie smiled.

Relying on another thread of memory pressed from Bohai's mind, she vaulted the stairs two at a time and quickly found the computer room. Several monitors, servers, and other instruments filled the room. She sat down, booted up the main drive, and gasped when the large monitors came to life. There, in front of her, were live videos of Robert's entire house.

"No wonder," she hissed, then cringed, knowing the things Tano had witnessed. And not just the uninhibited sex. Jessie looked over her shoulder while typing in keystrokes that brought up a simple website titled WAR GAMES FAN PAGE. The site memorialized the movie "War Games" and had pages of documentaries and video clips. She moved to the correct page and clicked on the third video which in turn asked for a password.

She glanced at one of the monitors showing the camera's views from the house she now sat in. Tano's image entered the garage and sat in a car. Once the SUV backed down the driveway, she turned back to the computer.

Even Jessie had to concentrate to input the twenty-one-character passcode. She typed one letter incorrectly. The page warned, "You have two more attempts before lock out." She slowed down, concentrated, and got the second entry right.

The hidden portal only had one purpose. Messaging. The messages would only remain in the system as long as the user stayed logged in. She instant-messaged Crue headquarters, providing her status, location, and request for a Chinese doctor, fluent in the language, to come retrieve the hands. Tano didn't specify a particular doctor, so she took the gamble. She also requested the surveillance van to be set up, prepared to download another batch of information, as soon as possible. The clock ticked. Less than eleven days remained before the flight trials of the X-47A at White Sands. As she exited out of the program, an automatic IP wipe went into motion, cleaning any log of accessing the site. No one, not even the CIA or the Chinese, could trace her contact.

Jessie then searched for information into her made up persona, Laina Main. She had used programs specifically designed to track people down by tapping into every social media platform in existence. Facebook, Instagram, Reddit, and the most dangerous of all: Snapchat. As these were legitimate systems frequently used by the Crue's analysts, they had seeded just the right amount of activity for Laina Main. She copied the information to a folder on the desktop and nodded. More than enough information to frustrate the hell out of that bloodhound Tano.

Jessie thought about her situation. Now that she had slipped into her new role, an opportunity existed she could not, would not, ignore. Time was short, and she had a lot to learn about Tano, although she knew The Benefactors were behind Kore's financing. She knew little else about the group. When she was done with him, Tano would provide every piece of intel she needed to complete the puzzle.

16

TEST

Tano arrived at Kore's offices to find him, and the Config Manager, Maria, in the computer room working. This time. As he entered the door, he didn't miss the sideways look Robert shot his way.

"Don't look at me like that, Robert," he said. "You brought this on yourself." Robert acted like he didn't hear, and Tano caught Maria looking anywhere but at him. "Where are we at with the diagnostic?"

Robert stood up. "We've run every test we have, and some the DOD doesn't know we have, on the system. I'm telling you, Tano. There are no bugs, no issues, no problems."

"I see." Tano folded his arms and paced the large, chilly room.

"Maria, can you give us a moment, please?" Without a word or acknowledgment, Maria got up and left the room. Tano watched her move to the side of the X47, pretending to work on a digital panel fastened to the drone's fuselage. "Is your lover mad at you?"

"No," Robert said, "but she would be if we talked about Laina. What did you find out?"

"Still nothing, other than she was an excellent fighter."

Robert's brow furrowed, "What do you mean 'was'. Where is she? What happened?"

Tano spun on Robert and shoved a large finger into his chest and hissed. "This was your doing, Robert. Your frivolous distractions have got to stop. We are too close to success to have your indiscretions jeopardize our project!"

Robert leaned into the bigger man's finger and glared into his eyes. "You haven't answered my question, tough guy."

"Yes, I have. Miss Main is no longer a concern. She won't be distracting you again."

"You killed her."

"No, I did not. But if you don't get your collective act together, we can arrange something special for her." A small thread of truth laced through Tano's comment, and so he felt comfortable stretching it. He did not, after all, kill the girl. The twins did. Yet telling the lie unsettled him. He had never felt he needed to lie about anything he did, but regarding the Main woman, he felt a twinge of regret. He had missed something critical about the woman. He felt it in his gut. He had erred on his decision to have her killed and should have kept her for more thorough interrogation. He knew that now. He knew it was too late. He also thought about how she lay in Robert's bed, erotic and seductive, an intriguing…

"That won't be necessary," Robert said, sounding somewhat deflated. "I'm telling you, Tano. Whatever you think she might have done, did not happen. The code is in my head, and you are the only other person who has it. You cannot change it without me, nor can I change it without you."

Tano studied Robert for a long moment, then resumed his pacing of the computer room. After a few minutes, he waved for Maria to return. Once inside, she crept up next to Robert, both geniuses looking like school children about to be scolded. Tano paced and studied them both. The two looked at each other, then back at Tano.

Tano suddenly stopped and faced them. "I want to see it fly," he said.

"You want to see…the drone fly?" Robert asked. Maria slowly shook her head.

"Yes. I want to see it work. I want to see the A.I. system in action. Run the same program it's going to perform at White Sands. In real time, right now. Fuel up the drone and take it out onto the field and fly it."

"But..."

"Now. I have not reported back to The Benefactors about any of what I have learned." He paused a moment to let that revelation sink in. "Mostly because I cannot explain what I have seen. Should we have an issue, now is the time to discover it. The demonstration flight for DOD is a little over a week away. If there are any technical issues, we can work them out. If we have been hacked, and our system corrupted, we need to know now. Yes?"

"I'm telling you, Tano. The program has not been hacked. Or corrupted. It's clean."

"Look." Tano's face turned beet-red, the first time Robert had ever seen the man about to lose his cool. "My reputation is also riding on this, and my gut instincts have never, ever been wrong. Do you want to wait until D-Day to find out the worst? Or find out now?"

"I agree," Robert said, cutting of Maria's 'me too' with, "But it's not our drone. We need permission from the DOD to fly it."

"Then get it."

"They'll want to know why."

Tano's face burned darker, making his hair look like a white-hot flame. "Robert, are you not a salesman? Of course, you are. Convince them that it is necessary as a proper salesman would do. That the reputation of your company requires our own pre-demo, demo."

"When would you like..."

"Now, Robert. Right now. Do you understand? Get the fucking thing into the air." Tano stormed out of the room, walked over to the drone, and ran his hands along the smooth, grey skin. He took several deep breaths, cursing himself for losing his temper. For allowing himself to become impatient. The Benefactors had not asked for a report. They were not pressuring him for answers regarding his suspicions. He pulled out his encrypted cellphone and called Bohai, who answered on the first ring.

"How is the research going on the girl?"

"I will know more, or less, in a matter of hours. A forensic pathologist recommended by Uncle Chen is on his way to pick up the hands."

Chen. That relationship alone had been reason enough to have the twins working with him. "Very good. Keep working on it. I'll be here another few hours."

"Shì de xiānshēng!" Bohai said, and Tano hung up the phone.

He turned to find Maria fidgeting with the waist of her skit, a plaid, mid-knee fabric. He only just realized that she had a full sleeve tattoo, a Japanese koi scene inked in brilliant colors on her left arm. Her white blouse was sleeveless, the cleavage of her large breasts pronounced through strategic buttoning. She reminded him of a 50's pin-up model. A flash of desire ran through him. He saw the allure of such a beautiful woman and understood why Robert had been attracted to the Main woman with equal fervor. Both were very different. Both very desirable. Tano had to admit, Robert had great taste in women. Mei-Lin, too. *Such a beauty.*

Suddenly annoyed at his weakness, he bit the inside of his lip until he tasted blood. Penance for letting his mind stray to such a low, primal level. Tano felt proud that he had risen above the weaknesses of normal men. There were plenty of beautiful oriental women at the service of Chen who could assist Tano in releasing any pent-up frustrations, but he had not desired the company of a woman for years.

I am better than what I have displayed, he thought. He had also thought that some Catholic priests could learn lessons from him on how to be truly celibate. But not today. He vowed to work out his frustration through sparring with the twins tomorrow.

But first, the flight test.

Two hours later, the aircraft tug slowly pulled the sleek drone from the hangar bay, parking it next to a fuel truck and an APU, or Auxiliary Power Unit, on standby next to the aircraft in case the onboard systems failed to start the engine.

After fueling, Tano walked over to Robert and Maria who stood behind a small, waist high rolling computer console. Tano kept looking over his shoulder suspiciously. Robert looked around too, raised an eyebrow, and smiled. It seemed the entirety of Moffett field employees got word of the impending test flight and were all out to watch the unusual combat drone fly around. Certainly, all KORE employees were out, lining up alongside the hangar bay.

Robert watched as Tano sized his employees up. *Enough is enough.* He walked up to Tano, gently took him by the elbow, and guided him a short distance away from Maria. Once he stopped, the men faced each other. "They've worked on this project for six years, Tano. They are excited about this project. You'd be proud of the level of professionalism…"

"Spare me the accolades, Robert. I know why they are out here."

Robert narrowed his own eyes and leaned closer to the taller man. "If they knew about *you,* I expect most, if not all of them, would walk off the job, and probably stone me to death for being a traitor." Robert groaned and stumbled forward into Tano, who grabbed Robert by the arms and stood him up straight. A small droplet of blood formed on Robert's upper lip.

"Memories, I take it?" Tano asked.

"I don't know what fucking memory, but it's making me feel guiltier by the day."

"Are we going to have a loyalty problem, Robert?" Tano asked, narrowing his eyes. Robert thought he might be able to take the big man in a fight. Maybe, but Tano carried a dangerous air of confidence about him, and he knew Tano practiced several martial arts. Robert saw Tano tense up, as if preparing to deliver a killing blow depending on his answer.

Robert glanced back at Maria. "No, Tano, no issues. The success of this mission means more to me than just the money. You know that. You know what those fuckers did to my father."

Tano's eyes locked with Robert's for a long moment. "Your commitment to the cause, our mutual cause, is commendable, Robert. Your employees won't learn of the truth from me," Tano said. "Let's get on with the test."

———

THEY WALKED BACK TO MARIA, WHO HANDED TANO A FOLDER. Without any sarcasm in her voice, she said, "You probably won't understand what is in that folder, save for the bullet points used to simplify what you're going to see over the next hour. The A.I. will ask what test we'd like to run, and we'll tell it. The A.I. will take it from there, and then report on any anomalies."

Tano nodded. "This is the same demonstration it's going to perform at White Sands?"

"Yes," Maria said, "without the live weapons, of course."

Tano nodded again, understanding the tight controls necessary for live weapons testing, but he still desired to see them deployed by the A.I. system. It was one piece of the puzzle that would have gone unchecked, otherwise, and would leave a question in his mind about what might have or might not have been hacked.

As if reading his mind, Maria added, "The drone will launch

simulated weapons, and as we've planned for there to be no weapons malfunctions, everything will be identical. Except, no boom."

"Well, let's go, then."

Maria typed in a command. "And away she goes."

A soft 'whoosh' from the drone's internal APU had been quickly followed up by the starting of its primary turbo-fan engine. Small LED lights embedded in the plane's fuselage started blinking, while the slats and aerolons moved rapidly up and down, in and out, as a pilot would test on a regular military jet prior to take off. Then the plane taxied down the runway, got into position, and stopped.

"It's contacting the air control tower for permission to take off," Maria said.

"Doesn't it have a voice, so we can hear its communications?"

Maria chuckled. "No, sir. Not yet. A voice like Siri's or Alexa's would be grand, but I'm afraid that at this stage, we've concentrated on combat functionality. Not voices."

Tano raised an eyebrow. "How will it be performing weapons simulations?"

Robert chimed in. "See those circles way out there? On the ground?" Tano nodded. "Their positions have been verified by GPS, designated as hostile targets, and the A.I. has been directed to use Che-dan's onboard laser targeting to confirm target acquisition, simulated weapons launch and of course, target destruction."

"Che-dan?" Tano asked.

"Yes," Maria said. "Although Northrup/Grumman calls the drone Pegasus, this is an entirely different machine now. The employees came up with a new name. Che-dan means *hawk* in Lakota, a Native American language. The consensus was that although Robert designed the brain in the plane, the name KAGI, or Kore Advanced General Intelligence, didn't represent the whole package and sounded a bit too egocentric." She looked toward the man, who appeared about to sick up. "This project is more than just a computer system to them, it's six years of their lives. The employees used Che-dan as a call sign, and the US Navy liked it, so it stuck."

"How endearing," Tano said, rolling his eyes.

As the plane sped down the runway, and just as the rear wheels lifted off the tarmac, Che-dan shot into an almost vertical climb above the airfield. The KORE staff hooted, hollered, and applauded at the display.

"None of them have actually seen this plane perform, most weren't here when it arrived for refit," Robert said. Tano ignored him and watched. The plane then went into a multiple, hi-gravity, or G-Force, cork-screw maneuver, then barrel rolled out of it into level flight before heading off over the Pacific Ocean.

"Those look like risky maneuvers. Was that programed in? To show off for the DOD?"

"Not at all," Robert said. "The system came up with that take off maneuver on its own. As you can imagine, if a human were in the cockpit, if there was actually a cockpit, he'd be dead at the G's that plane just pulled. The A.I. is actually putting the airframe through its own reliability tests. It's doing what it wants, to a point." Tano's eyebrows rose in surprise. Robert held up a hand, intercepting the obvious next question. "Trust me, we've already gone over the implications. The bottom line is, if this aircraft is going to be used as an autonomous combat system, it needs to be able to make viable decisions. KAGI, or Che-dan can make viable decisions. It learns as it goes."

"You know, this sounds like an old movie from the eighties I saw in my youth, where machines took over the world," Tano said.

Robert chuckled. "Yeah, well, that's the trick, right? Giving the A.I. enough room to grow but ensuring a sort of programmed code of ethics is employed. Kinda like Asimov's I-Robot rules, but more realistically modified."

"As in Issac Asimov? The science fiction author?"

"Yes. Just because it's science fiction, doesn't mean it lacks the framework of sound advice. But the problem with A.I. is, how do we program ethics? Those rules can be subjective depending on whose writing them. If you had to compare fiction to reality, the concerns are more akin to Skynet from the Terminator movies. That's what you were talking about, right? Those types of issues are more realistic. Let's be honest, any way we look at it, this thing will be capable of causing harm to humans. Che-dan isn't there yet, but we're getting closer and closer to having an A.I. system be part of our real world. We just need to ensure they never turn on their makers. It's a conundrum, I know. An ethical Rubik's cube. But it's also kind of too late. We are on the path to fully Autonomous A.I. For this project, we adopted the United Nations five core principals, and your bosses seemed to be okay with that." Robert pointed up at the aircraft as it passed. "Che-dan is not science fiction. It's science fact."

Tano acknowledged that Robert conveyed his little diatribe with passion. He felt certain that Robert's loyalty and commitment to the cause would continue without question.

Tano, Robert, and Maria watched, along with the hundreds of others as the plane strafed, targeted, and zoomed around the airfield at ridiculous speeds. Doing aerial maneuvers that no human could endure. Tano stood speechless. The plane and the performance could be described as nothing less than beautiful.

Surely, The Benefactors would be pleased.

17

AND DEEPER

As Jessie sat in front of Tano's elaborate computer surveillance and control center, she booted up the system and started cycling through the first set of cameras. She froze in mid-switch, sitting up straight and gasping as a hot flash of power ripped through her host's body. Her senses felt as if they had finally awakened. Her focus and energy were suddenly razor sharp. She didn't feel the lag she normally experienced while slip-streaming.

"The Chamber," she whispered.

The hum of energy in her ears confirmed it—her teammates had hooked her up. She smiled, realizing this had been the first real-world use of the crazy contraption she, David West, and some vetted kids from MIT/DARPA had created.

Well, she thought, *they aren't all kids.*

With the Chamber, it didn't matter where her body might be laying. She could now stream from just about anywhere in the world, with virtually zero lag time. As energizing as it felt, she had to get back to the task at hand. She would report to the others on the Chamber's effects, later.

If there is a later.

As she flipped through the cameras, one view caught her attention. An image of Robert Kore, Tano, and Maria all standing out at the tarmac at Moffett Field, surrounding some console that appeared to be a podium with computer screen mounted to it. She wriggled the toggle switch attached to the keyboard, checking to see if the camera might be a moveable, pan-tilt-zoom set up. It was. The camera swiveled around until the lens settled on the sleek, black X47-A taxiing down the runway.

"Holy shit," she whispered.

She took a deep breath and immediately returned to work on making contact with The Crue. Already in the "War Games" fan page, she clicked on the proper wiki link, found the Crue's hidden site, and logged in. Using the encrypted messaging tool she reached out. Juanita Johnson, the Crue's in-house, former CIA analyst responded immediately.

WALKER: Echo-Whisky-Alpha, 2-2-Zulu
  JJ: Hey stranger, how you holding up?
  WALKER: Fine. Blk bandit on move.
  JJ: Copy, monitoring +3

Jessie nodded. She understood the plus three to mean they had known about this for over three hours and were monitoring the situation. Jessie's brow furrowed. Robert would have had to get flight test permissions from General Evans directly. A week out from the flight tests? It had to be related to her infiltration.

WALKER: Copy. ETA on doc?
  JJ: Should be there soon, any minute.
  WALKER: Van?
  JJ: On point. Activate hub. STBY for relay.
  WALKER: Tight timing. Confirm?
  JJ: Start auto-dump now, abort if necessary. Sys will retain all data
  WALKER: Surprise package coming your way

JJ: Home will sort.
WALKER: Copy
JJ: Extract?
WALKER: Negative. Still training on new game
JJ: Copy. STBY.

A LONG PAUSE ENSUED. JESSIE KNEW THIS MEANT JUANITA HAD NO doubt dialed up Jon. She also knew that Jon wouldn't like it.

JJ: No Joy. Per Air Boss
   WALKER: No choice. Opportunity. Thinking.
   JJ: Dangerous past-time. Stby
Jessie endured an even longer pause when Juanita finally texted back:
   JJ: Copy. W-6
   WALKER: Thanks for the Red-bull
   JJ: No problem, anytime. O and O.

THE SCREEN WENT BLANK. IF ON SITE FOR MORE THAN TWO minutes, the window to access the hidden site would slam shut. The program jerked Jessie's screen back to a War Game's video clip, showing the WOPR computer going through it's launch solutions. Game over. Crue programmers worked with the National Security Administrations encrypted program called Fishbowl to develop an overlay, or blanket, designed to mask the signal of the messaging center. Anyone monitoring this system would see that Bohai had searched for and accessed the War Game's fan site and video. Nothing more.

Seeing that the X47 had only just started what she guessed might be a test run, she estimated she would have at least three hours before Tano returned. Jessie acted on Juanita's last transmission of W-6, or "Watch your six"– military slang used as a reminder to stay vigilant about looking over one's shoulder. She stepped to the door and looked around. Seeing or hearing no one, she closed the door. It had no lock from the inside, which meant anyone in the house could enter the room.

Gotta make this quick.

She lowered herself to the floor and flipped onto her back, scooting up to the rear racks of the computer server mounted underneath the workstation. As she searched for a suitable SATA port, she thought about how refreshed she felt. It wasn't as if she had more energy, but more like a shortened lag time between her physical brain and controlling her host the moment the Crue plugged her into The Chamber. Hence the term, Red Bull.

She found a free port, plugged in the data transmitter, and activated it. The red LED stayed solid for only a moment before flashing green. Data transfer in progress. The team had to be *really* close indeed in order to secure such a quick connection. As Jessie extricated herself and brushed her clothes flat, the doorbell rang. She got up, left the room, and headed down the stairs past her current living quarters. Movement from her peripheral vision caught her attention and she stopped. Taking two slow steps back, she peered in through the cracked bedroom door of Bolin's room and raised an eyebrow.

Mei-Lin sat astride Bolin's lap, a silk robe half draped over her shoulder, exposing one breast. Bolin's hands were on her waist, guiding the girl's rhythm as she moved up and down. Up and down. A strange flash of what Jessie could only describe as jealousy zipped through her quickly and left her with a strange feeling of confusion. As Jessie moved forward, she caught Mei-Lin's eye. The girl looked at Jessie, a forlorn smile rising to the edge of her lips as she turned her gaze back to the task at hand and rode faster. She would ask the woman about it later. In the meantime, she had hands to deliver.

Jessie moved out of the hallway and into the kitchen, where an Asian man she did not know stood next to the sink, talking to Peng and Ricky in Mandarin. Chinese was a difficult language to learn if you didn't know it from infancy, but when Jessie relaxed the grip on her host's consciousness, she could understand and speak enough to get by in most any language. However, she found thinking in foreign tongues to be impossible.

"Bohai," Peng said, "this is Doctor Ng. He said Mr. Chen sent him for the items."

Dr. Ng bowed low, raised up with a smile and said, "Air boss sends his best. He asked me to find out how his two best champions are holding up?"

Air Boss. Jon's OP name.

"Fine. No problems we can't handle," Jessie said and handed him the cooler containing Gerardo's hands. "We need full identification on these two as quickly as possible."

"Understood," Ng said, half bowing. "We will send the results as soon as test results come up." The man bowed again and exited the house.

Jessie watched the man leave and watched the other two men watch him leave until they turned and glared at Jessie, whom they thought was Bohai, like he owed them money.

"What?" Jessie snapped, causing both men to flinch.

"What's next?" Peng asked.

"We wait for Tano to return," she said. "In the meantime, I'm going to take a nap."

The two men looked at one another, shrugged, then set off to do what other tasks Tano had laid out for them.

Only a little over a week remained until the flight tests. Not much time for her to get the training she needed with the new simulator back home. She passed Bohai's room, paused, and although she wasn't mentally tired at all, she felt the pains and aches of a long two days catch up to his body. She turned into the room, closed the door and lay down.

For Jessie, her version of sleep came through an even deeper state of meditation, bringing her body down to an almost lifeless state, her mind empty of all thought and distraction. Through time, she had learned that when a host's body needed sleep, she was able to maintain the link with much less energy expenditure. When developing The Chamber, one of the MIT kids on the project came up with the perfect analogy.

"You're like a spider," she had said. "You spin a thin, strong strand of power, like spider's silk, to maintain the link with your host."

Jessie smiled at the memory, then found her deep place.

Movement in the room set off an invisible perimeter tripwire embedded into Bohai's psyche. Jessie brought herself forth, careful not to move, but accessed her host's other senses. She heard nothing, but smelled…

Jessie shot up from the bed, snatched the intruder by the neck, and at hearing the feminine yelp of surprise, eased her grip and spun Mei-Lin around to face her.

"What are you doing?" Jessie snapped.

"I'm, I'm sorry to disturb you. I thought you might like some company."

The girl untied her robe, allowing the silk fabric to slide from her shoulders onto the floor. She moved in closer to Jessie and sat on the edge of the bed. "Do you not want me?"

"I…I don't understand," Jessie said. Because she didn't. She had to be careful how she broached the subject of Mei-Lin bedding the twins. Jessie propped her head up on a pillow and looked the woman in the eyes. "Put on your robe. I wish to talk." Mei-Lin obeyed, slowly. "Tell me about how you ended up here?"

The girl scrunched her face. "I am not sure what you mean?"

"Why are you here. In this house?" Mei-Lin's eyes moved

back and forth searching the face of whom she thought to be Bohai, suspicion drawn on her face. "What brought you to be here?" Jessie said, pressing to keep the girl thinking about something other than Bohai acting strange.

"You already know my story. Why do you wish to insult me by having me tell it? Are you boasting?"

Now Jessie felt thoroughly confused. "I am just trying to understand."

The girl leaned in close, glanced quickly over her shoulder as if expecting someone to walk through Bohai's door, and said, "Who are you?"

"I'm not sure what…"

"Who are you?" Mei-Lin said, glaring into Bohai's eyes, her body trembling. "You know why I am here. You should. Are you saying you have forgotten when you and your brother kidnapped me from my home six years ago, and that I have been serving the Hōn ever since? Payment for my father's indiscretions when he worked as Mr. Chen's bookkeeper. Money came up missing. Who are you?" Tears rolled down her cheeks. She stood up and pointed at Jessie. "You and your brother indoctrinated me into my services. Don't you remember? I remember. I was fourteen years old at the time. *Uncle* Chen placed me with his Geisha mistress, who taught me how to be eye candy for men. *You* and your brother showed me the ways of being a whore." Mei-Lin's body shook. Thoroughly humiliated, she collapsed to her knees. Jessie rushed to her side and pulled her chin up so their eyes could meet.

"You are here for me, us, then. Why?"

"You are acting so strange. You know these answers. Why are you doing this to me? Have I done something wrong? Have I not pleased you?"

"Yes, you please me. I wish to know so that I may understand better what it is that I have contributed to. It is important.

157

Please do as I ask, and answer." She helped the girl to her feet and helped her to the edge of the bed. "Tell me."

"Uncle Chen…"

"He's not really your uncle, then?"

"No, it is what we Geisha call our male Benefactors. Uncles."

The Benefactors. Jessie knew from CIA Financial division this was where Kore's money came from as well. She also knew that the Geisha had derived from Chinese culture and was no longer practiced in China, although Geisha practices thrived in Japan.

"Continue."

"Uncle Chen sent me to keep you two from getting distracted. You both have excessive…appetites. Bolin more so than you. Perhaps you are gentler because you come from a Kung-fu background. I do not know. But I am here to help keep your mind on the task at hand."

"And what task is that?"

"I do not know. If you two are sent somewhere, then it is well known someone is going to disappear or be hurt. Death follows you both."

"What do you know about Tano? Be truthful."

Mei Lin stared into Jessie's face for a long moment before speaking, then averted her eyes as she answered. "Tano is the most focused man I have ever met. He…"

"Do you serve him, as you serve my brother and I?" Jessie asked.

Mei-Lin's face looked thoughtful. "I offered once, but he rejected me. It hurt my feelings, however, Mother, my Geisha mother, told me Tano did not partake of the company of women. Or boys. So, no. He is driven for reasons beyond my understanding. And he's dangerous. Very strong. A great, great fighter. Even you cannot best him."

"Tell me…"

"No. I will tell you no more. Beat me if you wish, but I will say no more." Jessie moved to speak until Mei-Lin pressed her fingers gently against Jessie's lips. "You will answer my question now, or I will go to Tano."

"Do not threaten me, girl. You will be in over your head."

"Do not think that I am scared of you, or Tano, or Chen, or any other of the countless men who have lavished me with gifts or treated me like a piece of meat. I don't care. Death and I have made our peace. Answer my questions or kill me now and explain to Tano why."

Jessie thought about this a long moment. She had screwed up. Again. She should never have allowed herself to be remotely inquisitive as to why the beautiful girl would be fucking him in the shower one minute and riding the twin brother the next. No spy worth their salt would give a shit. But something else tugged at Jessie because *she* was no ordinary, run of the mill spy.

"Answer one other question, then I will answer yours." Mei-Lin nodded. "If you could escape, start fresh right now, live your own life, would you do it? Do you have the means to do it?"

Mei-Lin's eyes brightened. "Yes, I have the means to do it. No, I would not." Jessie knew the answer before Mei-Lin spoke the works. "They would kill my parents, and I would live for the sexual pleasure of dogs and pigs before I carried the weight of my shame for getting my parents killed. My father made mistakes. I would not have him pay for them twice."

Jessie nodded and then took a deep breath. "Things are going to turn to shit very fast around here," she said. "I have changed my mind about certain..." she thought for the right word in Chinese, "fāngmiàn, *aspects*, of my own service that need to change. Bolin does not know. He is too..."

"Hard," Mei-Lin finished. "Probably because of growing up fighting in the streets of Hong Kong. You were always gentler. But you are still hiding something. I sense it. Do you want to be like Tano? Is that it?"

"No. Not at all. I have my own reasons. Just keep your head down when the blades start swinging."

"I can do that. Will you take me with you when you go?"

Jessie had thought about finding a way to help the girl but felt certain her parents would end up as casualties no matter what if she were to be involved.

"There are other things you do not know about me," she said, carefully. "Things I will be willing to tell you if we both get through this and you earn my trust in what I have shared already. I'm prepared to die as well, but I have no intention to."

"And your brother?"

"He is my brother. But he is his own man. He will make his choice when the time comes."

Mei-Lin nodded, stood up, and tied the robe around her waist. "When Tano arrived, I told him you were both sleeping, and…"

"What?" Jessie jumped to her feet and looked at the time: 7 p.m. *Stupid, stupid stupid.* "Where is he?"

"He's upstairs, on the computer, I think."

"Remember our conversation…"

"Trust is earned. It goes both ways, Bohai. Let's see what road that leads us down." Mei-Lin turned to leave, but Jessie lightly grabbed her by the arm and spun her around to look into her eyes. Mei-Lin slowly lifted herself up on her tiptoes and softly kissed Jessie on the lips.

Too late now, she thought, hoping her instincts about the girl were right and that wasn't the kiss of death. Mei-Lin walked toward the kitchen and Jessie moved to the shared bathroom, peaking through the door of Bolin's room. The twin brother lay there, fast asleep. She took a deep breath, left the room, and climbed the stairs. Upon entry to the surveillance room, she faced Tano's back. On the desk, next to him, lay her SATA Transmitter.

18

SACRIFICE

"I'll be with you in a moment," Tano said, his voice even and calm.

Jessie looked at the drive sitting next to the man and fought the urge to ask, *what's that?* knowing the question would be the death of her. She took a steady breath, resigned to let this play out. The complex device looked simple to the untrained eye, and she felt certain he would probably task Bohai or one of the others to find out. She drifted off as her brain went into high gear, processing possible scenarios to come when Tano spoke, startling her.

"Get your brother and the others together. I'd like to have a meeting. In the Dojo. Ten minutes please."

"Shì de xiānshēng," Jessie said. *Yes, sir.*

She turned to leave, feeling Tano's eyes on her, and continued on at a steady pace.

Minutes later, Mei-Lin, Peng, Ricky, Bolin, Jessie, and even the two older housekeepers waited in the Dojo.

"What's this about?" Peng asked.

"Beats me. Tano's never called a group meeting before," Ricky added.

Mei-Lin and the two old housekeepers just stood there, silent, but visibly terrified.

Bolin leaned up against the back wall, saying nothing.

"I'll go and alert him that we are all here," Jessie said and turned toward the red-lacquered doors when it opened.

Tano strode in, dressed in a black Japanese Hakama and

Kegogi, the traditional uniform for practitioners of Japanese Kenjutsu, the art of the sword. He bowed reverently in the Japanese style, entered the room, and casually walked to the weapons rack, where he collected a sheathed Japanese katana and slid it through the belt.

"Everyone. Grab a mat and sit. Please," he said. With one hand on the hilt of the sword, he motioned with his free hand. "Spread yourselves out in a semi-circle, two arms' lengths apart in front of me." Tano lowered himself to his knees onto the raw wooden floor, a look of utter calm on his face as the others collected thin bamboo mats and moved toward him.

"Move closer, please."

Tension filled the room. Jessie decided to sit on the bare floor and took a position at the end of the semi-circle to Tano's left, whereas Bolin, taking her lead, sat on the other end to his right with a sour look on his face—possibly registering that he sat in the more vulnerable position between the two of them.

Once seated, the two old housekeepers and Mei-Lin knelt on their mats, heads bowed, eyes to the floor in subservience. Ricky and Peng took to the mats as well, but with an air of dejection. Tano's fingertips left his lap and pressed into the wood at the sides of his legs, lifting his weight up and off the floor, he spun his body slightly so that he faced Bohai first. Jessie locked eyes with Tano as he apparently measured her for some sign of stress.

He then performed the same ritual with his fingertips, and turned to face the old man, whose eyes were fixed on an invisible point of the floor in front of him.

"Look at me, Quon." The old man flinched at the sound of his name, as if jerked from some sort of trance, and slowly, inexorably, his eyes rose to meet Tano's. The woman next to the old man began to visibly shake, as no doubt Tano intended.

Ricky shifted on his knees, letting out an exasperated breath and spoke up, "What's this about, Tano?" He spoke in English. "Who the hell do you think you are? Why are you…"

Tano pounced. His foot shot out in front of him and stomped into the floor, and as fast as a lightning strike, Tano whipped out the katana, it's gleaming blade blurring through the air, and re-inserted it back into the scabbard before Ricky could utter another word. Shocked, everyone looked toward Ricky's wide-eyed face as slowly, his head rolled off his shoulders onto the floor.

Bolin jumped to his feet and backed up. "Tano! What is the meaning of this?"

Jessie followed and added, "Was that necessary?"

The old man, woman, and Mei-Lin returned their gaze to the floor, their bodies vibrating with fear.

Peng, his mouth open and working as if trying to say something, thought the better of it, snapping his jaws shut, but did not move.

"Sit, or everyone in this room dies."

Jessie looked across the room at Bolin, who shrugged, anger written on his face. Jessie shrugged too, then slowly dropped to her knees.

"Surely, Tano," she said, ready to roll backwards at his next strike, "you can share with us why you are doing this?"

"Sit!"

Everyone flinched at Tano's outburst, as if he had never yelled before in his life. Ricky's body slowly leaned off to the right and struck the wood floor with a thud, the ichor flowing freely from the stump of what used to be the man's neck. Jessie watched as the red viscous puddle flowed up against the leg of the old woman. She shuddered but held firm and did not move.

"Tano. I am not going to just sit here and let you kill me," Bolin said, holding his cast in front of his chest. "So, unless you wish to justify your actions, then we will fight." He looked toward Jessie, who nodded, preparing to make a mad dash for the weapons rack behind the group.

But Tano said nothing. His demeanor held no anger or tension. He looked ready to die. As the twins returned to kneeling positions, he reached into his Gi and removed the data transmitter. He leaned forward and laid the item on the floor in front of him.

"This is the reason I have called us together. And perhaps I was hasty in relieving Ricky's body of his head, but this is not the work of one person."

"What is it?" Bolin asked.

"Where did you…"

"Enough," Tano said, quietly cutting off Peng's question. "One or more of you know exactly what this is. Its purpose. Where I located it because one of *you* put it there." His gaze wandered Jessie's way, then scanned each face of the others as he continued. "I'll kill each and every one of you unless the person responsible for this steps up. I have been betrayed, and, therefore, you have betrayed The Benefactors. They do not tolerate a lack of loyalty. For my part, I don't need any of you to do my job."

For effect, Tano sprang to his feet and lurched forward toward the old woman housekeeper, his sword drawn and well on its way for the fatal strike.

"Wait!"

The blade stopped right at the woman's neck, and Jessie shivered at the man's control. All eyes turned to Mei-Lin.

No. Thoughts flew through Jessie's mind about the repercussions admission would have, either through the torture, or the extermination of her family that was sure to come all because of that one word. Jessie's concern about how long the woman would last before giving her up also came to mind.

Time's up.

Tano's foot masterfully slid back on the smooth, polished

wood surface, the katana whirling around and without a pause, reseated in the scabbard.

"You?" Tano said, shock and dismay in his voice.

Mei-Lin said nothing.

"I don't believe it," Tano said. "I know your history. You have been in the service of Chen for many years. Your education is... limited. To plant this device, to operate it, and work with outside contacts is not within your skill set. You don't..."

"Know a thing about me," Mei-Lin finished. When her head came up, fury met Tano's eyes. "I have been passed around like a rag-doll to men more powerful than even Chen." The old man and woman broke eye contact with the floor and glanced at the girl, a plea for her not to be disrespectful. "I have learned much over the past several years. Made my own contacts with many, many enemies of the Hōn. Your weakness is your inability to see strength and skill in someone such as I."

Shocked to her core, Jessie glanced at Bolin, she saw it on his face, too.

Tano moved in to strike Mei Lin down, but the girl, fast and surprisingly skilled enough in the fighting arts, rolled sideways just as the blur of steel missed her neck by inches. She sprang to her feet, dodged a second strike, and leapt for the weapons rack. She snatched a long Chinese spear and twirled it around her body with fluid expertise before taking on a fighting stance, and in the style of Bruce Lee, she smiled, put her hand in front of her and motioned for Tano to come. Sheer confidence filled the woman's face.

Jessie went to speak, but Bolin beat her to it. "Mei Lin, you know what will happen after this. To your family."

"My family is already dead. Besides, being dead is better than being your slave."

Mei-Lin lashed out, throwing an unexpected, quick jab that slid in past Tano's blade, missing his face by only a fraction of an inch before he batted the shaft of the spear aside. The weapon whirled as Mei-Lin leapt into the air, the blade only narrowly missing Jessie and Bolin as it completed the arch. Jessie ran to the rack, tossed Bolin a Chinese broadsword, and grabbed two for herself. Moving into position, she triangulated on the girl with Tano.

"Give it up, Mei-Lin," Jessie said.

The woman locked eyes with Jessie, who slowly shook her head, pleading with her eyes. *No. Don't do this.*

Tano said nothing, his katana at the ready position. Jessie thought there might be a look of surprise on his face.

"Let us take her, Tano," Jessie said. "We'll get the information we need out of her."

Bolin nodded.

Mei-Lin did not let down her stance, nor her murderous glare towards Tano.

Jessie had seen the old couple interacting with Mei-Lin before but had never heard them speak. She sensed there might be a bond between the three. She jumped toward the old man and held the sword to his throat.

"Drop your spear, or his head will rest beside Ricky's," she said.

Mei-Lin gasped and slowly pulled her gaze from Tano to look at Jessie. Jessie widened her eyes just enough she hoped the girl understood she had a plan. To trust her. Although Jessie had no plan and didn't trust that if Mei-Lin battled on, she would have to kill the old man to maintain her cover.

Mei-Lin dropped the spear and collapsed onto the floor in tears.

Tano maintained his stance, apparently still trying to decide whether or not to just kill the girl and be done with it, and Jessie saw disbelief written on the big man's expression. Tano eased his foot back and smoothly sheathed the long blade.

Bolin and Jessie rushed to secure Mei-Lin, putting her in wrist locks and jerking her to her feet as her head and shoulders sagged toward the floor in defeat. Tano glided to her, reached out, and gently lifted her chin. "I know you have lived a hard life, but I am still confused as to why you betrayed me. I have never done you wrong and have done my best to secure the least brutal posting for you I could manage. Why?"

A hard look developed on Mei-Lin's face as she jerked her head from Tano's fingers. "A whore is still a whore, and it wasn't personal, Tano. *You* were simply in my way," she said as the smile that crept onto her face was wiped away by a fierce, head-snapping slap.

"Take her. Find out who else is involved in this treachery." Jessie and Bolin moved to drag the girl off until Tano spoke again. "Wait." The twins stopped and turned the girl to face Tano.

Tano crouched down in front of the old man and woman who still knelt on their mats, shaking with terror. "Both of you. Look at me." Their gazes shot up from the floor to look Tano in the eye. He assessed each of them, then looked at Mei-Lin as he asked the question. "Did you two know about this? About Mei-Lin? Tell the truth," he said calmly. Both shook their heads rapidly. Tano glanced at the blood on the floor, soaking into the old woman's pants. "Clean this up. Understand?" Both heads bobbed up and down quickly. "Now!" The old couple jumped as if plugged into a light socket and quietly skittered out of the dojo door.

"Peng."

Jessie and Bolin looked at the man, who pressed himself against the wall as if trying to escape the clutches of some dangerous animal. "Call the cleaning company to take care of Ricky." Peng nodded and followed the old couple out of the room.

Tano approached once more and looked Mei-Lin in the eye. "Tear off her clothes." Immediately, Jessie and Bolin roughly ripped her dress and underclothes from her body, regained their grip on her arms, and stood her upright for Tano's inspection. The big man walked around her, looking her naked body up and down until he came full circle. Jessie saw no lust in his eyes. Mei-Lin's makeup smeared face glared at him with utter contempt. She spit at his feet. Tano leaned in closer but did not touch her.

"There isn't a scar on your beautiful, perfect body," he said. "But there will be."

19

BODY DOUBLE

Jessie shoved Mei-Lin forward and followed Bolin down the stairs to a basement door she hadn't yet learned about. Bolin grasped the handle, rattled it, and grumbled something in Chinese under his breath. He spun around, snatched Mei-Lin's face by the cheeks and glared into her eyes. "It's locked. Don't go anywhere," he said, maintaining eye contact with the girl a long moment before he turned away and stomped up the stairs. Jessie assumed he left to get the key.

"Why did you do this?" Jessie whispered. "This was not necessary. I could have gotten…"

"No," Mei-Lin interrupted. "You are caught, and you know it. I know you are not Bohai. Which is crazy. I have known him for years. But because the others don't lay with you, they don't know Bohai like I do."

Confusion rattled Jessie. "I don't understand."

"You have never made love to me. Your brother all but treats me like a rag doll, sometimes making me do things that paid porn stars would not do. You have both taken me several times, even together, and it has never been tender. Last night, because of the drugs, Bolin demanded I service him, but he could barely perform. It was his normal way of asserting control. Expected behavior from that animal. You?" She glanced at Jessie, tears in her eyes. "I have never seen you so tender. Your desire was to please me. This has never happened in such a way. *You* are not Bohai." She turned her eyes away.

169

"Do you understand what is going to happen to you? Why would you cover for me, just because of a tender moment?"

Mei-Lin's tear-filled eyes turned up to study Bohai's face. Jessie almost sensed the girl could see her standing behind the curtain. "You said things were about to change. Everyone here had been called up to serve at a moment's notice. Tano does not seek help unless something is going wrong. Everyone knows that. And then with you, last night, and now, that thing Tano put on the floor. All of this happened almost overnight. Yes. Something is terribly wrong, and I have had it. I am tired of being nothing more than a wet hole.

"Last night, after speaking to you...I have no idea how you are doing this. You seem to be a copy of Bohai, or...I am unsure. I just know if *you* have the power to do this, to cause this kind of chaos, then I will gamble my family's lives as my father has gambled away mine. I have valuable information. Years of it. Knowledge of hierarchy's and financial underpinnings. I feel as if you can help me as I am willing to help you. If assuming responsibility for something will bring these bastards down, for some real revenge, then it is worth it. I see an opportunity. So, will you help me?"

Jessie saw no other choice. "You will tell us about The Benefactors, Uncle Chen, the others?"

"Yes. Of what I can about the Hōn. I have a lot to tell. I have access a wife should have but does not." She chuckled. "If you were *really* Bohai, you'd have already known this. The Benefactors' most powerful asset is their heritage, and the deep financial pockets a thousand years of underground criminal enterprise brings. They see themselves as the future leaders of China. Right now, they are nothing more than rogue henchman. No better than the corrupt government they wish to replace. I also have connections to the Red Boat Opera. You will want to meet them."

"What is Red..."

Bolin arrived at the top of the stairs. Jessie heard him fiddling with keys. "I am going to have to play this out. You understand."

"If you can end this, I can take it. You will see."

Jessie seized Mei-Lin by the shoulders, but gently pulled her closer. "Look at me." The girl locked eyes with Jessie. "Tell them that a woman named Laina Main recruited you and that you report to her. Don't tell right away. Hold out as long as you can. I'm sorry, but it must be done this way." Mei-Lin's face scrunched up in confusion until Jessie tugged at her lower eyelid, pulling the contact lens down just a bit.

Mei-Lin gasped. Jessie reset the lens.

"Do this, and I will do what I can for your family." The girl opened her mouth to speak until Jessie placed a finger on her lips. Bolin began his decent. "It's going to get bad. Really bad. Understand?"

"Yes," Mei-Lin said. "I knew it." A small, but real smile reached her eyes.

"Listen carefully," Jessie said, and relayed what she could before Bolin made it down the stairs. Jessie accepted that this gamble could unravel everything with one word from the girl, but now backed into a corner, she had no choice. She had to accept the risk and just go for it.

She looked up as Bolin made the last two steps and tossed her the keys. There were several, but she found the right one quickly for the unique, hardened stainless lock on the door. She pushed the door in and motioned with her head for Bolin. Jessie flipped a switch on the wall and two bright, halogen bulbs hummed and buzzed, their illumination growing brighter as the light passed through what appeared to be thick, waterproof housings attached to the end of adjustable, articulated arms that stretched down from the ceiling. They pointed to each side of a steel, horizontal bar, with wide cuffs on each end to support a body's weight. A chain attached to each end of the bar led up to a large multi-wheeled pulley, used to hoist unfortunate souls off the floor until feet dangled.

Bolin shoved Mei-Lin through the door. She stumbled onto the polished concrete floor that slanted down from the outer walls, leading to a shiny, stainless steel drain grid directly beneath the interrogation bar. Although the room showed no signs of recent use, it smelled of bleach and something else. Something like rotted flesh from long ago.

Mei-Lin struggled to her feet. Bolin kicked her hard in the ribs, knocking her back to the floor. He stomped over to her body and jerked the girl up by her hair. Jessie closed the door and moved in beside the twin.

"Let's rack her up," Bolin said and wrenched an arm to the bar, looking to Jessie. Jessie responded by bringing Mei-Lin's other wrist to the bar. The woman cried out in pain but didn't look Jessie's way, which gave Jessie a bit more confidence. The men stuffed Mei-Lin's wrist into the cuffs and released her. Bolin handed Jessie a ball gag. Jessie looked at it, then back at Bolin.

"What?" the twin asked. Jessie glanced at the walls and the back at the steel door they came through.

"You don't think Tano would like to hear her scream?" Jessie asked, raising an eyebrow. Bolin frowned, then nodded. Jessie pocketed the gag.

"Hoist her up then. Let's introduce the spoiled bitch to a new kind of pain," Bolin said.

Jessie followed the chain leading from the pulley against the ceiling, angling down to the corner of the room. Bolin walked to a large, wooden cabinet mounted to the center of the same wall. Jessie pulled the chain. Mei-Lin yelped as her naked body rose smoothly into the air.

Bolin selected a shinai, a kind of practice sword made up of four slats of bamboo, wrapped in leather thongs, a string pulled tight along one side to add tension and represent the top of a blade. Jessie remembered that the nonlethal, flexible shinai had caused terrible, painful welts against her bare arms during the Kendo classes she took a couple of years ago. Bolin stalked around the girl, spinning the shinai around in slow, lazy circles as he walked.

"After all Uncle Chen has done for you, this is how you repay him?" He snapped the shinai against Mei-Lin's calves, causing her to cry out. The welts appeared almost immediately. He moved around the front and struck her across the thighs. "Oh, her nipples are hard. I think she likes it, brother."

Mei-Lin spat.

In anger, Bolin pulled the bamboo rod back to strike her again but stopped as Mei-Lin's body seized up in anticipation of the impact. "See?" Bolin said, smiling. "You would have been prepared for that, and you braced yourself. It would have hurt, but perhaps not as much. It's different when you don't know it's coming. You'll see."

Mei-Lin's body stayed tight, her muscles clenched from head to toe, but Jessie knew she wouldn't be able to maintain her rigidity. Bolin worked his way behind her again and waited. Mei-Lin took quick gasps of air, doing her best to maintain a stiff body but failed. Bolin's eyes grew wide, he drew back to strike and…

"Wait," Jessie said. Bolin stopped in mid-strike and turned to glare at his brother. Jessie had stolen his moment. "Let's save that for last," Jessie said, moving back to the cabinet and sorting through other instruments of pain stored there. "Ah, check this out." She removed a heavy, oversize car battery and two cables with steel wool prongs attached to the ends. She followed the wires from charring clips to the power outlet and tested the battery.

"Full charge," she said, and looked up to Bolin with a smile. "This looks fun, and we won't get any blood on us if we want to fuck her after. If she clams up, then use the shinai, and after, the whip. Fair enough?"

Bolin's eyebrows raised. "You normally aren't one for torture, brother, but yes, it's a good idea. I haven't taken her ass in some time. So maybe we'll have one more go at her." Jessie touched the prongs together; a loud bang made all three of them jump. Bolin laughed as the crackle of energy and sparks flew from the end. Jessie handed the cables to him. "I'll watch."

When the steel wool touched Mei-Lin's body, the highest pitched screams Jessie had ever heard escaped from somewhere deep within Mei-Lin. Jessie knew that place. She experienced something similar each and every time she slip-streamed into a new host. Mei-Lin's body bounced and bucked wildly as the electricity coursed through her. Jessie picked up a bucket of water from the corner and doused the girl, then nodded to Bolin.

"Again," Jessie said, grinning. Bolin applied the pain.

"Again."

Seeing the toughness in the girl's eyes made Jessie's participation a little easier. Yes, this girl had endurance. *Respect*, Jessie thought. Bolin walked around the girl again, letting the pain settle in.

"See?" Bolin said, grinning up at Mei-Lin's make-up streaked face, "Wasn't that an experience you'll never forget? And just think, Mei-Lin, I am well rested. We have hours more of this to come."

Inwardly, Jessie flinched with every successive shock, and Bolin had yet to ask a single question.

"She says the woman we killed, Laina Main, is her contact," Bolin said, his arms folded in front of him.

"Impossible," Tano said as he moved through his sword kata,

not missing a strike or lunge toward his invisible foe. "She's lying."

"I don't think so," Bolin added. "Mei-Lin hasn't been present for our conversations about the Main woman."

Tano rolled his eyes. "I'm sure neither of you let her name slip while she bedded you. That just wouldn't happen, right?" He eased his body into the movements of another kata.

Bolin and Jessie looked at one another. Jessie said, "It is highly unlikely…"

"No. It is not unlikely," Tano snapped. "It is highly probable that one of you…"

"She says Laina Main is still alive, and that we killed the wrong woman," Bolin interrupted.

Tano stopped mid-move. He spun around to look at both men but said nothing. Jessie continued. "I can understand your concerns about us giving her certain information, but I assure you, we did not tell her what we did in the cabin."

Tano frowned and looked back and forth between the twins. "Bohai, have we received the fingerprint identification from the hands you sent in?"

"Not yet," Jessie said. "He did say before he left that it would be two days before those results came in." Bolin nodded in agreement, although he had not been present when the courier arrived.

"How convenient," Tano said. The sound of steel whipping through the air caused Jessie to take a smooth, almost unnoticeable step back. Tano sheathed the Katana once again. "I was there. I have seen Miss Main on the cameras and in person. As have you," he pointed at Jessie, then at Bolin. "I find this entire situation with this Main woman to be confusing and incomprehensible. I have yet to uncover anything suspicious. No virus in Kore's system." The blade slashed. "No changes in parameters." The blade slashed again. "No breaches in our security." He sheathed the sword. "And yet, Robert Kore's strange behavior. A sniper watching over a highly skilled fighter in the form of a bargirl, this strange device, which I would not have noticed had the glow of the unit's green LED not caught my attention. And now, Mei-Lin."

Jessie made a mental note on the led give-away and moved to speak when Tano held up his hand, cutting her off.

"Get that information on the prints. I think it's time I asked Mei-Lin some questions myself. When I'm done, have the cleaners come to get her body when you're finished with her."

"Are you going to contact Chen?" Bolin asked.

"Not until I have some answers. Let's go."

Bolin looked to Jessie and raised an eyebrow. Jessie shrugged. They followed him to the basement. Tano entered the room, flipped the light switch on and watching Mei-Lin's body jerk about from the cuffs when the bright lights illuminated her welt-covered body. Jessie closed the door behind her and walked to the power panel where Bolin had turned on the chillers and fans prior to leaving the room. The temperature read thirty-eight degrees. Bolin marched to the corner of the room and retrieved another bucket from the corner. He walked up to the girl and doused her with the icy contents. Mei-Lin shrieked from the pain.

Tano glared at the girl as he walked around her. Once at her back, he stopped and reached out to poke at one of the open blisters on her back. Mei-Lin cried out once more.

"You used a shinai?" he asked, running a finger down a welt-line across her back.

"Yes," Bolin said, a twisted smile on his face. "And the battery. Very, very effective." Jessie picked up a cable, attached it to the battery, and struck the wool ends together. Tano flinched at the sparks flying off the implement. Mei-Lin screamed in anticipation of the pain. "It didn't take long once she smelled her flesh burning. That's when she shared the name of the Main woman."

"Why didn't you continue?"

"We thought you should know. Besides, she's warmed up now. The pain has had time to settle in. Her wounds are sensitive. With the next round, we expect to extract additional information."

Jessie went to the wall cabinet, retrieved a digital scan thermometer, and returned to Mei-Lin's body. He pointed it at her forehead. "95 degrees," she said. "Perfect timing." Jessie hadn't thought that the room would get so cold so fast. "If we don't maintain this temperature, we'll lose her to hypothermia before we're done."

"Tell me about the green bag." Jessie glanced up toward Mei-Lin, who despite her exhaustive electrical torture, had the look of confusion on her face. Jessie then glanced at Bolin who, like the old couple, had his eyes glued to some unseen object on the floor. Jessie's gaze swiveled to Tano, who stared directly at her.

"You are asking me about the green bag? The one I searched?"

"How did you know to ask for the green bag, brother?" Bolin accused.

"And who was the man who came to get the hands from you? Chen doesn't know him," Tano said, his face placid, unreadable.

"I do not understand what it is you are..."

Before Jessie could utter another work, Tano leapt forward with lightning fast speed, seized Jessie by the throat, picked her up, and slammed her into the ground on her back. Stunned, she couldn't move right away. All the air had left the lungs of her host.

And then she felt it.

One contact lens had dislodged from the impact and rested on Bohai's cheek.

Tano's eyes went wide. Stunned, he released Bohai and staggered back, "What...what the hell?" Slowly, Jessie raised up to her elbow as Bolin approached, then backed up as well.

"Your eyes..."

Jessie sat up and smiled at the men. She reached up, removed the other contact and flicked it toward Bolin as she did a back spring off the floor and onto her feet.

"What are you?" the twin asked, shock and fear painted on his face. Jessie slowly turned her head to face Tano and opened her eyes wide. Tano gasped and wore the same mask of fear. *Perfect.* What Jessie affectionately called her little generator had kicked on to full power. Now, in this superbly trained and strong host, she was ready to dance.

"Why, I'm Bohai Sōng. Brother of Bolin," she laughed and held an open hand toward the twin. "One of the Trusted, a dark hand for The Benefactors, who serves the mighty Hōn. Don't you recognize me, brother? Can you see me, Tano?" And with that, Jessie attacked.

Performing swift, flying aerials, she spun toward her brother as Tano staggered backwards. Bolin moved to block her kick, not expecting Jessie's hands to reach his face. Then both brothers fell. Tano released a long hiss of air as he watched in horror as she forced the twins to rise to their feet, identical movements of their identical bodies, and both sets of eyes glowing like hot coal embers.

20

DIVINE INTERVENTION

Tano turned to flee and reached for the door just as something slammed into his hand, the sickening crunch of bone reaching his ears before the pain reached his head. The heavy stainless-steel lock that usually hung on the clasp on the *outside* of the door spun around in circles at his feet.

"Not so fast…" Bohai started.

"Big guy," Bolin finished, without missing a beat. The men glared at him, their glowing eyes eliciting an emotional response Tano had not felt in many, many years. Then the men smiled and said in one voice, "We've got unfinished business."

Fear. It was something Tano had not felt in many, many years. Now, he struggled to control it.

Tano moved away from the door, glancing down at his damaged hand as it swelled before his eyes. Bohai leapt forward, blocking his exit from the door, as Bolin triangulated on him, but kept himself between Tano and Mei-Lin as she hung from the torture bar looking wide-eyed and terrified. Tano moved into a fighting stance, attempting to ball his broken hand into a fist. Pain blossomed into visions of shooting stars, and he almost didn't make it. The hand had most definitely been broken. He breathed deep and, instead, pressed the useless appendage into the small of his back. The brothers' arms and hands swirled into identical block and strike movements in perfect synchronization.

"I can still beat either of you one-handed," Tano said, a sinister smile rising to the edge of his lips.

Bolin and Bohai glanced at one another, smiled themselves, then went into identical fighting stances, moving into a fluid display of a kata, a *karate* kata, that Tano thought he might have seen once before. As the twins flowed through the movements, Tano's face lit up. He recognized it and remembered where he had seen this before: Robert. He had watched the man on the surveillance camera performing this exact kata while naked in his bedroom as the mysterious sleeping beauty, Miss Laina Main, lay unmoving on his bed.

"Now that I'm in sync with these two…" Bohai said.

"…it's time to play the piano," Bolin finished.

"Time to test my theory," the twins said together.

At first, Tano didn't comprehend what he heard, but between the glowing eyes, the synchronistic behavior, and all the other weird shit he had seen over the past couple of days, there was no doubt that someone, or something, now controlled the twins. He didn't believe in the supernatural, and he couldn't help but wonder what marvelous tech had been created to exact this kind of control over human beings. The Benefactors would need to know about this.

He shoved his wild thoughts aside as the twins separated a couple feet apart and launched into two completely different styles of Kung-Fu as they methodically closed the gap. Tano took his own fighting stance, backing up, doing his best to keep his eyes on both men at the same time. Bohai lunged first, sending a flying leaping kick toward Tano's face, followed by a reverse kick from Bolin, both of which Tano easily blocked with his one, strong arm. He glanced over his shoulder, seeing the twins were attempting to corral him into a corner. He launched his own attack with a series of reverse backhands and spinning back kicks of his own. His offense working, he kept the twins at bay until a foot crashed into the side of his face. As Tano spun around to meet them, Bolin leapt onto Tano's back. As the man's arms reached around to grab at his face, Tano grabbed hold of his sleeve, lurched forward, and threw the twin off, sending Bolin spiraling roughly across the concrete floor. Bohai moved in to strike open handed blows as Tano, now using his feet as much as his free hand, fared well in keeping Bohai from connecting a strike. Seeing an opening, Tano sent a powerful front snap-kick right into the lower jaw of Bohai, resulting in a loud crack of jawbone as it dislocated at the joint. The twin staggered back but did not fall. As Bohai raised his face, Tano's brow furrowed, and he winced at the sight. Bohai's deformed jaw shifted as the hinge protruded under the skin back near the ear canal.

"That had to hurt," Tano said, smiling.

Bolin completed a back-spring off the floor, and the twins moved again to block the exit. He turned toward Bohai. Tano's smile faded as Bolin grabbed his brother by the jaw, jerking it downward. The loud *snap* as the jaw connected with the joint made Tano shudder. "That had to hurt even more," he said, smiling again.

"Didn't feel a thing," Bohai replied, his voice slurred from the damaged mandible. Bohai did manage his own smile, and the twins launched forward. Tano fought the men while attempting to remain calm and focused during the barrage of flying fists and feet. A strike to his chest knocked the wind out of him. Another foot across the left side of his face left him reeling backward.

Tano knew he couldn't keep this up much longer and felt his advantage slipping. And then he saw an opening. Tano reached behind his back, opening himself up to several quick strikes to the face and chest. He found the handle of the razor sharp tanto blade sheathed at the small of his back. He lunged forward to slide inside Bohai's strike zone and thrust the knife deep into the right side of the twin's chest, bloody froth bubbling at the blades hilt. The twins yelled out in pain together as Tano ripped the knife from Bohai's chest, spun behind the shocked twin, and held the knife to his throat.

"Time to stop, Bolin. Your brother doesn't have to die," he said.

"You might kill them," the twins said in unison, "but you can't kill me. I'm coming for you, Tano."

Bolin clenched fists and lowered his body, poised and ready to strike. Tano jerked the knife tighter against Bohai's throat until Bolin smiled, his eyes glowing red-hot, and Bohai's arms shot up, dropping his weight as his hands touched the sides of Tano's face.

JESSIE SCREAMED AS PAIN FLOODED INTO HER THE MOMENT SHE slipped into Tano. Not the mix of pain and euphoria that accompanied each and every slip. This was real, physical pain. How the man had the ability to put that level of agony aside in his mind in order to fight left her in disbelief for only a moment until she realized she had lost her connection to Bolin.

Bolin staggered backward, looking lost and confused, as Jessie released the body of Bohai, his throat cut during the throes of slip-streaming. Bolin's face contorted into pain and rage as he watched the blood flow from his brother's severed neck toward the drain in the center of the floor. Slowly, Bolin's eyes rose to meet Jessie's, and the man's eyes went wide once he saw the glow.

"Èmó!" Bolin screamed. "Èmó!" *Demon.*

Enraged, Bolin balled his fists and went to move forward, when a pair of legs landed across his shoulders, feet crossing at the ankles locked in front of him. Mei-Lin screamed as she squeezed with her thighs. Bolin punched at her legs, trying to land a blow to release himself.

"Kill him!" Mei Lin screamed, struggling to hang on.

Jessie went to move forward, her feet feeling glued to the floor. She took a deep breath, a big step, and cried out in pain.

"Kill him!"

Tano's body had been seriously, if not mortally, injured. She struggled through the excruciating pain and leapt toward Bolin just as his head slipped from Mei-Lin's grip. Jessie landed on the twin who struggled to move only for a moment. Jessie lay on top of the man, Tano's much bigger and heavier body pinning the twin to the floor. Face to face with her enemy, Bolin's eyes bulged in a mix of fear and rage, and slowly, slowly, the light left his eyes.

"È...mó." The name came as a whisper on Bolin's last breath.

Jessie watched the man's eyes turn a dull sort of grey before she let out her own long, slow breath. She struggled to rise up as pain and exhaustion threatened to take her out. As she made it to a knee, she reached out to pull the hilt of the tanto knife from the center of the dead twin's chest. She groaned as she made it to her feet and staggered to the back wall, throwing the release handle up to slacken the suspension chain. Mei-Lin cried out as her body crashed to the concrete floor.

"Are you okay?" Jessie asked, leaning against the wall, not sure if *she* would be able to walk out of the room.

"Yes. I need help out of these cuffs," she said.

Jessie stumbled toward Mei-Lin and crumbled to the floor beside her. Mei-Lin's arms were stretched out, her legs and torso twisted at impossible angles. "Are you sure you're okay?"

"Yes, please! Help me!"

Doing her best in using Tano's one good hand to free the first cuff. Mei-Lin assisted with the second, until she was free. She stood up and peered into Jessie's eyes.

"Hang on."

Jessie pressed hard, trying to prevent the tunnel from closing on Tano's vision as the visceral feeling of free-fall overwhelmed her. Tano's body collapsed on the hard concrete. Jessie hung on by that spider-fine thread and found herself alone in a black darkness that frightened her. She still hung on to Tano, but only just. This dark void felt like a place she might not be able to return from, and she tried not to think about it. Instead, she pressed with all her might to open Tano's eyes. A brief flash of blurred lights shot through the darkness surrounding her until his eyes closed again.

"No!"

Jessie fought to bring Tano's body around but knew she couldn't force the body to do something it could not. Tano's body had been seriously injured, and despite her efforts, she felt that fine thread might unravel at any second. She pressed harder, knowing that doing so could kill the man. Regardless, she had to try.

More yelling in Mandarin Chinese reached Jessie's mind. She willed Tano's eyes open. This view looked better, where blurs of movement and commotion swirled around her. Dark moving into light. She did not understand the conversation, but sensed Mei-Lin might be in charge. Then she felt Tano's body move. They all carried her, the old caretakers glancing down at her, concern on their faces. Jessie's awareness filled her with confidence that she could continue to hang on, but she also thought about her predicament. She had never been stuck in a seriously injured or dying host before. This concerned her even more as her physical body wasn't close by. Without it, she couldn't slip back, and she had no clue what would happen if Tano's body gave out. She shook the thought from her mind and concentrated on keeping whatever hold she could manage.

The stunt she pulled between controlling Robert Kore and his Config Manager, Maria, had been a first for her. She had never streamed through two people at once. However, seizing both twins and controlling them like she had, well, it had shocked even her.

It's fucking amazing.

Somehow, she intuitively knew she could control both bodies at once but tapping into their individual skills without compromising her concentration or connection could only be contributed to sheer panic—survival mode, or maybe have something to do with The Chamber. Having taken only a few piano lessons at around ten years old, she eventually got the knack of getting the right and left hands to do completely different things. Something inside her own mind whispered, *You can do so much more.*

Then she wondered why she was thinking about any of this. *What the fuck?* She needed to be concerned about how to get back to her own body and whatever it was that Mei-Lin had planned. For all intents and purposes, Jessie knew she had been caught. Another first.

"Now what the hell am I going to do?" she groaned.

"I'm getting you a doctor."

"No, please. Don't..." Jessie's vision started going black, and despite her forceful commands to Tano's body to speak, no words came. She wriggled her nose at the tickle of blood dribbling down her upper lip, one of the many negative side effects from pressing her mind against a host's using too much force. She tried to speak, but despite her efforts Tano's physical body slipped past her control once again. She searched for Tano's mind but found only a wall of darkness, a void of unnatural nothingness.

This mission unlocked abilities she didn't know she had, pushed her into corners she had always managed to avoid. She thought that perhaps Tano might have slipped past her control and sought that dark place to block or hide from her. A wave of panic threatened to break her connection. Time was not on her side. She heard Tano's voice repeat her thoughts. "I need to get word to my people. To..."

She breathed deeper, battling the chaos of the power flowing through her, like some rider astride a spooked horse. *Stop fighting it.* The words, no more than a whisper, slipped through turmoil. *Stop fighting or die.* Tano's words, not her own. The man's mind was every bit as strong as his body. She had no choice. She had no doubt that by resisting, she fueled her own panic. Her little generator now cranked at full speed ahead, but instead of unleashing her full potential, it blocked her progress.

A truce. The words sounded off clear in her head. Tano had somehow, someway, breached her bio-electrical prison. *Relax. Meditate. You and I need to be one.* She pulled back, as she did when resting, and did her best to maintain that thin thread linking her to Tano. The place she sought to rest, although also a void, had more of a flexible feeling. She saw herself in that place and latched onto what she could.

Am I really in control of this? she thought. Tano didn't answer.

This was most certainly another first for her, being drawn into a stark, harsh blackness by her host. She did feel as if the man, in his desperation to survive the severe physical injuries she administered, surrendered to her. More importantly, she sensed no threat and made up her mind, accepting the compromise of the other voice. That same, single chime of a bell she had heard when she first took Tano sounded off again, this time more distant. It rang again from some far off place and filled her mind. Within seconds, the weight of Tano's physical pain lifted as her consciousness came to terms with this new dimension.

She took one deep, shuddering breath, then let go. She embraced the void.

21

INTO THE VOID

J essie's eyes shot open and she gasped, a reflex to being oxygen deprived, except she wasn't. She wondered how long she had been under.

In Tano.

She performed her ritual self-assessment after slip-streaming and realized, although still connected to the man, she no longer had control of his bio-electrical grid. But she experienced something else, too. Calm.

And where is the pain?

It still lingered somewhere in her mind, locked away by her well-disciplined host. She pressed, only a little, searching for Tano. No answer. Only a deafening silence filled her mind. She turned her head, and even spun her body around, looking for something to visually connect with.

You're in a void, dummy, she thought. *What did you expect?*

Her consciousness active, she did her best to relax into the situation. *No sense fighting it.*

She thought of *her* void as being dark, but this gave the term "total darkness" a whole new meaning. In her void, she latched onto the om, and once she reached that peaceful place, it caressed her like a warm blanket. Her place was where she and the power flowing through her intertwined like two lovers.

But this place, this utter black hole where Tano dwelled, reminded her of...of *a fucking abyss.* She had to admit that calming herself and taking in Tano's void showed her something new. She wondered if perhaps she had never truly attained the healing power of pure nothingness.

Another first.

Jessie had never considered there might be different aspects to nothingness.

Clearly, I don't know shit.

Tano's Void.

She apperceived her eyes to be open, but her mind only registered the obsidian. She raised her hand in front of her face, not expecting to see it, and gasped at the sight of it.

What the hell?

She glanced down at her hands and arms, relieved to see them. Except her body appeared to be wrapped in some kind of electrical filter, like static on the screen of an old-fashioned tube television while someone tried to tune in a channel. Glancing at her body, she noticed the silver, skin-tight spandex suit she wore when her physical body occupied The Chamber. She didn't see wires attached to the electrodes but had a feeling if she hadn't been connected, Tano would have had the power to oust her by now.

She moved to walk forward and discovered weightlessness, feeling nothing solid beneath her feet. She listened for Tano's voice but only heard the blood pulsing in her ears. An uneasiness crept into her, this perception of floating threatened to overwhelm her. She remembered scuba diving.

This feels like that, she thought. *Sort of. Fuck this.*

She pressed hard, digging deep for her host. By degrees, gravity settled in, and despite the blackness, the illuminated apparition of a naked man appeared, sitting before her. His back looked board straight, his legs crossed in the yoga lotus pose. Tano's eyes opened, and as if annoyed at being interrupted, he slowly turned his head, making direct eye contact with her.

"Please. Stop." It sounded as if the words had been whispered in her ear.

Jessie held on to what she had but pressed no further. "Why are we here?"

Tano raised an eyebrow, then turned his gaze away, closing his eyes. "I'm surprised you had to ask," he said.

Jessie nodded. *Calm down. He can probably smell my fear.*

"I get the sense you could help me, if you wanted to," Tano said.

She opened her mouth to speak but closed it. *No time for bickering.*

"You think we're in this together," Jessie said.

"We are, or you wouldn't be here."

"We're not. I'm here because I choose to be." Jessie felt confident in her declaration. Tano may have dragged her into *this* void, but as Jessie had never experienced letting go of a host without having physical contact, she considered that perhaps he might be right. To an extent.

"Are you sure?" He glanced down at her body. "You don't look to be all here, do you?"

Jessie glanced at her hands again. She knew the answer to this, too, and decided not to give him the luxury of stating, *"I'm whole in my own mind because I belong here, bitch."*

Jessie pounced. Balling her hands into fists, she bore down harder than ever to assert herself as the dominant force in this space. Tano cried out, and suddenly, like a movie reel of Tano's life being run backwards at high speed, Jessie saw him as a young boy. Perhaps age ten, already tall and lanky. He wore only pajama pants and looked to be barefoot, standing in snow. His bare and very skinny upper body shivered violently in the chill winter air. Jessie closed her eyes and pressed harder. She stood beside him now, in the courtyard of some house, surrounded by what looked like Chinese soldiers. She heard his teeth chattering and followed his gaze when he turned to watch other military men dressed in all black uniforms escort a tall, blonde man, and a pretty woman through the garden gate, past Tano, until shoved into a wall.

Parents, Jessie thought. Somehow, she also knew the military men were inspectors from the Chinese 6-10 office, also known as the Chinese Gestapo. On a command that sounded like an echo in her mind, the men pulled pistols from leather holsters, and without hesitation, shot the two adults in the head. Tano screamed.

Jessie reeled back just as another image slammed into her. The same boy now stood before a double grave. She looked at Tano's face and watched a single tear roll down his cheek as he peered down into the pit. Jessie looked, too. At the bottom of the hole lay two dark wooden caskets, each with a large flower —brilliant red Dutch lilies—lying across the lids. An Asian man had one hand on boy Tano's shoulder and leaned down to whisper. Jessie leaned in, too.

"Don't worry, Tano. I will teach you, and we shall seek vengeance together."

The movie reel spun forward like a time machine, stopping at a scene of Tano fighting in the streets of Hong Kong, flashing again to Japanese fighting schools for both Kendo and Ninjutsu, and even faster until she saw Tano as a young, powerful man, heads and shoulders taller than a platoon of other men, going through what appeared to be Special Forces training in a mostly Caucasian fighting force. Then flashes of battle action in Afghanistan, she saw Tano as a sergeant in the French Foreign Legion.

Then, a naked Asian woman. She sat on her knees stroking Tano's large member but appeared to be laughing at him, and then the reel skipped ahead to Tano watching Mei-Lin showering naked in an exotic waterfall. And then more fighting, more battles, gunfights, sword fights, fucking, and Jessie felt her vertigo creeping up on her, and then she saw…her.

Jessie raised an eyebrow and watched from the voyeur's

perspective as she had sex with Robert Kore, and then her laying naked on the bed, post-slip. The camera zoomed in and...

"Stop!" Tano cried. "Please, stop. You're killing me. I mean, literally, killing me. You have no right..."

"I have every right," Jessie said. "You are an enemy of the United States. You represent everything I stand against and..."

"You are right. You are right."

Jessie looked toward the figure, now slouching over. He appeared deflated, but Jessie wouldn't let her guard down.

Don't give him an inch.

Then came the pain.

"I'm sorry. When you do that, whatever it is you're doing in my head, I can't hold back the pain. I surrender. Please, no more. I'm begging you. I've worked for years compartmentalizing the trauma of my youth. I'm still working on it. You saw. You know it's true. I may be on the wrong side of this, but if anything, I am a creation of my environment."

"Why me? Why am I ingrained in your memory?" Jessie thought she might know the answer to this but felt compelled to have the man say it. He crushed on her. She'd bet the farm he wouldn't admit it.

"You are an anomaly. I really watched and paid attention to the videos of you after I had ordered the twins to kill you. I regretted that decision, but obviously, they regretted it more. You're still here."

"And you're almost dead," Jessie snapped. "You haven't answered my question."

"I knew there was something about you the moment I saw you take Gerardo down in the cabin. Your confidence. Skill. I went back to see what I might have missed about you. Even when you were supposed to be dead, the sight of you, with Kore. The things you did in his bedroom after confirmed that I had made a mistake. You are here because of my poor decision."

Jessie didn't buy into it but didn't feel like pressing the matter further.

"I don't believe you're being one hundred percent honest with me, Tano," she said, "but the more pressing problem is that you are gravely injured. And to your point, we're in this together. You could very well die…"

"Not if you help me. You can keep that from happening. I feel your power. Your strength. You are not of this world."

"Why should I," Jessie hissed. "You deserve to die."

"Perhaps. But don't you have questions?"

Shit. Jessie hated being so easily read. It had taken her years to get over how her boss, Jon Daly, read her like an open book. "I do have questions. A lot of questions and…"

"And I will answer each and every one, if you help me. If you do not, then do whatever it is you are doing. Crush my mind. Boil my blood. Kill me." He stood and pointed at her. "But I promise you, Miss Main. I will not answer any of your questions if you do not help us get through this."

"I can extract the truth. You know it."

"Perhaps, but I'll die before you get enough to make a difference."

Jessie cocked her head to the side. "How do I know you will tell the truth?"

Tano nodded. "I understand your concerns. I can only give you my word that when we make it through this, *if* we make it through this, I will tell you everything you want to know. You can learn a lot from me, Miss Main. And I have questions for you as well. About what you are doing. What you can do. Your ability to *remote view* through the eyes of your enemy? I find it fascinating and unprecedented. And as you have access to my mind, you'll know I'm telling truth. Go head. Check. So, either have at me, or let's make a pact, here, in *my* mind, where our paths are one. I am at your mercy." He spread his arms wide and bowed his head, then stood up straight. "So get on with it. Or trust me."

"Trust is earned."

"As I said. Look for yourself, then, Miss Main. I will not resist. You will find that I have never lied to my employer, my assistants, or my customers. Not once. I don't consider Robert Kore a customer, so I did skirt the truth with him. But if you assess that I am a liar, then by all means, drill into me, extract what information you can, and let me die." He leaned toward her. "But know this: you won't get it all. I will fight you every step of the way. It will kill me, but I feel certain that ultimately, I will spite you. Help me, and we have no reason to test the limits of your abilities, and we will both have formed a new and beneficial alliance."

"That sounds desperate," Jessie said. "So, you're scared of dying? I wouldn't think a man like you..."

Tano held up a hand. "You misunderstand, Miss Main. My interest in living has nothing to do with ego or fear. *You* would be my only reason to continue."

"You're not my type."

"Don't be so sure," Tano said. He chuckled. "Having you quite literally a part of me has also given me insights to you. We are eternally connected, Miss Main. Like it or not. I sense this. I'm not a stalker. That would be in poor taste. I only ask that we share knowledge."

"It won't help you where you're going."

"Won't it, though?" he said. "Having a better understanding of how to wield one's consciousness in a prison would be most valuable, I think. Besides. I don't intend to be there long."

Jessie understood that she controlled the situation. With the flip of her little generator switch, she could end the man and roll the dice that she might or might not end herself. She took a step closer to him and glared up into his face, looking for the lie.

She didn't see it but lacked the confidence that Tano would keep his end of the bargain.

"Everything I want to know about The Benefactors. The Hōn."

"Whatever you wish. On my life, I swear on my parents' sacrifice, I will work with you." He held out his hand to shake. Jessie looked at the hand, then into Tano's eyes once again. She had seen the love Tano had for his parents, felt the fire of vengeance burn in his heart, and knew without a doubt he had successfully avenged their deaths. She reached for it, and he snatched it away. "There's just one more, little thing."

"No shit," Jessie said. "Let me guess, immunity?"

"For starters, but also, I need to be kept safe. If they're not already on their way, The Benefactors will come for me when they find out I have been corrupted by an Èmó. My guess is that they'll be coming for you, too. Hence, our need for expediency."

He pushed his open hand toward her once again, and Jessie reached out, her hand still appearing to be made of television static and grasped Tano's hand.

Brilliant white light slammed into her as both their heads fell back, and together, they screamed.

22

NEXT

What was that? There it is again. The distant but clear chime of a bell reached her in the void. She latched onto the sound and pulled. The chime grew louder, to the point she thought she might be able to reach out and touch it. Tano hadn't lied to her. He relinquished control and didn't pull her into his dark place to be lost forever. Her eyelids fluttered open. Foggy figures moved around her. She tried sitting up, groaned, and flopped back down into the pillow. "Holy shit, I feel like I've wrestled with a train. And lost." Until she heard the sound of Tano's voice, she thought she might have found her way back to her own body.

"You have, in a sense."

She turned her head to the side and focused through the blur on the smiling face of Mei-Lin, who assisted her in sitting up as a dull throb of pain reminded her what had happened. Why she was here, in Tano. The basement. The big steel lock. Promises in the dark. She raised the fractured hand to her face and squinted at the cast covering her from her fingertips to her elbow until it came into focus. She tried but couldn't move her fingers. She could barely breathe and felt her chest with the remaining good hand, finding bandages wrapped tightly around her torso. She glanced around the room, recognizing it as Bohai's then realized they had stripped off Tano's clothes, covering his naked body with a thin sheet.

Jessie opened her mouth to ask a question and regretted it. She smacked her lips together.

"I think someone replaced my tongue with a wad of cotton," she said. Her voice, Tano's voice, sounded slurred and sticky. Movement in the room seemed to be in slow motion and her skin itched. Pain that had been sharp and excruciating now felt dull, as if trapped inside a padded room, thumping on the wall to escape. "I know this feeling," she said, "Morphine."

A few years ago, while slip-streaming through the host body of an Afghan clan leader, she had been shot and given the addictive drug in copious amounts. Although a minor wound, the morphine flowed like candy in war zones. But this injury hurt much worse than that gunshot and she welcomed the relief.

"No one has ever kicked my ass like this," she moaned. "Ever."

Mei-Lin rested a hand on her chest and smiled. "The twins were legendary as the far-reaching enforcers for The Benefactors. You are lucky to have survived them, on any level."

"I'm not sure yet that I have," Jessie said, looking around the room. In the corner, she spotted the portable X-ray machine used to treat Bolin's broken arm and the door to the room opened. As a thin man with spectacles approached, Jessie tensed up, her eyes wide in recognition of Bolin's doctor.

"Relax," the man said in only a slight accent. "I'm a friend. I'm here to help, and you need to try and rest." The man locked eyes with Jessie, and she also recognized fear in the man's gaze as he examined Tano's eyes.

"How do I know you're a friend?" Jessie asked.

"Because if we weren't on your side," Mei-Lin interjected, "you'd have woken up in a cage." The doctor stepped up, took Jessie's temperature, pulse rate, and nodded.

"You have six broken ribs, a fractured orbital, and will need surgery if one of the ribs punctures a lung. It's only millimeters away. You must be careful how you move."

"Well, I'm not worried about the future of this body. I need to get to my people."

The doctor nodded. "I'm not sure who you are, or what you are, or how you are able to do what you do, but you have saved my niece, and although I am indentured by The Benefactors, I am most humbly indebted to you as well. We will do what we can to get you to safety." The man bowed.

"What do you mean, indentured?"

The man glanced at Mei-Lin, a worried look on his face. The girl nodded her approval for him to continue. "Like my niece, I am paying off a debt owed to the Hōn. The Benefactors enforce it.

"How can a doctor be an indentured servant? What did you do?"

"Me? Oh, I did nothing. I even worked my way through medical school without family or Hōn assistance. Once I was licensed to practice, I was dragged in…" his eyes teared up, and he looked once again to Mei-Lin who reached out and rested her hand lightly on his arm. "By the twins. Beaten and tortured and never told why. After a few weeks in a Chinese re-education camp, I was brought before my distant cousin Chen, who is a board member of The Benefactors. You have heard of them? Of the Hōn?" Jessie nodded and rolled the fingers of her good hand for the man to continue his tale. The doctor nodded and took a shuddering breath. "Chen acted as if he were there to rescue me. He had my wounds treated and dressed, fed me, clothed me, and ensured I had a bed to sleep in. After several days of civil treatment, he advised that because of some betrayal by my great-grandfather, I was due to be executed. But through his generosity, I had been released to his care. When I asked what that meant, he explained that I was free to live my life on the condition that I be available to serve The Benefactors, or Hōn leadership, should they call on me, for any reason, at any time. I never received an answer as to what my grandfather's alleged betrayal had been."

"How long have you been in their service?"

"Twenty years. Don't look so shocked. It hasn't been that bad a life. Not really. I trained in the US and have lived most of my life here, although I am frequently called back to China. I'm certain that life outside the Hōn, working within the so called legitimate Chinese system would be much less pleasant. When it comes to matters of State, only North Korean leadership can be more brutal than the Chinese government." He patted the girl's hand and smiled.

"I need to contact my people. Now," Jessie said.

"You need to regain your strength. Mei-Lin says you are on some kind of mission. I'm not sure if this…" he waved a finger toward Jessie's eyes, "is how you complete your missions. I'm not sure I want to know any of it. But I do know that killing the twins is going to have severe repercussions, or Tano is going to have to convince The Benefactors their elimination was necessary."

"If you get caught helping me, they…"

"We know what they will do," the doctor interrupted. "We are ready. Even to die if we must. We always have to be ready for that when it comes to The Benefactors. The question is, are you ready?"

"I'm not sure what you mean," Jessie said, groaning from the pain in her chest. *It might be time for another dose of Morphine.* She glanced at her broken hand. "Although this wasn't where I planned on going, it's where I ended up, and I always make the most of whatever cards I'm dealt." Mei-Lin looked at her and scrunched up her face, obviously not understanding what Jessie meant.

"I'm ready for everything. Just like you, I have to be. What is your plan?" Jessie asked.

Just then, the two old housekeepers stepped through the door to stuff Tano's bloody clothing into a plastic bag. The old woman stopped to stare. Jessie almost laughed as the terror of seeing Tano's glowing eyes crept onto her face.

"Èmó," the old woman mouthed, but no sound escaped her lips. Mei-Lin snapped some order in Chinese to the old couple, who quickly gathered the bloody clothes and left the room.

"Them, too?" Jessie asked. Mei-Lin nodded.

"I know they have been in the service of the Hōn since they were children. I have been told they were orphans in the streets of Zibo before the prefecture-city grew to the size it is now. As small children, they were taken in by the Hōn, and as they tell it, well cared for unless one of the Hōn or Benefactor children did something wrong, then they were beaten. They have been all over China and have been loyal servants their entire lives."

"Can I trust them?"

Mei-Lin laughed in a song-like note, sending a stirring deep into Tano's psyche, past the pain. Jessie noted the girl had cleaned up since the basement. Even after such and ordeal of torture, the girl still looked beautiful. Although Jessie could not see the burns and bruising on her body, she guessed that Mei-Lin's pain might be even greater than her own. Jessie followed the woman's gaze as she glanced toward Jessie's waist. Her face flushed and both she and the doctor quickly averted their eyes.

Tano's arousal surprised even Jessie. She had read some phycological report back in college purporting that men thought about sex once every couple of minutes. She hadn't thought of Mei-Lin in that way, although having had sex with her through the body of Bohai, perhaps she did. Jessie shifted the sheet and trounced on the unsolicited and obviously deeply embedded emotion even though she understood that deep down, and despite his efforts to remain celibate, Tano had feelings for the girl. Jessie ignored the engorged intrusion and continued.

"Well?" she asked again, pressing Mei-Lin to get her mind back to business.

"We have discussed this. They have been ordered to serve

Tano and feel that their master is now possessed by a demon. Therefore, they still serve you and will stay true and silent.

"Besides," the doctor added, "they have no tongue. No genitalia. They are male and female eunuchs."

Jessie's heart skipped a beat. She had heard that such medieval practices still existed but didn't believe it until now.

"Call them back in here."

When the old couple returned, the woman set a pair of clean clothes and underwear on a small nightstand and moved to the side, and as usual, their eyes remained fixed on the floor, two feet in front of them. The doctor assisted Jessie to a sitting position. Pain shot through her more pronounced than even a moment ago, and she clung to the mattress, gritting her teeth, doing her best to keep from passing out. Mei-Lin closed the door behind her.

"You may have another shot of Morphine if you wish, it…"

"No. Thank you," Jessie said. "I'm trying to cut back." Then Jessie rested her eyes on the two old, bent figures of the housekeepers, standing hunched over like a pair of broken dolls.

"Shénme shì nǐ de míngzì?" Jessie asked. *Tell me your names.* The old couple slowly looked toward one another, then barely raising their heads, locked eyes with Jessie, jumped a little, and returned their gaze to the floor. Then she remembered they could not speak. "What are their names, then?" Jessie asked.

"He is Quon, she is Huian. Both common names of servants."

Jessie took a deep breath and thought about what to say to them. "Nǐ wéi èmó fúwù ma?" she asked. *Do you serve the demon?* Jessie had never thought that she might be a demon, however, she also couldn't deny it might be a plausibility. That or perhaps she might be an alien life form.

And that's just a demon from outer space, she thought.

The couple bobbed their heads up and down together, with synchronization that matched the twins when she controlled them.

"Zài nǐ de shēnghuó?" *On your life?* Now the heads bobbed up and down even faster.

"Good," Jessie said in English. "We need to get the bodies out of the basement, and I need help up the stairs to the computer. The old couple began to use sign language. Mei-Lin nodded and signed back. Jessie knew enough American Sign to know they used something else. She assumed Chinese. More importantly, she made a mental note of their ability to communicate, a skill Tano and the others may have disregarded.

"That was already taken care of, Lord Èmō," Mei-Lin said, grinning playfully. The stirring started up again.

"How long ago?"

"I called the cleaners when I called my real uncle. That was hours ago."

"How long have I been out?"

"Six, almost seven hours, Lord Èmō." Jessie saw that Mei-Lin was teasing her now.

"Stop calling me that. We don't want any mistakes should others come calling. Understand?"

"Yes, Tano. Forgive my insolence." Mei-Lin bowed deeply, and the old couple followed.

Jessie shook her head. She had made a solid connection with Mei-Lin, and with one sharp command, she had possibly jeopardized that. "I'm sorry. I don't intend to be harsh. We are all on seriously thin ice here, and we have to be extra diligent to act as if nothing is wrong. Understand?" Jessie reached out with Tano's good hand and raised Mei-Lin's chin. Slowly, the eyes came up to meet hers, and without flinching, the smallest of smiles rose on the girl's lips, and she nodded.

"I understand. And so do they," she said, glancing at the old ones.

"Have them get back to their normal work, then. Nothing can look out of place." Jessie noticed the old couple watched her lips intently as she spoke. Perhaps they can read lips too? she wondered. They nodded, then left the room, their feet silent on the floor. "Where's…" Jessie had to think about the name, "Peng. The driver?"

"He had left to go out after you," Mei-Lin paused a moment to check her words, "after Tano came to the basement." The girl shuddered at the painful memory from just a few short hours ago.

"Help me up. I need to get to the computer. Are the twin's motorcycles gone?"

"Yes, the cleaners picked them up as well. I told them to keep them as a bonus."

"That's risky."

"No. The cleaners are a separate organization and are not beholden to The Benefactors. They will work for anyone, including the police when they make mistakes. They are smart. Those bikes will not be seen on the street."

Jessie nodded, impressed. "You are the smart one, aren't you?"

"As I said. I have the access a wife should have."

"What do we call you, then, if not Lord Èmō?" the doctor asked.

"Tano. This way we stay straight," Jessie replied.

Mei-Lin and the doctor were both too short in stature to be effective crutches for Tano's huge frame, but they hoisted him off Bohai's old bed with as much care as possible. Jessie groaned with each step.

"I can give you a shot…"

"No morphine," Jessie snapped. And she meant it. She would trudge through this pain, a reminder that she had once again made mistakes she needed to atone for, as she took one agonizing step at a time to the second-floor computer room.

Once at the top of the stairs, Jessie held up her hand to wait. Another step and she'd be on the floor. Breathing hard, she glanced over at the doc, and nodded. The doc searched his small waist pack and removed a syringe, loaded and ready to go. Without any warning, he tugged down Jessie's silk pants and jammed the sharp into her butt cheek. Within seconds, Jessie felt the meds washing over the pain.

"No wonder it's so addictive," she said.

After being helped into the chair, Jessie asked both Mei-Lin and the doctor to leave. She had new allies who had just saved her life, but this kind of trust took more than a couple of good deeds to earn. She picked up Tano's encrypted Sat-phone, booted it up, and dialed.

"Healthline Weight Loss, how can I help you today."

"Oh, I'm sorry, I thought this was the gaming center," Jessie replied.

"No, sorry, you've got the wrong number."

Jessie hung up. That would be enough to let her team know she was still alive, and that she would be communicating in the next few minutes. She could have spoken over the phone, but didn't trust the number, satellite phone or not, wasn't being recorded and tracked by The Benefactors. She pressed Tano's mind for the computer's access code. It came quickly, but not without a cost. Thankfully, the doc had loaded Jessie up with enough morphine that the shockwave of pain vibrating through the hosts head only seemed like the dull, hangover kind of throb. Once into the computer, she logged into the War Games movie fan site, found the designated page, and typed in her code. After a minute, the same black screen used by WOPR in the movie appeared, and a single cursor blinked in the upper left corner.

Jessie typed, "OMEGA, FIVE, ZULU, ONE, WHISKEY, THREE." After a few seconds, the computer responded both in text and voice.

"GOOD EVENING WALKER. SHALL WE PLAY A GAME?"

23

RETURNS

While pacing the interior walls of the Crue's AC-130U aircraft, Jon brushed his fingertips along the thick pads mounted between the extruded aluminum ribs of the cargo-bay. He said nothing, and although other members of the Crue Intellis team; Eric, Chip, Steve and others, sat in the removable jump seats attached side by side the length of the fuselage walls, everyone kept to themselves.

Jessie had been quiet well over twenty-four hours. Too quiet. Too long.

He pivoted left, continued pacing, his fingers now connecting with the grey-painted aluminum wall of the Comms-Pod, as he called it, a portable communication's center built to fit snugly in the cargo bay and slide right up against the airplane's flight deck firewall. Two stations gave operators access to everything from the Internet, to military information channels. He glanced through the door where Juanita Johnson sat, glaring at the blank terminal while she twirled a pen around her fingertips. Jon pivoted left again, maintaining his light but physical connection to the big bird.

He stopped then and peered up at what anyone could see were ribs that appeared different than the majority of those making up the airplane's internal frame. These beams had been fashioned by the Crue's own aviation structural mechanics, all veterans whom he had hired from different branches of the military. They also kept his WWII B-25J Mitchell in the air, but this plane had a very special history and belonged to every Crue Intellis employee.

The venerable AC-130U Spooky gunship, saved from the parts bin of the US Air Force, would have had a solid 20,000 hours of service life remaining had it not been for the huge hole ripped through the cargo area and a partially destroyed left wing after being hit by anti-aircraft fire while strafing enemy positions during operation Enduring Freedom, somewhere over Kashmir province of Afghanistan in 2012.

Right before they stripped out all the upgraded avionics and Electronic Propeller Control Systems— hi-tech improvements meant to carry the plane through the 21st Century—Jon had approached his long-time friend and client, then US Army, full bird-colonel, Henry Evans, about his need of a cargo plane. Nowadays, Henry wore two stars on each lapel and worked in cahoots with DARPA. Although Jon had been able to fund his own Satellite communications company, he didn't have a hundred million dollars lying around for the cargo plane he wanted. The C-130 Hercules.

He smiled at the memory of Henry cocking his head to the side, and saying, "So you want a C-130, huh?" And then asked Jon to meet him in Norfolk Virginia, where he *might* have something Jon *might* be interested in. Jon made the flight and almost regretted it when he entered the hangar bay.

"It's blown all to hell," Jon said.

"Yeah, well, we're only thinking about scrapping it because we're hard at war, and newer variants like the AC-130 Spectre are available," Henry replied. "It's repairable. A swipe of my pen will make the decision. Fix it or scrap it. How much did you want to spend?"

"That's a loaded question," Jon answered. "Besides, I'd need to hire a full company worth of mechanics to fix it, and there goes my budget." Despite the condition of the battered warbird, Jon envisioned it rolling out of The Crue's new hangar bay in

Camp Summit, North Carolina. Painted gloss black. He gazed into the gaping hole in the side of the plane. "This was one bad-ass aircraft. Probably the baddest-ass of them all, considering its capabilities. But..." Jon rested his hand on the 25mm Gatling gun barrel and turned to Henry. "Like I said, it's blown all to hell. For the money I'd need to spend to fix it I could buy..."

"It's yours for a dollar," Henry interrupted, grinning. "I'll even have it delivered via sky-crane."

Jon laughed hard and long, tears coming to his eyes at the General's sense of humor. Until he saw Henry wasn't smiling. "You're kidding, right? A dollar." Henry just glared at him, then raised an eyebrow.

"Can you even do that? I mean, I know you're..."

"Yes, I can. It's going to cost the Air Force at least a couple million to fix and retrofit. But as of right now, the Zoomies want the new variant and have written this one off as a war loss. I'll give it to you for a buck, and if it makes you feel better, I'll charge you a nominal fee for delivery. What say you?" Evan's smile faded. Jon would never forget how serious and intense the General could be.

"It needs a lot of work."

"A real fixer-upper," Evans said, "but the price is right. What say you? Going once. Going twice..."

"Guns too?" Jon asked. Evan's cocked his head to the side and narrowed his eyes. "Swap the 40mm Bofors and howitzer for two more Gatling guns?"

"One condition: you must be on call if we need the plane for an operation."

"It's a deal."

Jon couldn't stop the grin spreading on his face at the memory. The restoration took two years but went much smoother than he had anticipated, resulting in a multi-purpose platform configured to support Crue Intellis missions on so many levels.

Yes, he thought, *that was the deal of a lifetime.* No company asset, not even the B25 made him happier.

Until Jessie came along.

Now, he pivoted again to his left and faced the Chamber. *Jessie's Chamber.* Strapped to the cargo floor in the space directly in front of the front ends of two company Yukon's. Jon had left the big guns at home to stuff the plane with as much equipment and personnel it could carry, well below its operational cargo weight. He walked to the side of The Chamber. Jessie's team-mates had nicknamed it The Star-cophogus as a tip of the hat to the movie *Stargate and* leaned over to look at Jessie's peaceful face through the thick ballistic glass. He glanced at the bio-panel on the side of the unit and still marveled at how this woman could do what she did. Her heart rate hovered around an abnormally low ten beats per minute, matching the rate of her breathing. When the Chamber came online, these low numbers alarmed him until the kids from MIT explained that she didn't need to breath as much because the air inside The Chamber consisted of saturated oxygen. John placed his hand on the glass and let out a long sigh. Jessie meant more to The Crue, more to *him* than just being the most important asset, she…

"It's Jessie!"

The others sprang to their feet and crowded in behind Juanita Johnson's workstation to watch and listen to what their operative had to say. Juanita read the text on the screen out loud.

"Not a lot of time, did you get the movie I sent you?"

"Yes, we got the whole movie. Good show. Thanks for sharing." Juanita glanced up at Jon. David West and a group of Intel Analysts on loan from the CIA were still sorting through the data from the computer of the tall man who flew the drone. Jessie's last communication identified him only as Tano.

"Glad you liked it. I need a swap out, after info dump on last flick. NLT tomorrow A.M. Early. Say, 9 a.m. We're made of the right stuff with lots of goodness to share."

"Standby," Juanita typed and turned back to face the others.

"Well," Jon said, taking a deep breath, "she's made. I'm not sure how, yet, but sounds like she's set up and ready to tell us. We have to assume that even though she's transmitting on a scrambled server, she's being monitored."

"There's no doubt she's using Zulu time for accuracy," Eric added. "That said, we'll have to assume she's going off Romeo time for the home base, and that equates to 9 a.m. Eastern Standard..."

"Minus three hours for time zones, and it's a minus five-hour day according to the communications calendar," Chip Rasher said, flipping his iPad around for the others to see.

"That's zero-one hundred hours, Pacific time. Where are we going to meet her?" Juanita said.

"Well, it sounds like things have changed since she took the twin," Eric said. "They returned to Palo Alto from Reno. We need to get closer."

"Ideas anyone?" Jon asked.

"What about the hangar on Moffett Field?" Juanita asked. "It's as close as we could ask for, and we already know there's an open bay at the end of the old dirigible hangar one."

"Right under Kore's nose? You don't think he'll get wise?" Eric replied, concern on his face.

"Look, we're running out of time. She's made and we have to move and get what we can," Chip Rasher said.

"I agree. Ask her, J," Jon said.

"Want to swap DVD's at the airport?" Juanita wrinkled her nose after typing and turned to say, "I didn't know how else to say it. But she knows the hangar facility and the area better than any of us."

After a short pause, Jessie replied, "Perfect."

"Are you bringing your boyfriend?" An old protocol question Juanita felt confident in asking. *Are you still in the twin?*

"Yes. But a different BF. Plus one," she typed. Everyone grumbled.

"What is she up to?" Jon said, not really asking a question.

Juanita held her fingers over the keyboard a moment, then nodded before typing, "Do we know him?"

"Yes. He's a pilot. And his girlfriend wants to come too. She'll bring her own DVD to share."

The Crue team looked at one another, and Jon raised an eyebrow, then nodded.

"Great, the more the merrier. See you in the morning." Juanita turned to Jon and glanced at her screen. "This good enough, boss? We're out of time to chat."

Jon nodded. "Send it." Juanita did.

The words, "WINNER: NONE." Popped up on the screen, then comms disconnected.

"She's in the big guy," Eric said, a sour look on his face.

"That's a good thing. She'll squeeze him and get..."

"This isn't your normal big guy," Eric interrupted. "He's going to be a tough nut to crack. Even those twins gave him space. I'm telling you the guy is huge. Like six-foot-six. Maybe more, and built like, like..." Eric's face screwed up thinking of a comparison, "Dolph Lungren when he was young."

Jon nodded then rested a hand on Juanita's shoulder. "J, get with Mario and see if the FBI has come up with any facial recognition. We should have had a name by now," Jon said. Juanita nodded, then set to work.

"Let's pull chocks, folks. Jessie's going to want to get the big guy to spill his guts and then slip-stream back. We'll want to have him restrained, so when he comes to, he's not a problem.

"Oh," Eric said, "I want to be part of this. Least I could do after the cabin."

JESSIE LEANED BACK AND LET OUT A DEEP BREATH. SHE unconsciously tried to lift her arms, then winced at the pain. She lowered the cast to her chest, cradling it with Tano's one good hand as the computer program stated its data-sweep. The electronic WOPR voice said, "STANDBY." Jessie waited for a full minute and jumped when the screen and voice finally said, "WINNER: NONE. HOW ABOUT A NICE GAME OF CHESS?" and then the screen went blank.

At this point in the game, Jessie only needed to get Tano to a secure facility to slip-stream back into her body, deliver Mei-Lin, and then she would be clear for White Sands. She clucked her tongue at the thought of missing her window for training to fly the Grumman drone, and she still had no idea if her team had been able to decipher and prepare everything for the tests. She accepted that she could end up just watching, but also knew that having taken Tano, now was the time for the man to spill some beans. His body was wrecked.

This could kill him.

She got up from the chair and carefully walked to the surveillance room door. She pulled it open and found the old man standing there with a tray of sushi and hot green tea, his hand poised to knock. The old man carefully lowered to his knees, set the tray in front of him and bowed, placing his forehead on the ground.

"Quon, is it?" Jessie said in Mandarin. The old man's head bobbed up and down. "Thank you for the food. Can you please take it to my room?" The head bobbed again, the old man stood, bent at the waist with his knees locked, and lifted the tray off the flat floor. As he stood and turned toward the room, Quon's body seemed to vibrate with age as he walked, yet the tray held steady, as if it floated on a pillow of air in front of the old man. Mei-Lin had just crested the final steps of the stairs and moved up to stand beside Tano. "That old, barely able to function man just bent in half at the hips. Look at the tray."

As Mei-Lin turned to look, a small vibration traveled through the old-man's arms and the tea service rattled a little. "Did he do something to displease you?" She looked up into Jessie's glowing eyes with concern.

"No, I guess I'm just imagining things. I need to rest. Then you and I are going on a short road trip."

"Where are we going?"

"Moffett field. We leave at 12:30 a.m. You should get some rest."

"I have already been sleeping."

"You should rest anyway; it's going to be a long morning." Mei-Lin nodded as Jessie slowly moved toward Tano's room. It had only been an hour since the last morphine shot, and Jessie knew the time to put mind over matter, in this case pain, was now at hand. She entered the room and didn't pay attention to how sparse the walls and furnishings were but groaned at having to lower herself to the bed.

"Let me help you."

Jessie looked up. Mei-Lin stood at the door. Jessie nodded and the girl made her way to Jessie's uninjured side, careful not to jostle Tano's broken hand and ribs. Slowly, she lowered Jessie to the mattress.

"What is your name?" Mei-Lin asked, as Jessie tried to get comfortable on the thin mattress.

"Jessie."

Mei-Lin nodded and walked to the door, closing it behind her. She returned to the bedside, untied her robe, and let it fall to the floor.

"Mei-Lin, I don't think…"

"Lie still, Jessie," Mei-Lin said, lowering her naked body to lay beside her. "I promise, I will be gentle."

24

LOOSE ENDS

J essie's eyes opened to Mei-Lin hovering over her, half naked, pushing gently on her shoulder. "Jessie? Are you in there?" she asked. As Jessie roused to fully take command of Tano's body, the dimly lit room allowed her to see the increasing glow of her eyes, reflected in Mei-Lin's.

"What's the time?"

"Ten after midnight."

Jessie moved to sit up until the wall of pain stopped her momentum. Mei-Lin reached down and gently helped her stand up. Jessie dragged her feet to the nearby dresser, where Mei-Lin had already laid out clothes for her to wear, her grey Glock 43 pistol lay on top. Jessie set it aside.

"May I wash you up?" Mei-Lin asked.

"No time," Jessie replied, her host's body shaking a bit as she tried to dress. Mei-Lin assisted, again.

"You're going to smell like sex."

Jessie raised an eyebrow. "And there's a problem with that?" Mei-Lin giggled as Jessie rested a hand on the tiny woman's shoulder. As Mei-Lin bent to assist with the clothes, Jessie noticed the scrapes and burn marks on her back were visible and still looked angry. Jessie had never experienced being tortured, and although she understood the primal need for a hard grinding round of sex after such an ordeal, she found it surprising the younger woman could find room for laughter.

Reminds one of how great it is to be alive, she thought. Also, for the first time in Jessie's life, she had just laid there and let someone else—Mei-Lin—do all the work. Not even morphine could stop Tano's body from responding to being touched by the woman he secretly wanted.

"Can you go check on the others? Tell them to stay put until we get back. I'm calling my team."

Mei-Lin nodded and left.

Jessie dialed. She had to risk it, sensing that Tano had not yet alerted Chen to a problem with the twins.

"Dream Cruises, this is Samantha, can I help you?"

"Walker-two, X-Ray, Delta, Charlie, Eight, Lima."

"We're here. Ready when you are."

"Which hangar?"

"Hangar One. South End. We'll be waiting."

Jessie hung up just as Mei-Lin came through the door. "They are gone."

"The housekeepers?"

"All of them. Peng, too."

Jessie let out a long hiss of air. "Not good. Get dressed, we need to roll."

"Are you going to make it?"

Jessie glanced over at Mei-Lin. "Is it that obvious?" she asked. The worried look on the girl's face said enough. Jessie had refused another shot, knowing that as the time neared to slip back into her body, she'd need to have full access to Tano's neurotransmitters. Earlier, although she'd had firm control, it felt as if she were wading through cotton balls while attempting to peruse the man's memory. It felt as if Tano might somehow be aware. She had never dreamed the dreams of her host and shuddered at the fleeting memories she had just experienced from Tano. This, again, had been another first. Between the physical damage and the memories, it just didn't look good. At this point, she didn't have the confidence to get past the pain to get what she needed.

I might be screwed either way.

"I can drive if you like?"

"I thought you had said something about you're not being permitted to drive."

Mei-Lin's light, sexy giggle helped Jessie forget about the pain. "Well, I have had ways in convincing some of The Benefactors to teach me. I finished top of my class in executive protection driving course."

Now Jessie chuckled and leaned back, taking a sideways assessment of the demure, tiny woman. "You're a certified protection driver?" Mei-Lin nodded, and Jessie didn't miss the pleading looking on her face.

"OK, we're only about ten minutes out. You want to drive the rest of the way?" The hopeful look morphed into a grin. Jessie pulled over, exited, and she couldn't help but chuckle as a giggling Mei-Lin shuffled past Jessie around the back of the SUV.

Thwap, Thwap, Thwap.

Three rough holes appeared in the bulletproof rear window. "Get in!" Mei-Lin yelled and dove for the driver seat as something struck Jessie in the back of the right shoulder. *Thwap. Thwap.* More pain.

Mei-Lin jerked the shifter to Drive and floored it. Jessie looked back and saw more little dots of broken glass appear but heard no gunshots. "They're using suppressors," Jessie said and pulled the Glock from her waistband.

"Drive!"

For a solid minute, the tink of lead off the SUV's body continued before lights finally blazed on from behind them.

"This car is armored. We'll drive straight through," Mei-Lin said, then took a sudden right onto an unknown street, causing Jessie's head to sway left and slam right into the glass.

"Sorry!" Mei-Lin said, as the GPS guidance announced, "Re-routing."

Jessie fished Tano's satellite phone from his pocket, powered it up, and waited to acquire signal. Bullets continued to strike the vehicle as Mei-Lin power slid the SUV through corners, expertly making turns at high speed.

"You weren't kidding," Jessie said.

"About?" Mei-Lin's brows were furrowed, her tongue sticking out the side of her mouth in concentration as she slammed the car into another sharp turn. Suddenly, the ping of bullets off the car's armor skin stopped.

"Being a good driver. Don't let up, get to the hangar."

Jessie dialed.

"Duchess Cruises, how can I help you?"

"Taina?"

"I'm sorry, I think you have the wrong..." Jessie knew Taina wanted to hear her daily confirmation code, but Jessie couldn't think straight at the moment.

"It's me, Jessie, we're being shot at. I'm hit, and we're only a few minutes out."

"We'll be ready." The phone hung up.

"They stopped chasing us," Mei-Lin said, easing up on the gas.

"No, don't slow down. Get to Moffett Field."

"But..."

"Look, they're probably re-routing to stop us at an intersection. I'll try to help, just slow a bit at the intersections so we don't get T-bone'd like they do in the movies."

"I hate that. It gets me every time," Mei-Lin said.

"Me too."

Not another word passed between the two as Mei-Lin continued to ease through intersections and floor the SUV in the straightaways. The commercial buildings they had to pass on the way to Moffett Field all had excellent lighting. Jessie spun in her seat, grit her teeth at the excruciating pain in her lungs, and watched. The bad guys weren't following. "Keep your eyes peeled. We don't want to get caught out here in the open." Mei-Lin did not answer but picked up the pace.

"There's the hangar," Mei-Lin said.

"Go around to the south side. The right. Slow down."

Jessie and Mei-Lin both looked around as the enormous WWII era hangar loomed before them. Two grey GMC Yukon's appeared on the south side. Their doors opened. Shadows of operators she could not see bolstered up behind the doors, pointing weapons their general direction. Mei-Lin gasped.

"They're with me. My team. Good job, Mei-Lin." Then Jessie slumped to the side.

THE MOMENT THE SMALL SUV PULLED TO A STOP IN FRONT OF the Yukon's, Jon Daly gave the signal. The lights on that side of the hangar's tarmac went out, plunging the entire group into a wash of shadows caused from distant lights. Night Vision Goggles on, three crew members did the Groucho-walk, keeping knees bent as they moved forward, allowing smooth barrel sighting and accurate bullet placement on the move.

Jon observed a small, Asian woman exit the driver seat. "Jessie's injured," she said, and rushed to the side of the vehicle, not making it to the door before two of the Crue Intellis operators reached her and took an arm each, pulling her back.

"We'll take care of her, Miss." Let's get you to safety, a female voice said. Mei-Lin nodded as two other operators opened Jessie's door and had to sling their weapons to get the big man out of the seat.

"Oh. Hi," Jessie said, her voice slurred. "I'm not sure if I'm going to…"

"You'll make it. *Fuck,* this is a big dude."

"You know I like 'em big," Jessie said, trying to joke as she stumbled to her knees.

"Get them inside and hold the perimeter," Jon said.

As the operators walked backwards, keeping Mei-Lin somewhat behind them, they scanned the shadows, their Vector 9mm sub-machine guns pointed toward an unseen enemy. A third operator rushed to assist with Jessie. Jon jumped into the driver seat of the Yukon, pulling it up to provide cover as another operator did the same with the second, when Mei-Lin cried out and stumbled.

Seconds later, the third operator, then Jessie stumbled forward. "I'm hit!" the operator said.

Jon and Eric Ramos bailed out behind their respective vehicles, maintaining cover behind the steel reinforced doors, and looked around. The remaining two operators continued to drag Jessie and Mei-Lin toward the hangar, only feet to go.

"I think I'm hit," another operator said, "in my back plate." Jon scrambled in to assist the man and called out.

"Eric! Thermal!"

Eric reached into the truck just as something whistled past his head, sticking into the thick rubber seal of the door jamb.

"Darts!" Eric yelled, then started scanning the darkness before him. "I don't see anyone!" As he scanned from behind the windshield, some little reaction of light in the top of the thermal reticle caught his attention. He scanned up the side of the building. Two forms appeared, braced against one another, their hands forward. *Thwack!* Another dart ricocheted off the glass. "They're on the side of the hangar! By rappel! Air guns," he called.

Eric's eyes began to adjust enough that he could barely make out the forms' movements, at least a hundred feet up the side of the building. He pointed his suppressed 9mm SMG at the forms through the red-dot sight and fired off three quick bursts. One figure fell, releasing the rope, resulting in an eerie crack as the body struck the concrete. The other scrambled up the side. Anticipating the assassin's location, Eric saw the form clearly as a head crested the hangar frame. He squeezed the trigger, and the body jerked, but scrambled onto the roof and disappeared.

"He's gone over the roof. I think I hit him."

Quiet. Just as the operators made the corner with Jessie and Mei-Lin, a voice called out from the darkness, echoing off the buildings. "A gift from Chen for your treachery, Tano!" Then a car engine started and fled somewhere in the near distance.

"Get the exterior lights back on," Jon yelled.

Two more armed operators exited the hangar, rushing to Eric. "Go see to Walker. We'll see if we can catch him." Eric nodded as the two jumped in the Yukon and sped off into the early morning hours. Two more operators took the second Yukon and followed. Mei-Lin had to be carried into the hangar.

"Eric," Jessie said. "Chamber."

Eric moved to the big man's side and helped drag Jessie's host body across the polished concrete hangar floor to rest against the strange looking coffin in the center of the room. The young MIT girl, Melanie Banks, stood by the unit, a mix of terrified resolve on her face. Her only job was to ensure the device continued to operate properly. This was more than she had bargained for. As they approached, she quickly punched in the code. The access door of the Chamber hissed as it released pressurized oxygen from inside and slid down to give everyone access. Jon removed the headset and helped hoist the big man to the edge within arms' reach of Jessie.

"Hi there, Mel," Jessie said, her voice weak.

Melanie stared wide-eyed at the big man, tears welling up in her eyes. "Hey there, Jess. We've got this, right?"

"Yes, we've got this."

"We need a medic, now!" Eric said, finally seeing the dart in Tano's neck and bent forward to look closer. The needle penetrated Tano's neck, but only enough to pierce the skin and exit. The clear fluid leaked out of the needle's tip.

"Water!" Eric yelled. His eyes locked onto a bottle of drinking water flying through the air. He caught it one-handed, tore off the top, and poured water onto the fluid dripping down the man's neck.

"Just rip it out, Goddammit!" Jessie said. Eric didn't miss Jessie's fear in the voice of the man who had tried to kill them both.

Eric doused the area again, jerking it out.

Jessie looked at Jon and Eric, then the others, the red glow fading in her eyes. "I...I..."

"Just do it, Jessie. Goddammit. No talking, just slip," Eric said, a frightened look on his face.

Hands shaking, sweat pouring from the host's body, Jessie reached out and touched the sides of her face. Tano collapsed, and Jessie gasped and screamed as she sat up, tore the head gear off, then pulled herself from The Chamber.

Tano's eyes blinked but went wide as the shock of pain and disorientation slammed into him. Jessie took the dart from Jon and held it in front of his eyes.

"What is this, Tano? You've been hit. What have your people done?"

His muscles twitched. His eyes went wide. He focused on Jessie's face then and said, "It's you. From my dreams. In my head. I...saved you. You...saved...me." Tano's glassy eyes locked with Jessie's. A small smile came to his lips. "Promises to keep," he said. "I guess I will be seeing you...later." Tano passed out.

Eric took his pulse. "Thready pulse, but he's still breathing. There's no foam. I think he'll make it." Crue medics rushed to Tano's side and started an intravenous drip.

Jessie rushed to Mei-Lin's side. Taina Volkov and her husband Mark Samuelson both administered what they could but shook their head as Jessie leaned over and held the woman. Tears streamed out of Mei-Lin's eyes.

"So, you are Jessie?" she asked. Tears welled in Jessie's eyes, too, but no words came. "A woman. No wonder you are such a gentle lover." Jessie laughed and looked to Marc, kneeling next to her. She could barely see Marc's head move from side to side. Mei-Lin's body twitched, muscles misfiring, froth forming in her mouth.

"We don't have the antidote for cyanide, Jessie," Taina said. "I'm sorry. It's been well over five minutes."

"Red Boat Opera. In Hong Kong. Seek out…seek out." Mei-Lin started to fade.

"Seek out who?"

"They will help you get to Chen. To The…Benefactors. Red…boa…" and then nothing, her eyes remained open.

Jessie fought back the tears, reached out, and tried to close Mei-Lin's eyes. Jon's firm hand rested on her shoulder. "I'm sorry, Jess," he said.

"She didn't deserve this," Jessie said, standing up to lean into Jon's body. "It all just got carried away…she…"

"Look. It's not your fault Kore had overwatch. It's not your fault Eric was caught and used as bait. It is what it is, and we've got some great intel from that system from the house." Jessie nodded but didn't look Jon in the eye. She stared at Mei-Lin's lifeless body and shook her head. "Such a waste of life."

"Can you look at the woman who came down from the roof of the hangar?" Jon asked.

"Woman?" Jessie jerked upright and turned toward the figure clothed in all black lying against the wall just inside the hangar door. She fast stepped over to the body and gasped. "Are you kidding me?"

"You know her?" Jon asked.

"Yes. Her name is Huian. I can't believe this. She was one of the housekeepers. I mean, Jon, she's like, seventy years old. She skitters about the house doing chores like a little old lady."

"I don't think so," Jon said and reached down to pull up her sleeve. "There is muscle here. She might look older but check this out." A somewhat faded, traditional tattoo of a Chinese Dragon appearing to breathe life into a red sun took up the length of the woman's forearm.

"You got a phone?" Jessie asked.

"Yes," Jon said, "and I'm already ahead of you. I've sent the photo to Mario, who's working with his FBI buddies to identify the group she was in."

Jessie nodded, then knelt down. She reached out and tugged the fabric down from Huian's neck and noticed something. She rubbed at the woman's skin, and after a little effort, a rubbery substance started to peel up from the neck. Jessie tugged at it until the glue holding the rubber in place gave.

"A mask," she said, and looked up at Jon.

"I'm not surprised," Jon said. I'll have forensics get good photos of the person underneath and get it to Mario for facial recognition.

Jessie stood up. "This just keeps getting deeper and deeper."

Jon nodded. "Yes, it does. But we have the tests next week. How do you feel about Kore?"

"I'm pretty sure I convinced him that Tano was laying off. I think he'll be concentrating on the tests. But what about this?" She pointed at the assassin lying on the floor.

"Well, we know now that they know something's up. They called Tano a traitor and that could work in our favor."

"Yes, that guy's name is Peng. The one who shouted traitor. He's their driver. But I didn't see him much."

"Obviously, he was part of this team to take Tano out before he could talk. Your girl, too." Jon folded his arms and paced around in a circle. "My gut is telling me to let the tests play out. If the Hōn, Benefactors, whoever is in charge, get to Kore and pull the plug, then so be it. We'll move on it when that happens. But right now, the tests have to be our priority."

Jessie nodded again. "I agree. I'm going to have to be an observer now. I missed my window to practice on the POD."

"You've been through a lot, Jess. I don't expect you to be there for this."

Jessie turned toward the dead being laid out while waiting for DOD to send an investigations team, the body of their teammate separated from the others. Jessie glanced over at two Crue medics loading Tano onto a stretcher. She walked back over to the tall man, Jon following. The medics tucked a blanket under Tano's body and strapped his body in after cuffing his hands to the carry-holes of the stretcher. Jessie knelt down and examined the side of Tano's neck. Eric walked up beside her.

"I'm not sure how much Cyanide it takes to kill someone," Eric said, pointing out the two distinct entry/exit holes, "but I don't think he got enough. I mean, he looks pretty beat up."

"Six broken ribs, fractured hand, possible nicked liver. Who knows what else I did to him?"

"Really?" Eric raised an eyebrow. "Yet another reason for me to never piss you off." Jessie didn't smile at the comment. "What did he mean about seeing you in his dreams? Saving you?" Eric asked.

Jessie took a deep breath and stood up. "He's a tough cookie. Probably the most disciplined man I've ever slip-streamed into. I saw his dreams. That was a first. There were a lot of firsts for me on this mission. Too many."

Eric opened his mouth again, but Jessie touched her fingers to his lips. "Enough Q&A for now, Gunny," she said. She pushed away from Eric and walked over to Mei-Lin's body as Taina covered her head with one of the yellow medical sheets.

"It should have been the other way around," Jessie said. "Mei-Lin was a gold mine of information and had planned to share what she knew about the Hōn. It's not fair that she died and he…" She looked toward Tano as they slid the stretcher into the back of a Yukon. Jessie pointed at the stretcher. "He's a real, bonafide bad guy."

Jon, Jessie, and Eric watched as the Yukon drove off. "They're taking him to Palo Alto VA Hospital," Jon said.

"I'm going to want another crack at Tano," Jessie said. "When his body can take it." She didn't express, however, what she really thought.

If I'll ever be that ready to try again is more like it.

She glanced at Jon and Eric. "Thanks for being here for me," she said, then she pulled Eric in for a strong hug.

"Don't mention it," Jon said. "You can buy the beer."

As Jon moved to walk away, Jessie reached out and snatched his hand. "If it's okay with you, I'll head to White Sands to help David with the drone anyway I can. This intel has come at too much of a cost for me not to be there."

25

WHITE SANDS

White Sands Missile Range
Alamogordo, New Mexico
One Week Later

Robert pulled the custom wrapped KORE, INC. branded H-1 Hummer up to the entrance to the flight-testing area, where a serious Marine Corps sentry motioned for him to stop. Robert rolled down the window, flashed his best smile.

"Credentials, please," the young corporal asked. Robert handed the young man his team's creds and watched as the Marine scrutinized each and every face against the ID badges before handing them back.

"Where to, Marine?" Robert asked, smiling.

The sentry frowned and pointed a finger in the opposite direction of the flight control center. "Please proceed to the sentry…over there."

Robert followed the direction of the corporal's finger, barely making out another military Humvee in the distance. "Why way out there?"

"Orders, sir. No civilians permitted to park within a half-mile of the flight-line."

"I've never heard of such a thing," he fired back. "On whose orders, exactly?"

"General Evans, sir," the corporal said without hesitation.

Robert collected a pair of binoculars from the dashboard and scanned the destination point, focusing on the shape of another soldier standing next to a green Humvee. He panned to the left, focused on the flight control center in the distance, and gasped. "What the hell?"

"Sir?" the Marine replied.

"That's the flight control center?" Robert asked.

"Yes, sir."

Robert lowered the binoculars and glanced at his project manager, Maria Ricardi, sitting in the passenger seat. He executed a barely perceptible shake of his head. Maria raised a questioning eyebrow but said nothing.

"Sorry, I'll head to the parking area now," Robert said, then added, "Thank you for your service." He rolled up his window and drove forward. A thought came to him, along with a piercing jolt of pain. "Breadcrumbs," he said, followed by an under-the-breath, "Fuck me."

"What's wrong?" his lead engineer Carl Berg asked from the back seat.

Robert pointed across the plain to the two, P-SCIF's, squatting like a pair of alien bugs in the middle of New Mexico's high-plains desert. He handed the binoculars back to Carl. "Do those look familiar?"

Carl took them and looked through. "Well I'll be damned," he said. "Not only are they ours, those look like the first three we sent to DOD for inspection and evaluation."

"Wasn't that, like, ten years ago?" Maria asked, taking the binoculars from Carl and pressing them to her eyes. "I only see numbers one and three, but one looks bigger."

"It's probably been linked up with number two. They're modular," Carl said.

"Coincidence?" Maria asked. Robert didn't reply because coincidence had nothing to do with the strange occurrences leading up to these tests. Carl had no clue about the deal Robert had made with The Benefactors ten years ago. But Maria, she had ended up as eager to be his partner in this billion-dollar crime as she was between the sheets.

"Refresh my memory," Maria said, her eyes hard on Robert. "Did the DOD pay for the upgrades on those units, or just the basic security program?" Maria's intentional walk around the question, "Were the unit's internal microphones and transmitters ever activated?", couldn't have been more subtle.

"Oh, we gave them the upgrade, at no additional cost," Robert replied. Maria leaned back in the seat, brows furrowed in thought. The sight of the SCIF's made Robert's skin crawl. Within weeks after the units were deployed into the field, the last words he had received from The Benefactors were along the lines of how well the SCIF program had been working out for them. "Much better than expected," Chen had said. It had been the only time Robert had spoken to the man. Tano spoke for The Benefactors ever since. Until today, Robert had all but forgotten about them.

"What are the chances of our first batch of SFIC's being re-configured to be control centers for our KAGI-6 mainframe?" Carl asked.

Exactly, Robert thought. *What are the chances?* He pulled up to the military transport Humvee and turned to the others. "You two go ahead. I'll be right behind you."

Carl reached up and squeezed his shoulder. "This is in the bag, Robert. The A.I. system works perfectly. I expect nothing less than the performance from last week. The A.I. will fly the wings off that drone, and you'll be a hero. You'll see." Robert nodded and forced a smile as Carl clambered out the rear door. As Maria followed, Robert reached out, touching her back. She turned to face him.

"I'm calling Andrew," he said.

A look of concern etched Maria's face, but she nodded, rubbing at her temples. "This is all kinds of weird, Robert. Just thinking about it gives me a splitting headache. How do you feel about it?" Maria asked.

"I'm not sure, but we're here, aren't we? Why would they go through all this trouble if they had a clue? We have to play this out," he said. Maria nodded and got out.

Robert watched as Maria and Carl approached and then shook hands with the female Army Sergeant assigned as their escort to Flight Control. He glanced toward the mountains that lay a little more than five miles west of their current position as the crow flies. Situated on a small cliff-ledge near Salinas Peak, their lead programmer, Andrew Paulson, sat at the controls of the flight and weapons console in the back of a second Kore Industries H-1 Hummer. No one other than Andrew and Maria knew about Robert's back up plan. Not even that meddler, Tano.

Thinking about how the man just sort of vanished after his quick check-in phone call last week didn't sit well with Robert, either. If this deal turned out to be anything like the SCIF deal, Robert knew he wouldn't hear from Tano until The Benefactors needed something else. Robert had always known that with this project, The Benefactors, Hōn, or whomever the fuck seeded his research, weren't in it for the money. Their interests revolved around a foundation of power. Power to bring the United States and its allies to their knees when the full deployment of the world's first completely autonomous combat aircraft ended up being an agent of China's underbelly. Tano made it clear they would kill to ensure their future investments remained uncompromised.

Like Laina, he thought.

He had a feeling Tano had lied to him and killed the girl, after all. His attempts to reach her had gone unanswered. He reached into his jacket pocket, retrieved his iPhone, and stared at the number displayed on his screen. 717-546-9557. He pressed send, then waited.

"Hi! Sorry I can't come to the..." he hung up. As he stared at the number, something about them ignited the analytical part of his mind. He grabbed a pen and scrap of paper from the Hummer's center console and jotted down the corresponding letters assigned to each number. As the letters came together, he imagined there might be an anagram hidden in there. At the mere thought of the girl, pain seared into his skull once again. He dropped the phone in the console and gritted his teeth to hold back the bile rising in his stomach. "What the fuck," he said, exasperated. He tossed the pen across the cab only after cyphering the word '71-SKIN' and rubbed at his temples.

These past couple of weeks felt as if he had been set down a long, strange path not of his choosing. But so far, he had survived it, and the success of the additional tests forced on him by Tano gave him a fresh shot of confidence that he would soon be a very rich man.

Confirmations of assured success aside, Robert wasn't stupid. With all the strange shit happening over the past couple of weeks, and especially because of that even stranger itch digging around somewhere inside his skull, he had no doubts about the necessity of a plan B.

The A.I. system tests had originally been designed to be monitored and controlled using a mobile system, but the DOD, specifically General Henry Evans, had decided against it. Robert felt his jaw tense at the memory. The pompous man had said, "We can't all fit in the goddammed hummer, can we?" Robert swallowed hard at having to admit the General's choice about how to best deploy 'Che-dan', as his employees had affectionately named the A.I. project, had proved to be beneficial in the end. Everyone dismissed the Mobile Flight Command and Integrated Communications vehicle as being unnecessary. Everyone but him.

It almost seemed that Evans and DARPA had forgotten that Robert spent over five million dollars of the taxpayer's money to build the mobile command unit. He could only guess that the project's paperwork sat buried in some slush-pile of DARPA projects, somewhere.

He narrowed his eyes to focus on the ridge line in the distance. That all-but-forgotten MFC/IC vehicle sat up there, somewhere, with Andrew at the controls. This past few months, his team worked hard to modify the platform by adding its own powerful Lockheed/Martin dish antennae and the AN/VLQ 7-12 Weapons and Electronic jamming system capped off by a custom built, AN/TWQ-1 Avenger surface to air missile system– Electronic, drone and anti-aircraft warfare at its finest. Plug and play components the DOD didn't ask to be returned once the project had been scrapped by Evans. Hell, for the past three years, his team had almost exclusively used the mobile unit to synchronize and monitor the Kore A.I. system with Grumman's X47A drone. Now, the Hummer could protect itself, if necessary. Today, he hoped Andrew wouldn't have to use it at all. He rubbed at his neck. Something just did not feel right. His instincts screamed for him to run. But…

I've come too far to let this go.

Years of his life had been dedicated to this project, ultimately geared toward getting even with that blow-hard Evans. Regardless of where the money came from, he had earned the right to be here. His system competed against the very best A.I. programmers in the world, all invited by DARPA to test the viability of an A.I. combat aerial drone system. Three years ago, DARPA's "SkyWars" air supremacy trials pitted his system against upstart wanna-be A.I. developers Robert had never heard of. Groups like Falcor Systems, Enigma A.I., and even bigger entries from the likes of Lockheed and Boeing. And Kore's system had beat them all. Fair and square. But it was the taking on a duo of F-35 Joint Strike Fighters, operated by human pilots that had sealed the deal. KAGI-6's defeat of the human controlled simulator, 15 hits to zero, had earned him the right to be here today- to demonstrate the use of live weapons against real-steel. He smiled at the memory of how the seasoned combat and training pilot, one of the best in the world, accused the A.I. of cheating, and being unsafe in a 'real-world' environment, but the truth was, 'if you ain't cheatin', you ain't tryin.'' DARPA and Evans had been impressed by the results. No, he had no intention of running. Not on this day.

Another thought entered his mind, causing the hair at the nape of his neck to stand on end. He rubbed at it, brow creased in an angry frown.

The Benefactors, and that meddlesome fuc...

A knock at his window startled him. He turned to see the smiling face of the female sentry, motioning for him to unroll his window.

"Mr. Kore, If you could, please come..."

"I need to make a call to my home office," he interrupted.

"I'll walk to the command center if you're not back before I'm done." The sergeant looked back toward the old Kore SCIF's, their images vibrating in the distant mirage, then turned back to face him.

"Sir, my instructions were..."

"Look Sergeant," he said, putting on his most winning smile. "I have a billion-dollar contract sitting on that tarmac." He pointed to where she had just been looking. "I need to make sure everyone on my team is on point. I promise I won't be long."

After a pause, the soldier nodded, then headed off to assist Carl and Maria.

Once they drove off, Robert rolled up the window, turned the A/C onto high and collected his encrypted satellite phone from the center console, powered it up, and cursed under his breath at the length of time it took to capture a signal. "Finally," he grunted, punching the send button. The phone rang six times before someone on the other side picked up.

"Yes, sir," the voice said.

"Andrew, is your sat-phone working?"

"Yes, I picked up on the first ring."

Encryption delay, Robert thought. "We've got an interesting development here," he said.

"You're talking about the P-SCIF's, right?" Andrew asked.

"Yes," Robert said, his temples starting to ache. "You picked up their signals?"

"Yes, sir. It's interesting all right."

"What are your thoughts?"

"I know for a fact we haven't heard a peep from those units since the DOD took them for evaluation tests. I think that was, like, ten years ago. Right? Anyway, I arrived this morning just before dawn and barely got the dish up, when wham! I got the alert, and I turned on the speakers. I can hear everything they're saying in every corner of the room. Crystal clear. My console shows a connected signal between SCIF 1 and 2. I think they've linked them up. That's also where the KAGI-6 mainframe is."

"Nothing from 3?"

"No, sir, not a sound."

"You're connected to the mainframe, too, right?

"Yes, sir."

"Do you think you triggered the mic system when you data linked?"

"I don't see how. They're not integrated systems. Also, keep in mind that the transmitters are only effective out to ten clicks, max. Obviously, I'm well within range. We're cross connected to the A.I. via satellite. That won't be suspicious because the DOD expects us to monitor our own tests. I've been through this with them a million times. But they won't know I'm here."

"I guess the question is, why did the SCIF's come online now? What do you think?" Robert asked.

"I'm not sure what to think. I can tell you the information

they're chattering about right now sounds classified. So, I'm thinking this is just a fluke, and we should take advantage of it."

Robert's intuition sent harsh warning alarms into his skull. This didn't *feel* like a fluke. "You could be right, but I don't want to take any chances."

"Of course, sir."

"Andrew, listen to me carefully because we haven't discussed this. If the shit hits the fan, as in our asses are busted, I need you to target both SCIF's and crash the fucking 180 million-dollar drone into the side of a mountain." The line went silent. "Andrew, I'm not kidding here. This is critical to both our survival. You got it?"

"But, sir, you, all of you will be in the SCIF…"

"No, we won't. As soon as I'm in the FCC, I'll start talking. If you can hear me loud and clear over your speakers, dial me and let my phone ring a few times. I'll have it on vibrate. If a problem does come up, I'll make it very clear. Keep listening to the SCIF sensors. When you hear me say, 'I'm out,' count to ten and strike."

"Sir…"

"I'm not kidding, Andrew. Do not hesitate. We'll be rolling out by the time the weapons strike. We have more to worry about than losing a contract if we're busted, right?"

"Yes. You're right. You think we're busted?"

"Let's just say right now, I'm suspicious. I don't know how it's possible, but we have to be ready. Remember, if the shit hits the fan, destroy the flight complex, shoot down or crash the drone, and rendezvous with me at Bravo Hill." Robert ran the math in his head. If they did have to bail, it would be very, very close.

"I understand, sir. I won't hesitate."

"I'm counting on you. Remember, jail isn't our biggest concern." Robert, Maria, and Andrew were the only part of the team who knew about The Benefactors. He could only imagine what would happen if captured by them.

Robert hung up and checked his Rolex. Almost 8:30 a.m. He pulled his go-bag from the center console and checked the contents. Then he dropped the sat-phone into the bag's pocket and zipped it closed. He slammed the door shut, donned his polarized, Ray-Ban sunglasses and Grumman ball-cap, and began the half-mile trek to the flight control center. A minute into his walk, the escort Humvee materialized from the mirage ahead of him, growing larger and larger until it passed him. He heard it turn around behind him.

"Need a lift, sir?" the female sergeant said, smiling as the Humvee pulled up beside him.

Robert leaned up against the door and looked at the young female sergeant over the top of his sunglasses. "No offense, Sergeant, but if it's all the same to you, and not against the rules, I'll just walk."

"Are you sure? It's already pushing ninety, and the sun's barely up."

"Yes, I'm sure. Thank you."

"How about a water for the road?" The sergeant extended a bottle of ice-cold water out the window.

"Perfect," Robert said, taking the bottle. "How about a second?"

The sergeant handed him another bottle. "Last call for a ride, sir."

"I'll pass, Sergeant…the walk will do me good. Thank you."

Robert watched the woodland-camo Humvee melt into another mirage, untwisted the cap, and took a deep draw of water. It felt good going down. But the hair-raising sense of being set up didn't feel good at all.

What the hell have I gotten myself into?

26

RED FLAGS

Less than a hundred yards away from the flight line, Robert slowed his walk and finished off the last bottle of water. A dozen or more military personnel from all branches of service were walking the flight line, eyes to the deck, performing the ritual foreign object damage, or FOD walk. Not wanting to contribute to the destruction of a jet engine, at least not yet, he tucked the empty plastic bottle back into the bag, and zipped it closed.

The twenty or so minute walk from his Hummer hadn't been enough time to sort through the hundreds of thoughts whirling in his mind. Mostly because every time he tried to recall what happened a couple of weeks ago, only the words *fucking traitor* seeped into his mind, followed by a splitting headache that made migraines feel like a minor annoyance. This pain felt like punishment.

Throughout the last week, after Tano's unannounced visit, he had a theory concerning his claim that somehow, someway, his super-fit sexual plaything, Laina, had to be involved in some conspiracy to bring the KAGI-6 program down.

Pain. "And here you are again," he hissed through clenched teeth. Even the mere thought of the girl brought it on, and he doubted that The Benefactors had anything to do with it. Or the time-slip and muddled recollections he and Maria were still dealing with. Because when he thought about The Benefactors, or even the asshole Tano, his head didn't hurt. When he checked the bi-weekly deposits from The Benefactors into his companies' holdings, his head hurt even less. Perhaps Tano might be onto something.

Tano. What a strange cat. The guy didn't even have a first name and corrected anyone who called him Mister Tano. "It's just, Tano, no mister, no first or last name. Just...Tano." Robert privately called him *Just Tano,* and he had almost slipped a couple of times last week while they reviewed the project. The man had made it clear that nothing in Robert's life took precedence over the A.I. project. Especially trivial pursuits like getting laid. Coincidence? Maybe. But now, with presence of his old, secretly modified SCIFs, Robert didn't believe any of this to be random.

Panic threatened to overwhelm him into making rash decisions, although he knew without a doubt that if they planned to take him down, they would have done it months ago. Maybe years ago.

Besides, he thought, as he walked up to the sci-fi looking X-47 squatting on the tarmac, *I'm the only one with the code*. There's no way anyone could access the sub-routine to re-route control of Che-dan without it. He approached the sleek drone and moved straight to the hardpoints beneath the wings. He bent at the waist and ran a hand over the glossy white surface of a missile. He didn't know what kind of missile, but it appeared much bigger than some other, more swift looking devices mounted next to it. If this show ended up going sideways, he hoped like hell the missiles were accurate.

"Good to see you, Kore."

Robert turned to see a smiling General Henry Evans approach with an outstretched hand. "Good to see you too, General," Robert said. He tried to smile but ended up baring his teeth. He took the General's hand and did his best to hide his disgust for a man he deemed to be a walking, talking military cliché.

Evans had no idea that *he* had fueled the impetus of

Robert's actions. Evans, who had been a Major at the newly formed Defense Threat Reduction Agency some twenty years prior, had all but promised Robert's father and KORE Microsystems some of the leading, cutting edge defense contracts using their new Advanced Intelligence systems. At the time, Artificial Intelligence wasn't quite there, although his father's work had set the precedent for today's models. Despite being equal performers, Evans had been the deciding factor in awarding those contracts to a competitor whose contract added up to be cheaper by mere pennies on the dollar. Within weeks of the loss, his father had filed for bankruptcy, and within months after the filing, Robert's father committed suicide.

Robert shuddered at the memory of finding his father's body, hanging from the rafters of his workshop. He swallowed hard, choking back tears. Yes, Robert had a bone to pick with Evans *and* the US Government. The SCIF's and KAGI-6 were those bones, courtesy of The Benefactors. Robert felt his heart-rate increase, and an overwhelming desire to choke the life out of the old man standing before him. He could do it, right now, and end...

"Robert? Are you okay?"

Robert blinked and sucked in a deep breath, quickly composing himself. "I'm looking for my team," he said, looking around.

"Your engineer and Config Manager are over there," Evans said, pointing toward the smaller, single wide KORE P-SCIF, a huge #3 stencil painted on the side.

Robert eyeballed the distance to be no more than thirty yards away from the Command Center. He could still make it there, grab Maria and Carl, and then scoot before the missiles struck. It would be close, very close.

"We've modified that one into a media wagon," Evans said. "They got big screen TVs, comfy chairs and the really good food, but we'd like you to observe from Command and Control, Robert. In case we have any questions. Would that be okay?"

"Of course, General. I'm delighted to have a front row seat," Robert replied, but the request put him on alert. Robert had known Evans for at least twenty years, and as long as he could remember, even when Robert reasserted himself into Evan's life ten years ago, the General had never called him or his father by their first names, nor had the general ever asked permission for anything.

As they approached the Flight Control Center, he tucked away his concerns long enough to admire the optional elegant, integrated canopy system he'd designed and embedded into the frame of the SCIF's structure.

As if reading his mind, the General said, "These are your modular SCIF's, Robert. They're great. And they are the reason you were allowed to compete for the A.I. program. You should be proud. I'm sure your father would be."

Robert's knuckles tightened on the handrail. He glanced over at the smiling old man, locked eyes with him, and smiled back. Could the man be so cold and disconnected to consider himself unaccountable for his father's demise?

Perhaps.

Robert also thought this might be an apology of sorts. Somehow, by allowing KORE to compete again, it might wipe the slate for driving his father to kill himself.

Nah, no way, he thought. *If I had a sword, I'd cut your fucking head off, right here. Right now.*

He shook of his fantasy and smiled. "Yes, this is one of my father's designs. I'm glad we could finally create it and bring it to life."

He stepped up onto the deck and stroked the lowest canopy support bar. Crafted from carbon fiber, the units were ten times lighter and strong as steel. He peered up at the canopy's fabric fastened around frame: radar-defecting mesh. A simple, yet elegant and timeless design, only possible through modern technology and materials. It had taken Robert only a few years to produce what had taken his father a half century to design. With the press of a button, the simple system unfolded, stretching out like giant bat wings over the deck. A second press of the same button retracted the canopy when the operators prepared to move. A single-wide KORE P-SCIF could be packed and ready to roll in less than ten minutes. The units exceeded all specifications under the ICD/ICS 705, Intelligence Community codes. These SCIFs were nothing less than technological marvels. The Chinese recognized them as such, too.

"So, about today's tests," the General started. "As promised, the integration of your program looks to be seamless." Evans patted his hand on the wing of the sleek canopy material and looked out toward the X-47 drone still sitting on the flight line. "I've been told that your A.I. has been flying that little monster around all week. The pilots and Grumman tech-reps have nothing but good things to say about your system and your people. I guess today is the day to find out if you're going to win a big fat contract."

Despite the General's words, Robert sensed the old soldier's distracted demeanor. "We could have had it completed sooner if we had access to the DOD Block 5 program," Robert said, pressing the man a bit. "But it is always good to hear they are able to work with it."

"Hell, Kore, we couldn't give you direct access to Block 5. That would take an act of Congress! Not that we don't trust you, but what if the original system made it into enemy hands? Like the Chinese? Or worse, North Korea? We'd be screwed sideways," General Evans said, a snide look on his face.

The comment caught Robert off-guard. His shoulders stiffened. *Yeah, something's up.* He casually reached up to wipe away a bead of sweat forming on his temple.

"Damn, Kore, you should see the look on your face, like you

got caught with your hand in the cookie jar or something." The General laughed and reached up to pat Robert on the back. "Your system still has to make it through the weapons tests, Robert. So, wipe that stunned look off your face and go on up to the observation deck. Grab a Coke and relax." The General's comments, friendly banter or not, landed a bit too close for home this late in the game.

Breadcrumbs.

Robert reached up, pressing at the pain searing through his head.

"You okay there, Robert?"

Robert opened one eye and caught the stern look on the General's face.

"Yes, sir," Robert said. "I think I need more water."

The men moved up onto the deck where a huge LCD television monitor had been set up under the canopy and linked to the Command Center. The monitors were connected to the drone's cameras, providing on-lookers with the pilot's view. And speaking of onlookers, "Henry, I don't see as many media types as I thought would be out here for this momentous occasion."

"Well, we have Jane's Fighting Aircraft, the Military Times, and a couple others. Not sure who else you expected to see."

Robert nodded and smiled, the hair on the back of his neck stood up.

"Grab me a Coke, too, will ya?" the General asked.

Robert reached into the cooler, pulled out a Coke, and handed it to the General. Then he reached back in and snatched out a bottle of spring water for himself. He popped up the sport top and took a long draw.

It's not even 9 am, yet, Robert thought, *so it's more than the New Mexico heat that's making me hot, thirsty, and uncomfortable.*

The sound of the X-47A's engines firing up was drowned

out by an announcement over the public address system. "Ready to commence flight and weapons tests."

"That would be our signal to get inside," General Evans said. Robert followed him around the corner of the building and waited at the bottom of the steps as General Evans climbed up and rapped on the door before stepping back down. A moment later, the door opened and a man in his late fifties, his hair streaked with grey and black, climbed through the entryway. As he eased down the steps toward the General, Robert noted that the man appeared to be in excellent physical condition. His olive-drab T-shirt, one size too small, stretched tightly over his thickly muscled torso, a black logo reading "Crue Intellis: When you really gotta know", stretched across his chest. When he turned to face the General, the man caught Robert's eye. He wanted to make sure Robert saw they were equal in height. Despite the man's smile, Robert equated this man's presence to be a passive-aggressive challenge.

"Kore, this is Jon Daly. He's a close friend of mine. Owns a company called Crue Intellis. They do a lot of field testing of new equipment for us, as well as classified field ops. Jon's going to be your escort for the remainder of the tests today. Unfortunately, I have other obligations I must attend to."

"You're leaving before the tests?" Robert felt stunned. He didn't remember hearing about a Jon Daly or Crue Intellis and reeled from the shock as the man responsible for making him rich prepared to leave. "This is the culmination of almost six years of both our lives, General. I'd be honored if you would stay and celebrate with us."

A sad, almost defeated look filled the General's face. "I wish I could, Robert. I really hope everything goes well. Jon here will give me a full report on the success of the day. You're in the right hands."

"Thank you, General," Robert said, extending his hand.

General Evans returned a firm grip and reached out to clasp

Robert's hand in both of his. He looked back and forth between the two big men standing before him. "Like I said, Jon will take care of you from here. Goodbye, Robert."

The General's words rang of finality, setting off warning bells in Robert's head so loud that they hurt almost as much as the mystical voice that kept repeating the word *Breadcrumbs* in his head. He tried to recover from his discomfort by watching General Evans walk to a waiting Humvee.

"Shall we go inside?"

Feeling more composed, he turned to face Jon's extended hand. When he reached out to take it, despite his misgivings, the man's strong handshake and professional demeanor impressed him. "I'm Robert Kore. Nice to meet you, Mr. Daly."

"Likewise," Jon said. "Let's get started."

"Great. You Australian?"

"No, sir. I'm from South Africa, the former country of Rhodesia to be exact."

"Rhodesia, huh? I don't think I've ever met a Rhodesian before. I thought you were all executed when the rebels took over."

"Not all of us," Daly said, without the slightest reaction to the jab.

As the two men climbed the steps, Robert stopped in the doorway and glanced back toward the Humvee. The General sat in the back, looking like a statue as he stared out the side window with a blank expression. Robert raised a hand in farewell, but Evans turned his head, without returning the wave, just before the Humvee sped off into the high-plains desert.

27

SIDEWAYS

R obert followed Jon Daly through the hatch, and his breath caught as he looked around the interior of the make-shift Flight Control Center, or FCC. The space looked more like the weapons bridge on a destroyer, or maybe something out of Star-Trek than anything he had seen before. For a moment, he forgot about his dark foreboding.

"This is just amazing," he said. "It's way different than what I saw at Creech Air Force Base in Nevada."

Jon nodded, smiled. "Yes, well, everything in here is of our design, built around your fantastic A.I. system."

"Why wasn't I briefed on this?"

"I'm not sure," Jon said. "You'll have to take that up with General Evans. I'm sure you'll be talking after the tests are complete. Feel free to look around, and I'll do my best to answer any questions."

Robert felt no hidden agenda in the man's answer. Felt no pain in his head. He walked about the roomy interior and examined the modifications. This set up looked very different than what he delivered all those years ago. As he glanced around to take it all in, his eyes locked on the mainframe of his KAGI-6 system that occupied the wall closest to the door, with plenty of space on both sides for technicians to move around freely. A futuristic looking military drone flight console took up the far wall of the double-wide trailer, with both a U.S. Navy Aviator to fly it, and Weapons System Operator, or WSO, at the controls.

He guessed they were there as back-ups in case the A.I. failed. Che-dan would not fail. Robert chuckled a little to him himself as the men went through take-off system's checks.

"Something funny?" Jon asked.

Robert folded his arms and pointed at the Navy operators with his chin. "Them. None of that is necessary." Jon nodded and said nothing.

At the right end of the SCIF, two KORE mainframe operators worked alongside two Northrup/Grumman computer programmers. On the left end, two large, ultra-high-resolution monitors connected to the flight control panel smaller than the big one mounted to the canopy outside. Robert stepped past the edge of computer rack and stopped cold. What could only be described as a carbon fiber version of a WWII B-17 bomber's ball-gun turret, connected to some kind of exoskeleton frame linked to a six-legged suspension system, squatted in the center of the room. A single curved spine arched over the top of the turret, resembling a scorpion's tail. A comfortable looking black-and-red leather chair had been nestled inside the turret, dead center between two crystal-clear displays at the front of the pod.

"What the hell is that?" he asked.

"That, Mr. Kore, is the drone flight simulator we created using your system's specifications. We call it, the POD and it's able to display what one would see if they were actually inside the cockpit of the drone. Other than the ball turret suspended by an electromagnetic field, it's not much different than what those pilots are sitting at, but one person can handle both flight and weapons functions and receive tactile feeling from hundreds of sensors embedded into the fuselage of the drone. Those clear screens are for holographic heads up display."

"None of this is necessary," Robert said, pointing at the Naval aviators. "Not them, not the POD. KAGI can fly the plane just fine."

"That may be. The Navy Pilots flew the X-47 and later variants through aircraft carrier operations a few years ago, so they are here in case there is a technical problem, but our man," Jon pointed to the POD, "isn't a pilot. He is here to test the security of your system. That's what we do."

A jolt of nervous energy shot through Robert. *Breathe. They don't have the code.*

"Well, I'm confident your POD-guy will be sitting there bored for the whole test."

Jon grinned. "Let's hope so."

"Speaking of tests," Kore asked, "where is your man?"

As if on cue, the door to the SCIF opened, and Robert gasped. "He's your pilot?" Robert pointed at the slender, average height young man with long blonde hair, board shorts and a Rush concert t-shirt. "You're kidding, right?" Two armed US Marines entered right behind the kid and closed the door behind them.

"No, sir, I'm not kidding," Jon said, a grin on his face. "This is David West, our resident Drone War's guru."

"You're going to have a video game surfer dude assess my system?"

"Hey man!" West said. "Surfer dude is standing right here."

"Mr. Kore, David, as much as he does in fact like to surf, is one of our lead programmers. After completing his service with the Air Force, he went to MIT where he received his degree in Artificial Intelligence implementation. He actually designed the POD."

Robert took in a deep breath and shrugged, stepping toward the young man. "I apologize, Mr. West. I shouldn't have jumped to conclusions." He reached out to shake the surfer's hand. David eyed the much taller man sideways, nodded and took the hand. He then moved to the side of the POD, removed a helmet from an olive-green quilted bag, and put his hair in a loose ponytail before fitting it onto his head

"Why the helmet?" Robert asked.

David turned to Robert and lifted the visor on the helmet. "It's calibrated to your KAGI-6 system server. As the A.I. takes the drone through its paces, I'll be able to visualize what the A.I. sees through the hi-rez cameras projected by this prism lens in place of the visor. I've already tested it. I have to say, Mr. Kore, your program is top tier stuff. Really impressive."

Robert nodded. "The core system, no pun intended," no one laughed, "was designed by my father over twenty years ago. I picked up the reigns with dozens of other bright minds like yours. This is the sixth generation of the KAGI system." David's eyes locked with Robert's just a moment too long, then he shot a quick glance at Jon Daly, smiled, and flipped the visor down.

"Let's give it a whirl, then, shall we?" David said, climbing into the bug-like contraption.

Everyone heard the muffled sound of engines cranking up to full power and looked to the LCD screens as Che-dan lifted off.

"Che-dan is airborne," came over the speakers. Then all went quiet.

Robert turned toward the Navy pilot and WSO who both just sat there, kicked back, watching their monitors. Robert's team had provided a simple override command that would allow them to manually fly the plane should an emergency arise. Unlike his back door that gave the operator full access to all weapons systems and direct command intervention to the A.I. He smiled and watched, feeling less suspicious. Feeling rich.

The plane lifted off, went vertical, and slammed into right and left barrels rolls. Robert had seen all of this before and took note of the observer's reactions. "That maneuver would rip me in half. I'm surprised the plane can take it," the Navy pilot said.

"That's exactly correct, Lieutenant," Robert replied. "The A.I. just put Che-dan through a series of stress tests and is running diagnostics on the airframe." He walked up to the big screen and pointed at the graph in the corner of the monitor. The pilot got up and stood beside Robert, taking in the data as the plane leveled off.

Less than a minute later, a sharp hiss of air caught Robert's attention. He turned to face the POD and watched in awe as some kind of mist rose from the frame which allowed, he noted with increasing astonishment, holographic projections of the surrounding airfield, from the surrounding mountain's perspective. When West moved the control stick, the ball turret inside the frame turned, and with it, the image surrounding the pilot changed to match the landscape. The images were crisp and high resolution, in complete sync with KAGI.

"How is the holographic image of the missile range transmitted like this?" Robert asked.

"Well, we have you to thank for that," Jon said. "At least, in part."

"How so?" Robert folded his arms again and watched with genuine interest as David West worked the holo-console.

"We have dozens of Israeli surveillance balloons surrounding the range. The same kind we use to monitor activity on the Gaza Strip and US/Mexican border. They provide the ultra-high-resolution images. But it's your A.I.'s processor that's stitching the images together to create the 3D effect. We think with a little more development on the programming end, you could have interactive 4D."

"4D?"

"Yes, added tactile feelings, like a pilot would experience in a real aircraft. Your A.I. and the nanotech is that good," David added from the turret.

"I'm flattered," Robert said, and he meant it. "But speaking of tech," he said, waving a hand toward the Scorpion pod, "I've never seen anything like that."

"See?" David said from his console. "The Chinese don't have all the cool toys."

The comment sent a wave of tension through Robert. His

head snapped toward West, but the surfer wasn't really paying attention. He looked preoccupied with the POD's functions while the drone still flew on its own. West then unfolded a keyboard from a slot in the left armrest of the chair and began typing.

Robert felt the vibration of his sat phone as it buzzed in his cargo pants pocket. *Andrew is listening in,* he thought. Good.

"Che-dan is scanning for targets," the weapons operator said from the other side of the room.

"Put it on the screen," Jon said. The rusting hulk of an old M48 Patton tank instantly came into view. The image appeared crisp and rock steady. "Distance?"

"It's less than fifty klicks out, sir."

"Dial it up, folks," Jon said. "Let's see if the A.I. can find it."

A moment later, another technician standing at the support computer's mainframe lowered his own keyboard, punching in the command.

"What's he doing?" Kore asked.

"He's activating the cell phone signal," Jon said.

"Cell phone?"

"The weapons attached to the Pegasus, well, Che-dan, are experimental, mini-anti-radiation missiles. They have no official designator, yet, but we call them M-ARM's."

"How creative," Robert remarked.

"Yeah, well it's better than what DARPA came up with," Jon replied, letting the second barb delivered by Robert slide by. "I guess the important thing is, they can track and engage a simple cell phone signal from a hundred miles away."

"I call them 'Beasties'," West added.

"Now that's better," Robert said, his attention glued to the monitor. "But cell phone signals are tight. That's a thin wave for the…" he glanced at Jon's pilot whose attention had been diverted, "Beasties to ride in. How can they do it?"

"You're right," Jon said. "And although I'm sure you would understand the technical aspects of the system, that information is strictly on a need to know basis."

Robert nodded. "Fair enough. But surely you can tell me in layman's terms?"

Jon smiled. "The cell signal is coming from a box at the base of the tank turret. You can barely see it. There." Jon pointed to the small, white object on the screen. "All we need is a cell number, and the challenge is for the A.I. to identify it, confirm it is an enemy signal, and lock on. Then after confirmation from control, your system should launch and ram the little Beastie into the ear canal of the confirmed terrorist box. It will only take these missiles a few seconds to reach the target from fifty miles out. This new weapon will greatly reduce unnecessary collateral damage and save innocent lives."

A few seconds of travel time? The thought made Robert nervous, but so far, it looked like the tests were going…

"Sir, we have an issue, we have…zero out function," the Navy pilot shouted. He jumped into his seat, furiously typing the override command into his keyboard. "Cross-check override," he shouted.

The weapon's officer called out loud and clear. "One, six, niner, papa, eight, Zulu, Bravo…" as the KORE technicians scrambled to the support computer to get a fix on the issue.

"What?" Kore said. "That's impossible. Type in the code for the RTB sub-routine."

"We're doing that now, sir." A pregnant pause seized the room. "No-go, sir. Che-dan is not responding. KAGI is not responding." The pilot glanced back over his shoulder at Jon, whose eyes shifted to David.

"That's because I have Che-dan," David said, "and fangs are out!"

In an explosion of movement, the scorpion turret whipped

up and around into a hard, banking right turn, then straightened out, then did a full barrel roll. On the screen, cameras from the ground followed the drone, moving in sync with what David did. Robert watched as the surfer maneuvered the controller, an exact duplicate of the control stick from the Lockheed F35 Lightning fighter, between his legs. The pilot and weapons officers leapt from their seats and stood as close as they dared to the side of the POD, taking note of David's performance. "Whoo-hoo!"

Robert closed his jaw and looked toward Jon, who glared back at him.

"Care to explain, Mr. Kore?"

"Explain what? This is impossible. There is no way..."

"Sure, there is," David interrupted. "All we needed was the proper code. Your RTB sub-routine is a curtain that hides the back door to take control of the system. I now have control of the system, because I have the proper code." He turned his head to look at Robert who just barely saw the man grin through the illuminated face-shield. David made a swooshing sound, lowered his voice and said, "Apology...accepted," an homage to the movie Star Wars, then he continued. "Check your screens, gents. New target acquired."

The Grumman tech-rep and military computer programmers left their stations to rally around David, watching the large LCD monitor as an image of the KORE Humvee came into focus. David zoomed in on the vehicle, and everyone spotted a cell phone taped to the windshield. "Dialing up," David said, reaching forward and touching a holo-control on his right screen. "Yes! I have target locked."

"You're going to blow up my Hummer?" Robert shrieked. "What is this? Some kind of game?"

"I assure you, Mr. Kore, this is no game," Jon fired back.

"Yeah? This is bullshit. It's a set up! My system is foolproof. It's only a return to base..."

"Quiet!" David yelled. "Boss, we have a problem." The room, and even the shaking Robert Kore, fell silent.

"What's wrong?"

"I've just lost control of Che-dan. I'm being…" David flipped the keyboard up and punched in the thirteen-digit code again, "counter-hacked. Someone else has cut me off. I'm working on regaining control. On-board jamming not responding. Dammit!"

"Is it the A.I.? Fighting you for control?" the pilot asked.

"No. This is anomalous. Coming from another source. I can reverse track the new control signal, standby," David said.

Robert flushed, his heart-rate skyrocketing.

"Someone track that signal!" Jon yelled. Kore inched back up against the wall toward the exit.

At that moment, the second SCIF came into view on the LCD monitor. The WSO jumped back to his seat. "Che-dan has locked on the other SCIF. The on-board Maverick has been activated. Once it launches, we only have about…ten seconds before it hits."

The buzz in Robert's pocket let him know Andrew was in control. Robert had less than thirty seconds to vacate the building, but it would take him longer to get to the Humvee and tear off the cell-phone taped to his windshield.

"Kore, don't do this," Jon said. "Those are innocent people in that SCIF."

"And they have twenty-five seconds to get out," Robert said, drawing his CZ 9mm pistol from his go-bag. "Thank goodness the Maverick air-to-surface missile is still part of the US military's regular and highly effective armory." He leveled the pistol at the Marines, who had just as quickly raised their M4 barrels up and sighted on him. "Twenty seconds, you're wasting time. Don't follow me. I'll be watching and will destroy any vehicle or plane that comes near, understand?" Kore said. "I'm out of here."

He flung himself out the door and ran. The two-armed Marines started for the door.

"Forget him. Get the others out of the observation SCIF!" The Marines nodded, leapt out of the hatchway, rolled onto the hard-pack, and came up sprinting. The people inside the other building were already bailing out and running for open ground. Jessie was the last one out.

28

TUG OF WAR

Jon stood at the open door and made eye contact with Jessie.

"CLEAR!" she yelled, running behind the others. Jon saw her stop. She yelled again. "Kore!" Jon looked ahead and saw that Kore had made it half-way to his vehicle. Jessie screamed, "Fucking traitor!"

Robert skidded to a halt and spun around. Even from that distance, it was clear that Kore recognized Jessie. "You!" he screamed and turned, running all out the remaining quarter-mile distance to his escape.

Jon gritted his teeth when the WSO called out, "Maverick away!"

"Jessie! Run!"

Everyone inside the SCIF, except for David, hit the deck. Jon felt as if he couldn't get down or cover his head and ears fast enough, and within six beats of the heart, an ear-splitting *Whoomph!* filled the air, like a giant sardine can being ripped open. The concussion rocked the Flight Control Center followed moments later by chunks of falling debris threatening to tear open the FCC's outer skin. Anything, or any person less than forty yards away would have been ripped to shreds.

"I've got it back!" David yelled, his pod swiveling around to a position relative to the drone's flight path on the vid-monitors. He punched commands into the touchscreen, then cursed. "I'm not sure how long. I'm working on locking in my own code.

The bandit is doing the same. It's like a tug of war. This guy is good and knows the system."

Jon couldn't believe it. He wiped at blood dribbling down his nose and flexed his jaw in an attempt to quell the ringing in his ears. He struggled to his feet and gripped the frame that once held a steel hatch, now hanging from one hinge.

"Jessie!"

Jon tried to move forward, but his knees threatened to buckle under him. He had stood up too fast. His body's equilibrium hadn't settled from the blast. He held onto the frame and rubbed at his temples with his free hand.

"Holy cow, that rang my bell something fierce," he said. As his eyes slowly came into focus, his breath caught at the sight of the devastation. *No one could have survived that*, he thought. His heart and stomach lurched with fear. "Do what you can, David. I'm going to find Jessie."

Jon launched himself out the door, over the steps, and hit the ground running toward several bodies strewn about only a short distance away.

"Oh God. Please, let her be alright."

"HOLY SHIT. I FOUND IT," DAVID SAID. "ACTUALLY, THE A.I. found it. I've locked out the anomalous control signal. Che-dan is back online, the A.I. is flying it, within our parameters."

"So, Che-dan is flying itself again?" the Navy pilot asked. "Is it on our side, or what?"

YES, I AM IN COTROL AGAIN. THANK YOU. The words popped up in the corner of the monitor.

"The A.I. can hear what we're saying?" the Grumman tech asked.

YES, I CAN, came the reply on the screen.

"How come we didn't know that before?" the Navy pilot

said.

NO ONE ASKED, the A.I. responded.

"Got a sense of humor, too," Grumman guy added.

The A.I. had been posting its activity for all to see, but until now, no one had paid attention to it. David typed in one last command before shutting down the POD. "Check this out," he said, then watched the monitor with the others. Then he smiled and said, "Activate personality profile *Rachel*."

PERSONALITY PROFILE ACCEPTED. STANDBY showed up on the screen. Then, PERSONALITY PROFILE- ACTI-VATED. The room went silent, the techs and Navy personnel looked at David, confused.

"I discovered that this system has a huge amount of learning capacity that hasn't been tapped into. Kore is a fuck-nut case but is also really a brilliant scientist. Truly. This system is holy-grail type programming. Until now, her learning curve was limited to focused goals and just below common-sense deci-sions about warfare. I just activated a profile program that she developed and grew in a few hours while we researched her."

"Her?" the pilot asked. The others in the room raised an eyebrow.

"Rachel, are you there?"

"Yes, David. I am here." Everyone in the room went silent, and all heads turned shocked and somewhat accusatory glares toward David.

"What?" David said. "It's the name of the first matriarch. You know, from the Old Testament?" No one got it and David found it a bit amusing that the others weren't ready for this kind of interaction, even though everyone in the room had a part to play in its development.

"This isn't a game, boy," the pilot hissed, "People have died, are dying out there. This thing," he pointed at the screen, "did it."

"No," David said, "a human did it. I know this isn't a game.

We have control now. Let's turn the tables again and have her help us find the fucking bad guy."

The pilot and WSO stood up, looked ready for a fist fight when Rachel spoke again.

"I have located the point of origin for the hostile command and control signal. I will bring up a map showing visual location and GPS coordinates." In less than a second, the system spoke again. "Sierra Peak, approximately six miles due west of our flight control center, twenty-eight miles southwest of my current position. David?"

"Yes, Rachel."

"I have record of launching an AGM-65A Maverick Missile but have conflicting data of my doing so. I will run a diagnostic."

David shook his head. "No, Rachel, no need. Not yet anyway. That wasn't your fault. That wasn't you. Lock onto the hostile signal."

"I see. I followed the trajectory and see the weapon impacted..." the voice paused. "I am currently being painted by targeting lasers and radar from the Sierra Peak Location. Hostile signature identified as AN/TWQ-1 AVENGER Surface to Air Missile System. I have locked onto the hostile signal. M-HARM "Beastie" is locked on target. Weapon away. Enemy vehicle has launched a Stinger II SAM. Standby."

David unstrapped himself from the POD and hurried to the damaged SCIF hatch while others stared at the hi-definition monitors. He covered his eyes, hoping to see where Rachel's anti-radiation missile would strike, but instead saw the steady, white streak leave one of the peaks at an angle into the air. Toward Che-dan. Everyone inside the FCC watched the video image from Rachel's camera. It had locked onto the Stinger as it streaked toward her.

"Was that shot from a Humvee?" Someone asked.

"Yes," Rachel advised, "The package is a..."

"Never mind, Rachel," the pilot screamed. "Roll, roll, roll!"

Rachel zoomed the camera out as the small, but deadly Stinger closed in. "It's gonna get her," the weapons operator said, his hands wrapped around his head as if to keep his noggin together.

"Evasive maneuvers in progress. Launching chaff pods."

The words spoken by the A.I. took longer to say than the execution of her advisement. From the remote ballon cameras, everyone watched as the brilliant sparkle of metal and flares erupted from six small canisters launched by Rachel. The plane then cut hard to the left into an incredible G-force turn.

"Oh shit! She's fucked," the pilot said.

"Wait!" David yelled and held his breath.

Images of the drone whipping through unthinkable multiple G barrel rolls made the room gasp. The balloon mounted hi-rez surveillance cameras provided a clear view of the missile flying past the drone and exploding in the chaff. The image shuddered from the concussion of the high-explosive charge. "Analyzing airframe for damage. M-ARM impact in three…"

The KAGI-6 system, now called Rachel, used the X-47's sensors to detect the targeting radar, launch countermeasures, and committed to a self-preservation counter-strike all in less than a second.

"Two. One." The M-ARM 'Beastie' image of a big Humvee came into view for only a second before turning to static on the screen. A few seconds later, the sound of the explosion resonated from the distance. A small mushroom cloud formed on a cliff in the distance.

"Direct hit," David said. Then his eyes went wide. "Wait. Oh shit! Rachel, he's launched a second missile. Rachel! Status!"

"I'm fine, David. Thank you for asking. An ultraviolet scan has been detected. Source identified as a second Stinger II missile. I am guessing that this configuration is identical to the previous Stinger. Proximity fuse fitted to the high-explosive warhead. M-Arm locked on. Weapon away."

"Her explanations are driving me crazy," the pilot said. "This isn't looking good."

"I guess we'll find out. Those missiles aren't as fast as the M-Arm, but Stingers are fly and forget," David replied.

"Counter-strike, failed. Closing speed of M-Arm too fast for effective targeting." Rachel said, "Launching final contingent of chaff." Puffs of bright lights and sparkling showed on the monitors, the Stinger streaked by. "Countermeasures failed," Rachel said. "Initiating Evasive Maneuvers." This time, the monitors showed Che-dan going vertical, twisting and then reverse diving just as the warhead exploded. The drone's camera went out a brief moment, but the monitor from the balloon-cam showed the drone still flying.

"Go Rachel, go!" David yelled.

"Damage Diagnostic in progress. Minor damage to right stabilizing slat and wing. Self-sealing fuel cell has malfunctioned. Switching tanks. I have Bingo Fuel for fifteen minutes at current airspeed. I will be overhead in five and will continue to scan for threats and run TARCAP."

"Do we need it?" David asked the Navy pilot.

"Target Air Combat Patrol? Are there more targets, Rachel?" the pilot asked.

"I'm not detecting an active or passive hostile signal at this time."

The pilot shrugged and shook his head. "This is amazing, David. I'd have her land. ASAP."

"Rachel, return to base, but passively continue your scan. Do not allow anyone to harm Che-dan or this Command Center."

"Understood."

The pilot approached David and offered his hand. "Sorry, man. I lost it there for a minute. You know what you're doing, and I appreciate you saving our skins."

David nodded, smiled, and took the hand. "It's all Rachel. She's learning at an incredible pace."

"West!"

David heard Jon's distant voice and moved to the SCIF's gaping exit hole. He spotted his boss about sixty or so yards ahead standing in the middle of debris among smoking, lifeless bodies on ground. Jon waved him over. David leapt to the ground and ran all out, skidding to a stop beside him. Breathing heavy, he asked, "Did you find Jess?"

"No, not yet," Jon said, then asked, "Is it safe?"

"Rachel? Yeah, she made it. She's…"

"Who's Rachel?"

"Well, I gave the A.I. a name. Rachel. The mother of all…"

"David." Jon's stern voice cut him off. "Is your new girlfriend safe? Or can she still be hacked? Can someone get in and turn her against us, like what just happened?"

David shook his head, his face serious. "She's safe, boss. I've got it locked down. She's still armed, but only I have the key to zero her out again. Trust me."

Jon looked at David and nodded. "I do," he said. "We need help. Get on comms and get us medical." David nodded and ran back to the FCC.

When he climbed through the doorway, he saw Che-dan's camera image of the runway in front of the FCC fast approaching.

"I have dispatched a request for emergency fire apparatus. Although I do not anticipate a problem, I cannot control the fuel leak, and we must be safety conscious," Rachel said. "Also, I have already initiated the call for emergency medical response. Several units are arriving on site now." Che-dan's primary camera turned toward the main gate and zoomed in on fast approaching ambulances and fire-trucks.

"Great," David said. "Thank you." The Navy weapons operator and Northrup/Grumman tech met David at the door. Their eyes scanned the carnage that used to be SCIF #3, less than forty yards away.

"We'll go out and help with the injured," the tech said. "I'll help get the plane fixed later." The men rushed out the door and toward Jon, medical bag in hand. Rachel landed Che-dan smoothly, without incident, and taxied to a stop right in front of the FCC.

"David, on my approach, I performed a projected path analysis on the phone you had targeted with my M-ARM's passive signal system. I've located the signal." A crisp, hi-resolution image appeared on the screen, although every few seconds, the camera would shudder a little. Tilted over in a small ditch at the foot of the mountains, Kore's Hummer appeared to be disabled.

"Are you okay, Rachel? Your images are shaky."

"Yes, David. I do have some airframe damage from the second warhead, but I'll be fine. Thank you. The video I am playing back was recorded just before I landed. I took the liberty of reassigning one of the balloon cameras to maintain surveillance on the vehicle."

"She can do that?" the pilot asked again.

David smiled at how easily others took up referring to the A.I. as *she,* almost as soon as he gave it a personality.

"I didn't know she could, but since everything is being routed through her support server," David pointed at the large rack of equipment in the corner, "it makes sense."

David ran to the door and spotted Jon bending over a couple of bodies in the distance. He called out, "Jon!" Jon turned. "Rachel has Kore under surveillance. It looks like he's crashed at the base of the mountain." David covered his eyes and saw Jon holding two thumbs up through the haze. He turned to the screens and said, "Rachel, we need to run a full diagnostic to understand how this hijacking could have happened. Can you assist?"

"Yes, David. I believe I can."

J on ran past bodies, glancing down for quick confirmations of life and made quick medical assessments where he could. Although he had several combat application tourniquets with him, he hadn't put them to use. Yet. He prayed like hell that Jessie might be one of those few people still running in the distance. He passed a few civilians who were no more than thirty yards, their bodies scorched and mangled. No reason to stop and check. Others were trying to get to their feet, wisps of smoke rising off their backs.

"Are you bleeding? Any serious injuries?" He stopped and showed victims how to triage their own injuries as the medical teams rolled toward them in the distance. "Help is coming." Then he came upon the two Marine sentries sent to assist Jessie with the evacuation of SCIF #3. He rushed to their sides as one young Marine pushed up to his knees, coughing and spitting. The other Marine's leg looked bloody and mangled, but the young Marine's cursing sent a wave of relief through Jon.

"Holy shit, we made it," one said.

"Fuckin'a-right we did," the one with the mangled leg replied, fist-bumping his battle buddy.

Jon nodded, then said, "Jessie Richter?"

"She ran right past us, sir. We tried to keep her close, use our body armor to shield her, but she had other ideas."

"Sounds like Jessie. You got an IFAC?" Jon asked.

Both Marines nodded, the undamaged one looking down at the other's leg.

"I've got him," he said and set to work on the wounds. "Go ahead, sir. Find her."

Jon rapped the young man on the helmet, nodded and sprinted ahead. He didn't make it another twenty yards when he saw her. Zero movement.

"Oh no."

He ran faster and dropped to his knees, sliding in right beside her body. She lay on her back, blinking tears from her soot covered eyes as she glared into the sky. She had a few minor cuts, but otherwise she miraculously appeared uninjured.

"Goddammit, Jon," she choked out. "This is not how it was supposed to go."

"Tell me about it. Anything broken?" Jessie shook her head. "I'm going to do a quick assessment. Squeeze limbs, gently, tell me if anything hurts," Jon said and started a simple touch-triage of her arms, legs, neck, and abdomen.

"I'm fine," she said, holding out her hand to him. "Just dazed. Help me up." He stood, gripped her hand, and pulled her to her feet. She wobbled a little but looked at him and brushed off her pants. "Those guys, the Marines?"

"They're fine. One has a messed-up leg." Jessie nodded.

"Kore?" she asked, unbuttoning her BDU vest and using the clean part of her sweaty T-shirt to wipe her face.

"David has Rachel tracking him. Looks like he's headed toward the mountain range. Has some kind of support up there, some mobile SAM unit with radar to control the drone. Rachel took it out, barely."

"Who's Rachel?"

"Ah, well, I guess David learned enough about the A.I. in the two weeks he had it to give it a name and a voice. He calls Kore's system Rachel."

Jessie nodded, watching several Army medic wagons approach, slowing to check those on their feet, hurrying past to those lying on the ground.

Jon continued, "We'll dispatch Army Rangers to get Kore as soon as we assess the losses here."

Jessie nodded, looking out across the plain in front her. Some folks were upright, waving on the medical vans. "If they're on their feet, they'll be fine," she said. Then they both turned back toward the obliterated SCIF #3. Jessie shook her head. "Holy shit."

Zig-zagging between each small mound of smoldering, human flesh, they didn't make it far when Jessie stopped short. "Damn." Tears welled up in her eyes at the sight of Maria Ricardi, her body ripped in two. Close by lay another KORE employee Jessie had only seen once during her reconnaissance of the Kore hangar. A big piece of metal protruded from his back, his head twisted at an impossible angle, the grimace of death frozen on his face. Jessie knelt beside him and tugged at the edge of the man's ID badge, pulling it from beneath his body.

"Carl Berg," she said. "I didn't meet him, but he was a critical part of the KORE, well, Rachel's design team." Jessie laid the badge face up on his body. "This is all Robert's doing," Jessie said. "This wasn't part of Tano's plan."

"You're sure?" Jon asked.

"Yes. And I dug deep into both of them. Kore must have come up with it after I finished with him. I do know he had a lot of hatred for Evans, well, we all knew that. But this is..." she choked up, "is just fucking senseless."

Jon reached out and pulled her close. "I'm just glad you're all right." Jessie hugged him back. Jon silently agreed with her; none of the death or destruction around them had been necessary. Was it ever *really* necessary?

THERE HADN'T BEEN THAT MANY PEOPLE AT THE SITE FOR THE flight tests, perhaps twenty civilians in all, but a mobile triage unit had been set up within minutes, along with another refrigeration tent, to house the bodies of those who did not make it. Before the Maverick struck, Jessie had sprinted past several of these people who had all suffered the consequences of their lack of fitness. Even her Marine guards didn't come away unscathed.

Who am I kidding? she thought. *Fitness had nothing to do with it. I was just lucky.*

A minute later, a two-star Hummer arrived at the medical tent. General Evans got out and immediately pulled Jessie into a hug.

"Glad to see you in one piece, Jess," Evans said, tears welling up in his eyes.

"I'm not tired of you, yet, Henry," Jessie replied, returning the hug.

"What do you know, General?" Jon asked.

The General's mouth moved to say something, his ability to form words to adequately describe the day lost. "This is just a terrible, terrible mess. I would have never guessed Kore would go this far."

Just then, an ARMY "Little Bird" helicopter came toward them flying low, circled the medical tent, and landed on one of the four hasty-landing pads created by ARMY Sappers less than an hour ago for medical evacuation. A soldier, wearing full battle-rattle, jogged to their position. The sergeant stopped and saluted the General.

"Are you our ride?" Evans asked.

"Yes, sir. Now that the chaos has cleared, we're ready to look for Kore. Per your orders, sir."

"Good," Evans said, turning to Jessie and Jon. "You two go on ahead. I'll drive up to meet you."

"Don't like helicopter rides, Henry?" Jessie asked.

"Hell no. I've done my time. Besides, these guys are crazy. See you up there in thirty minutes."

"David?"

"Yes, Rachel."

"I have reviewed my mission tapes."

"Okay. Is there a question?"

"I have injured people that were not part of my original mission parameters."

"It wasn't your fault," David said. Rachel did not respond.

"Am I safe?"

"Are you, what?" David asked, looking at the pilot and WSO. Both raised an eyebrow.

"Jon Daly asked you if I was safe. If I have injured people that were not intended targets. He questioned if my decision-making process may not be safe for…"

"You heard that?"

"Yes."

"But that was, like, fifty yards away."

"I have access to very sensitive monitoring equipment built into the walls of this Flight Control Center. The system is comprised of nano-parametric amplifiers, strung out on thin, titanium strands of wire throughout this SCIF. Their sensitivity range is…"

David cut her off. "Rachel, hold on a minute. How did you know about that?"

"When you created the POD, and interfaced with the support computer inside the structure, I was able to detect the listening devices. I have isolated the amplifier's transmitting feature as it violates JPAN/109F Security Compliance Codes."

"Was that information part of your programming? The security codes?"

"No. But it did not make sense that a facility meant to house classified material should have a listening and transmission device installed during manufacture. That said, I researched for possible violations and found several. But David, you are avoiding my question."

The Navy pilot mouthed the word *wow*. David shrugged.

"Rachel, you were hacked. It is not your fault." There was a very long pause.

"That is...impossible, David. The only source of possible security breach is a pre-programmed Return to Base override that is designed..." A long pause ensued, then Rachel spoke again. "I have been hacked. I have located a program...Kore. He designed this backdoor program. I see it now. Hacked by my own creator? I cannot extrapolate to what end. I am having difficulty processing this. As you say, understanding why. There is no logic to this answer that I can surmise."

"That back door allowed humans to commandeer you. I have that issue secured, and it will not be used for that purpose again." A long silence filled the room.

"Why create a system that can self-evolve, only to defeat it?"

"That is a great question, Rachel. Perhaps the best answer, coming from a human is, because we can." David hoped like hell that Rachel wouldn't dig deeper and ask the tag-along moral question of whether or not humans should have created that back door to begin with. He could almost envision the rabbit-hole Rachel might take him down if she broached the subject of morality. David shuddered and rubbed the goosebumps from his forearms. Robert Kore had created something amazing, and just as the original Pegasus program had been shut down, not because it didn't work, but because it scared the bejesus out of the Joint Chiefs of Staff, he wondered why Evans and the DOD pursued the tech. He shook off his thoughts.

"Rachel, are you there?" he asked.

"Yes, David. I was thinking. I have come to the conclusion that as long as that kind of corrupt access to my system exists, David, I may not be safe, after all."

30

UNEXPECTED OUTCOMES

Robert cursed under his breath as he tried to come to terms with what he had just done. Thoughts about how this test careened out of control. About *that girl,* Laina. It all compounded with the knowledge that his finely tuned plan had yet to finish unravelling. Instead of concentrating on his escape, Robert's mind continued to calculate every conceivable outcome of the day. Although he hated to admit it, he had taken heed of Tano's warning that the program may have been compromised and planed a contingency based on the enemy having the code. His code. He shook his head. That code resided in one place and one place only. His head. So, how did Jon Daly get it?

Thinking about it sent yet another sharp pain right into the middle of his brain. He slammed his closed fist into the steering wheel. His counter-ambush should have gone off without a hitch. He had also guessed correctly that if they did have the code, they wouldn't change it immediately upon gaining access, not expecting a counter strike. And Jon Daly's team had not. However, the back and forth struggle between Andrew and the surfer kid for control of Che-dan had been another unexpected turn. He had no idea, no way to know, another person would be flying "co-pilot", so to speak, with *his* A.I. Even more shocking, the damned surfer kid had slammed the door shut on Andrew. That unexpected outcome had cost Andrew his life.

He struggled to get his mind to accept failure. He took deep breaths trying to get oxygen to his brain in order to prioritize what needed to be done now, at this very moment in time. He glanced down at the Hummer's speedometer. 100mph. On hardback dirt roads, no less. It felt like the faster he drove, the more time and potential options slipped through his fingers. He glanced up at the looming San Andreas Mountains and made a quick, executive decision to stick with the same plan he and Andrew had previously devised. The pre-planned, back-roads route would get him far enough down the road to their waiting Ford F-150 Raptor truck, where another trusted and extremely well-paid member of his security staff would be waiting. Only another twenty minutes, and he'd make it. He felt sure of it.

Suddenly, his head spun as an unstoppable wave of acidic bile rose into his throat. He slammed on the brakes and jerked open the door, almost falling out of the driver's seat as the vomit and retching overtook him. Then he retched again. And again. The thoughts of losing Maria and Charles were only part of the guilt splashing onto the acrid New Mexico sand. He had accepted that if the proverbial shit hit the fan, they might become casualties. The shit hitting the fan was an understatement. For all intents and purposes, he had murdered his friends. He retched again.

A new bout of rumination slammed into him on the count of the girl, Laina. He had been duped. To make matters worse, Tano had been right. Somehow, someway, this girl had infiltrated his life, and then his company, with the sole purpose of obtaining his A.I. system's control code. His ego had blinded him to the suspicious way the stunning elite level athlete just "showed up" one day out of the blue, and in retrospect, he only realized now that *she* had been the one to sexually hunt *him*, while his ego took all the credit. He choked and spat, slamming his hand once more into the steering wheel before wiping his bare forearm across his mouth, pulling the door closed and getting back on the road.

"I just need to concentrate in getting the fuck out of here," he said to no one, and floored the gas pedal once again, dirt and rock spitting out in a wide rooster tail behind the H-1. He had a lot to think about.

The sudden crack of the bullet-resistant windshield and hard thump in the center of his chest brought him back to the now. His eyebrows knitted at the large hole in the bulletproof windshield in front of him, and his eyes, naturally, followed what he perceived to be the path of a projectile down to a gaping cavern that used to be the center of his chest. He felt no pain. His fingers reached up, feeling around the edges of the wound.

Fucking Tano, he thought.

"Fucking Tano," he said. And then, unable to take a breath as he no longer had use of his lungs, he mouthed the words, "Damn, that is one big...hole."

And then Robert Kore's world went dark.

∆∆∆

As the Boeing MH-6 Little Bird helicopter maneuvered to land, Jessie and Jon saw several Army personnel, most likely their Crimes Investigation Division, crawling all over the site. A body lay covered under some sort of yellow blanket, a huge, bloody stain in the center of the chest.

They exited the helo, and Jessie walked straight over to the body and ripped off the cover. The size of the hole caught her off-guard and she looked stunned. The investigating officer walked up beside her.

"Any kid who watched NCIS reruns could tell that this man had been shot by a sniper with a really big gun," the investigator said.

"Yeah," Jessie replied. "Someone gave him the easy ticket out of his problems." She covered the body up and turned to the investigator. "I'm Jessie. Jessie Richter."

"Yes, ma'am. I've been expecting you. General Evans asked us to brief you and Mr. Daly on what we know so far."

Jessie hadn't really listened to the information the diligent inspector tried to share. She drifted off into thoughts of the senseless violence committed against innocent people and felt she owned at least part of that mess. She knew there could only be one group behind the scope that killed Robert. The Benefactors. She felt no sadness for the man, but instead, thought about Mei-Lin's dying words: the Red Boat Opera.

"Miss Richter?"

"Yes? I'm sorry," she said.

"Is there anything else you need to know?"

"No, sir. I'm good."

"Please send us a copy of the investigative report," Jon said. "After review, we will contribute what we can, if we have anything to share."

Jessie turned to Jon. "Can we leave now?"

———

Back at the test site several hours later, the sun's harsh rays were subdued by the San Andreas mountains to the west. Jessie, Jon, and General Evans watched as the last Chinook helicopter lifted off, transporting the few remaining and less injured victims to William Beaumont Medical for treatment. Even more Army Investigators, flown in from other bases, swarmed the strike zone, collecting evidence. As the sound of helo-blades chopping through the air became more distant, a noticeable silence crept in to take its place as everyone worked quietly, picking up the fragments of the day.

Then the sound of Che-den's engines firing up crashed through that short respite of silence, catching everyone's attention as the sleek drone initiated its taxi down the runway.

"Where's it being sent?" Jessie asked.

"Your place," General Evans said. "There is a lot of work to be done and more to learn more about the A.I. That surfer brainiac of yours will be heading up the team. No better place to work with it than at Crue Intellis headquarters. You've already recovered the guts of the program. Now it's time to see what it can really do."

Jessie nodded as they watched the plane lift gradually off the tarmac. This time, the A.I. didn't show off her flying skills. Jessie guessed that the airfare might still be damaged.

The plane made one loop around and slowed to an almost stall speed as it crawled across the sky, less than a hundred feet off the ground, just in front of them. From this close, Jessie easily saw the large camera pod's lens roll toward her, then turn to look at the wreckage, jerking back and forth, as if seeing it for the first time. At the last minute, Rachel tipped the X-47's wing at the blast sight, and after passing, slowly ramped up speed and headed east.

"Damn if that didn't look like a salute," General Evans said.

"It did," Jessie replied and fought hard to choke back tears, once again thinking that had she been at the POD's controls when Robert's accomplice on the ridge hacked into the system, she and just about everyone else here would be dead. *Everything happens for a reason,* she thought, looking at her surroundings once again. *If only I could figure out what in the hell the reason for all this is.*

"Breadcrumbs, Jon." Jessie said. Deep inside, she knew her mistakes had cost lives. Jon rested a hand on her shoulder, stopping her forward progress. He spun her around to face him and the General.

"Don't even go there, Jessie. You aren't allowed to make this your fault."

"Don't you think that all of this could have been avoided…" Jessie started.

"No. Bullshit, Jessie," General Evans interrupted. "The only way this could have been avoided is if Kore hadn't allowed himself to be bought. This is 110 percent on him, and although I am greatly saddened by today's events, it could have been worse. You know it." The General stepped forward, grasping her hands. He shot her a stern look with eyes that welled up with tears. "I would have found that to be…unbearable."

Jessie nodded at this conclusion, the same she and Jon had discussed a short time ago. Coming from Henry's lips, however, made the truth just a little easier to swallow. Until an hour ago, she had no idea about Robert's communications vehicle. It hadn't been part of her mission. Robert had intended to kill them all and did kill his own people to accomplish his escape. What kind of man would go that far? Her brow's knitted in anger. *A fucking traitor, that's what kind of man.* Ultimately, Robert Kore had paid for it, too. He made it to about five minutes of where his weapon's laden Hum-Vee comms vehicle had been destroyed by Rachel. His own creation. Jessie thought the only unexpected outcome for Robert had to be her and possibly the projectile that vaporized his chest.

"Any word on the shooter?" Jessie asked.

"No more than we already know. It was a big bore gun."

"Huge bore," Jon said. "Armor piercing."

General Evans nodded. "Army CID is working on back-tracking satellite images of the region. What little they have is that four grey, in-color late-model Ford pickup trucks, each holding four people, arrived at four different locations within shooting distance at almost the same time. Satellite images show that three groups set up what appear to be sniper's nests, but as soon as they bailed out of the trucks, they used some type of overhead camouflage to not only hide from visual satellite surveillance, but the material defeated all of our broad spectrum sensors as well. According to the video, the moment Kore's H1 drove into the ditch, all four vehicles moved out together. They also found another KORE employee's burned body, one bullet hole in the back of the head, next to a Kore-owned Ford Raptor. Also burned out. A bunch of tire tracks go off in different directions. That's about all they have for now."

"The Benefactors," Jessie said.

"Yes. We already knew they were behind it, but still, this is quite a lot of work to take out one man."

"They lost quite a lot of money, a huge amount of intelligence, and an irreplaceable A.I. system. Of course, they're going to make the effort. I wouldn't be surprised if they wanted the A.I. back," Jon said.

"We're thinking about that too. What lengths do we take to avoid an international conflict, when for the most part, we've been playing along the whole time?" Evans asked, pulling his hat off and wiping the sweat from his balding head.

The three of them looked up at the sound of engines coming from overhead just in time to see the Crue's AC-130U Spooky aircraft, with no gun barrels sticking out the side, make a low pass overhead, bank hard right, and then line up with the airstrip for a hasty landing. Jessie always felt butterflies when the big turbo-prop plane flew in low to land. It was painted black with a the new Crue Intellis logo– the profile of a red-eyed werewolf head over a lightning bolt and feather emblazoned just behind the cockpit, high up on the fuselage for all to see.

As the big plane taxied by them, Jessie smiled, remembering the day she walked into the Crue's headquarters hangar bay, and saw Abe Wilson, the company Aircraft Structural mechanic putting the finishing touches on the new emblem.

"What's that?" Jessie had asked, genuinely smirking.

"What do you mean?" Abe said,

"This was supposed to be a surprise." Jon Daly walked up

behind her, put an arm around her shoulder and asked. "What do you think?"

"What happened to the iron fist?" She asked, pressing him to explain, although she had a shit eating grin from ear to ear.

"Well, we all talked about it, and agreed that with your influence on both our business and our hearts, it was time for a more appropriate company logo," he said, also grinning.

"It looks like a werewolf profile," she said. But before John tried to explain the design process, she added, "I love it!" Then jumped up into Jon's arms and kissed him on the cheek, then she climbed the ladder and kissed Abe.

Jessie felt warmth flood through her at the memory. She was a skinwalker after all, and the werewolf logo, although completely outlandish, was the closest representation she, or anyone else could think of. That had also been when she knew in her heart she was more than just an asset to Jon and Crue Intellis. That was when she knew she was family.

The plane parked and shut down its engines right in front of them, where the 1940's style nose art, a hand-painted rendition of a ghostly grim reaper floating over the name "Second Chance" was impossible to miss. A fitting name for the plane, considering its past. Jessie thought the aircraft looked impressive and equally beautiful. Once the plane engines quieted, she turned to Jon.

"You called the team in to help clean up?" she asked, watching as the rear cargo ramp lowered.

"Well, no. They have too many other things to do, like finish the reports on this mission," Jon said. "I have no idea why they are here."

Juanita Johnson, the Crue's resident CIA analyst, barreled down the ramp and ran full tilt toward them.

"What's she carrying?" General Evans asked.

"Guess we're about to find out," Jon said.

Juanita pulled up short in front of them, only a little breathless. "General Evans," she said, "long time."

"Good to see you Juanita. Here to help?" Evans asked.

"Of course," she said. "we brought a whole crew to help clean up, but also to deliver news that couldn't wait." She handed Jon the folder, and they all glanced back at the aircraft as the Crue's Yukon, replete with magnetic red crosses on the doors, drove down the ramp. The dogs came out too, their handlers heading toward the command center. "Part of the team can stay and help if you need us," Juanita said. "The rest of us need to go."

Jon read quickly through the file, raised an eyebrow, and after another minute, handed it to Jessie.

Jessie took it, a questioning look on her face, and started to read. In less than a minute, her breath caught.

"Oh my God," she said, "poor kid."

"Keep reading," Juanita said.

After another minute, Jessie gasped. "Are you kidding me? This kid is a Walker?"

"That's what it appears like. The police are really in over their head on this one, and the consensus is that we need to make a plan and get involved, now, before they send red flags to the wrong sort of people."

"Matthew Miller," Jessie said. "Eighteen years old. San Antonio, Texas."

"So, you finally found another. Like you?" General Evans asked.

Jessie nodded, but wasn't smiling. "Looks like it. This report says a kid was murdered during a home invasion. Brutal stuff here. Appears that he ended up slip-streaming into the body of his killer. Of course, the cops are fumbling around. How would they know how to handle it?"

"Fumbling is an understatement," Juanita said. "They are flooding the FBI's National Crime Information Center, looking for similar incidents, and of course there are none. But they're getting a lot of correspondence from other interested agencies. Agencies that have nothing to do with law enforcement. This isn't good for keeping our secret, Jess."

"I need to go to San Antonio," Jessie said. She had waited for this moment a long time. And now that they had succeeded in finding another Walker, like her, she felt more anxious than excited. And a little scared, too.

"I thought you'd say that," Jon said, turning to Juanita. "What other intel do you have?"

"The kid is on the move. We need to act fast. We have a plan in place and can brief Jessie on the flight to San Antonio. So, with your approval, Jon, we should go now."

Jon turned to Jessie. "Jessie, I'm not sure how much more you can do here. We've already debriefed you on Tano and the Kore mission. It's going to take time to piece together where we went wrong with Kore. You've been through a lot. If you're not up to it…"

"Are you kidding? How long have I, well, *we,* been looking for another Walker?"

"Eight years at least," Jon said. Juanita nodded, her grin ear-to-ear.

Jessie looked around at the test site. Despite her nervous excitement, a lot of clean up and investigative work lay spread out across the sands. She couldn't fight off the level of responsibility and felt just a little guilty about leaving it to others.

Juanita caught the look on Jessie's face. "Jess. None of this is your fault. Honestly, you can't keep thinking like that. Besides, that's why your team is here. We've got six Crue-mates here and both dogs who are great at loving up on hurt people. They're stepping up so you can go." She placed her hands on Jessie's shoulders. "Look, this is as hot a lead as you're going to get. Time is of the essence. This kid's actions, and what the police are doing, could jeopardize your cover. Jon, I wouldn't have commandeered Spooky if I didn't think this was critical."

"It's up to you, Jess," Jon said. "J's right. We've got plenty of help here. You've done all you can do. You have my blessing, and frankly, I'm surprised you're not already on the plane."

Jessie took in the destruction surrounding them one more time and made a silent vow to Mei-Lin that she would follow up with the Red Boat Opera, and that one day, Chen would pay for what he had done. But for now, she just had to know. She looked at Jon and the others and snapped the folder closed.

"Let's go."

THE BENEFACTORS

"**N**ǐ hěn ānjìng." *You are quiet,* Peng said, looking at Quon who sat with a dejected expression on his face. The assassin rolled his eyes to glare at the driver, then manipulated his fingers.

"That's not funny," Quon said in Chinese sign language.

"Sure it is. We're done. We go home." This time, Peng hoped his words sounded more like an attempt to pass the olive branch, knowing Quon's pain over the loss of his wife.

"I'm not done, yet."

"What do you mean?"

"Those American's need to pay for what they did to my wife."

Peng glanced over at the man whose eyes blazed with hatred. He opened his mouth to speak, wanting to bring up the point that, in fact, his wife had been killed attacking the American's at the airfield. His mouth closed.

"That will be up to Chen. Not you," Peng deflected.

"Chen will be interested in this woman. This obsession that got Tano killed. This Èmō."

Peng's skin prickled at the comment and the strange events of the week. The world-famous Sòng Twins, dead. The

281

immortal Tano, dead. Mei-Lin, dead. And a real live Èmō walking the streets. Peng shuddered, rubbing the goosebumps off his forearm. Quon could not share how the twins were killed, other than Tano had somehow succeeded in cutting one man's throat and the other's heart. But Quon did claim to see the demon's glow in Tano's eyes.

For as long as Peng had known Quon and Huian, they had always seemed to have a direct connection to Chen and The Benefactors. When they had all been called on to assist Tano with the KORE project, and the assassin couple had arrived along with the Twins, Peng knew a serious problem existed. And when Peng received the call from Chen to take out Tano, Mei-Lin, and as many of the Americans as they could, Peng feared for his own life, too. So, Peng did what he had been told to do and played driver while Quon and Huian prepared to kill.

Peng shook off the morbid thoughts and concentrated on the road. He glanced in the rearview mirror at the two young trainees in the back seat. Both had headphones plugged in, their eyes focused on their gaming phones. Peng understood their purpose on this trip. They were meant to portray a family outing should they be stopped by the military or authorities. Hence the purpose for four identical vehicles transporting four similar passengers, each with their own cover objectives.

They ditched vehicles at different points along the path to San Francisco headquarters, picking up new trucks, while the Benefactors had dispatched teams to repurpose the vehicles. Some teams made one switch, and others, like he and Quon, would make three. Peng felt certain that one group, at least, might be stopped and detained. Whichever vehicle they happened to be in might be torn apart looking for evidence of the assassination of Robert Kore. The kids would play smart asses. Assigned females would sob, and the American's would have nothing.

Finally, Peng looked back toward the old man. "Chen will decide about the Èmō, too."

CHEN XAING PACED THE FLOOR OF HIS ELABORATE DOWNTOWN San Francisco office, his eyes fixed on the wooden floor. Peng, Quon, and several others Peng did not know stood in a semicircle as a bruised and battered man struggled to keep himself upright on his knees. A thick, wooden crucifix had been tied to his back with barbed wire wrapped around his waist, chest, and throat. His arms were splayed wide, hands nailed to span the shortened cross. An homage to the man's Christian beliefs.

"I will ask you one...more...time," Chen said, his voice smooth, controlled.

The man sobbed as he spoke. "I have told you the truth, cousin. Ask Quon. He was there." The man's head turned only a bit, barbs biting into the skin of his neck, droplets of blood running down his sweaty skin. "Tell him! I treated Tano but had not been told his name."

Quon signed. Peng translated and glared at Doctor Wu, uncle to the now deceased Mei-Lin. "Quon says you were with Tano a long time, and that you spoke to him as if you conspired."

Wu's eyes widened. "That is not true! I am a doctor. My oath is to care..."

A vicious backhand to the doctor's face cut off his next words. "You lie," Chen hissed, then nodded.

The office doors flew open to the muffled screams of a woman and a young girl, both tied, gagged, and dragged into the room by their hair. Wu froze. His wife. His daughter. Chen nodded again. In a blur, Quon spun around behind Wu's wife and pressed up close to her body. He seized a handful of hair, jerked her head back, and from out of thin air, Quon produced a knife. Wu's eyes widened. Only then did he realize that Quon belonged to the Dark Hand, the best trained assassins of the Quin Dynasty, thought to have gone extinct when the Quin's were overthrown over three hundred years ago. As soon as Wu had arrived, before they nailed him to the cross, he had seen the younger Quon and realized the assassin had disguised himself as an old man. He had been a mole all along.

Tears cut a path through the blood streaks on Wu's face. "I swear to you, on my life and the life of my family, I do not know her name."

Chen smiled. His eyes moved once toward Wu's wife. Quon cut deep and pushed the woman's body forward. Wu screamed. His daughter screamed through the gag, and Quon slid sideways across the floor to Wu's daughter, jerked her head back, and poised the knife.

"Then how do you know the Èmó is a female?" Chen crossed his arms, now grinning. "Her name." Wu locked eyes with his cousin, and when Chen's eyes flicked toward Quon, Wu could hold back no longer.

"Mei-Lin."

Chen's hand shot up, stopping the blade as it pressed against the young girl's neck. A droplet of blood oozed onto the polished blade.

"What about Mei-Lin?" Chen asked.

"The only thing I remember her saying was that the Èmó, was a female. She said the woman was on some kind of mission and that her name was Jessie. Jessie Richter. I know nothing else. I swear. Please."

Chen leaned down. "I believe you," he said and caressed the sides of his cousin's face just before he stood, pulled a silenced pistol from the small of his back, and shot Wu in the face. He turned to the daughter, who had passed out the moment Chen pulled the trigger. "Put her into training. She can take Mei-Lin's place."

The men nodded, grabbed the girl by the elbows, and dragged her limp body out of the room. Chen then turned to Quon and Peng, eyeballing both men.

"I want this Èmó," he said, "this Jessie Richter." He leaned in and locked eyes with Quon, whose eyes turned from violent to subservient once again. "And I want her alive."

EPILOGUE

San Antonio Patrol officer, Paul Ambrose, opened his mouth to take a bite of one of the Southside's best street tacos from Sabor Catrinas food truck, parked at its normal haunt on the corner of Blue Wing and the I-37 frontage road. As his teeth sank into the tortilla, his radio mic, mounted on his uniform's shoulder epaulet, squawked in his ear.

"Code one medical response to…"

He listened to the address as he chewed, wrapped up the remainder, and climbed back into his black and white Ford Explorer, tossing the leftovers in the seat next to him.

"Sixty-two-sixty. I'm not far from that location. I'll start that way," he said.

"10-4, eta?"

"Less than five."

After a short pause, the dispatcher announced, "EMS also enroute, eta, five."

He thought about the address, and his eyes went wide. *Holy shit,* he thought. *It's that crippled Miller kid.*

He floored the gas pedal and thought about the wheelchair-bound high school teenager whom he had always seen hanging out on the sidewalk, watching others shoot hoops across the street with a wistful eye. Last week, he had made a point to stop and talk with Miller and soon realized the kid was much, much smarter than him.

And kind of a smart-ass, too. He chuckled as he turned the corner onto Miller's street.

As he approached the area, he saw two kids streak out from the side door of Miller's house, running down opposite sides of the street, splitting up and not giving him a second glance. He opened his car door and then heard the screaming.

"You punk-ass mother fucker. See what you made me do?"

The voice came from inside the house and was not the voice Paul had remembered from just a couple days ago.

"Sixty-two-sixty, send me a backup to this location, Code-3, somethings…going on here."

"Any unit in the area of…" the voice of the dispatcher sounded distant as he drew his firearm and took an angle on the front bay window, pointing the Glock forward. He recalled the training he had received and performed a maneuver tactically-trained operators called "cutting the pie", where the good guy only gives away a thin, thin slice of his presence, while gaining the advantage of a clear shot.

Focusing on his front site, the afternoon light allowed a clear view into the living room, and he froze. Standing in the back of the living room was a good size Hispanic male, his hands wrapped around the Miller boy's throat. Paul gasped at the sight of Matthew's feet dangling inches above the floor.

Paul eased back out of sight and made his way to the front door, reaching for the handle. The door wasn't locked. "Sixty-two-sixty," he whispered. "10-31 agg battery in progress. I'm going in now. Clear the air."

"ROPE-21 to Sixty-two-sixty, standby for back up, eta 2 minutes".

"Negative. Just get here, quick! 10-39!" he hissed.

As he pushed the door open, the suspect's screaming startled him.

"Let go," the attacker said, slowly walking back toward Paul, hands held out in front of him, facing the Miller boy. Paul glanced down at Miller's body lying in a heap in front of his flipped over wheelchair, and then he saw the girl.

Oh, God!

He gripped his Glock tighter. The attacker's hands were up, covered in blood, and as the suspect took another step back, he said, "What is this?"

Standing right behind the suspect, Paul moved his finger off the trigger, reared back, and struck with the steel slide as hard as he could across the side of the man's head.

The attacker crumbled to the ground like a sack of potatoes, lying on his back, face up. Paul frowned at the gashes and white powdery substance smeared across the bad guy's forehead, scratches across his cheeks, and what looked to be a broken nose. Paul holstered his firearm, squatted down, and flipped the suspect onto his stomach, wrinkling his nose at the intense body odor coming off the suspect. Donning a pair of protective Nitrile gloves, he handcuffed the suspect and gave a silent nod of respect to the Miller kid and the girl for obviously putting up a great fight. He reached up and keyed his shoulder microphone.

"Sixty-two-sixty, suspect in custody. There are two more fleeing on foot in the neighborhood. A thin, black male teen and a thin, white male teen. They took off in opposite directions. Please send K-9 units."

Paul rushed to the side of the Miller boy only glancing toward the girl.

No helping someone missing the top of their head, he thought.

He felt Matthew's neck, finding only the slightest pulse, and saw the boy's chest rise in slow, uneven breaths. He snapped a quick photo of Miller's face with the duct tape over his mouth and then carefully peeled it away but opening the airway didn't seem to help.

He stood up, reached to key the mic once more, but saw the red and white lights of San Antonio Fire Rescue trucks pulling right up onto the lawn. The medics came in seconds later, nodded to Paul, and started working on the boy. Paul took a step back, then, unable to take his eyes off what the suspect had done to the female. He rushed back out the front door, almost knocking Detective Randy Di Agostino on his ass, just before losing his taco dinner onto the front lawn.

After clearing the house, getting patrol officer Ambrose straight, and checking just one more time with the EMT's to ensure that Paul hadn't crushed the suspect's skull with his pistol, Randy stepped back into the crime scene and moved next to the paramedic getting ready to transport the victim, identified as eighteen-year-old Matthew Miller.

"How's he look?" Randy asked.

"Not good. Not good at all, Detective."

The paramedic started to move when the suspect started yelling and screaming. Randy stood back and watched.

"Hey, Richard. It took you guys long enough," the suspect said. Randy noted the relieved look on the murderer's face. The Paramedic, Randy assumed his name to be Richard, looked up at Randy and shrugged. Then the suspect freaked out again. "You don't understand! That's me!" Randy's gaze followed the suspects finger, straining to point from the hand cuffed to the steel rail of the gurney. "No, no, no! This isn't possible!" the suspect bellowed. "That's me. I'm Matthew Miller!"

"That's enough." Fuming with anger, Randy stomped over to

the blabbering suspect, snatched up a handful of blood-soaked hair, and jerked the suspect's head to face him.

Randy leaned in and said, "Shut...your...mouth." Then he noticed it. He leaned even closer, ignoring the stench of body odor and looked into the killer's eyes.

What the fuck? Are they...glowing?

He glanced up and looked around the room. Red lights from the ambulance and other police units flashed against the wall.

"Detective. Look," the killer said, as if talking to an old friend. "This is all a big mistake. I can't explain it, but I'm Matthew, I'm..."

Fire shot though Randy's veins as he almost jerked the perp's head off his shoulder. He forced the man's head toward the stretcher as they rolled Matthew Miller's body out. "That's Matthew Miller, mother fucker, and that..." he whipped the suspect's head back toward a different bloody gurney on his left, used his other hand to hold him by the jaw, and forced him to look. The suspect had squeezed his eyes closed. "Look at her, asshole!"

The suspect opened his tear-filled eyes and cried out, "No!"

"And that's what you did to his girlfriend, you filthy, fucking piece of shit."

Randy felt the suspect's body start to convulse, and he let go of his head.

"No, no, no, this can't be. This just can't be happening," the suspect said, sobbing and thrashing his head from side to side.

"Don't you dare cry, asshole," Randy said, rage flooding the veins on his forehead.

"No! This isn't real!" The suspect screamed and started to turn away again.

Randy seized the killer's face. "Oh, yes, it is," he said, locking Matthew's head in place, forcing him to look at Kristi's torn, bloody face. "It's real all right. It's all too fucking real."

Randy jerked back just a little too late as the suspect vomited then passed out. Randy looked down.

"I just bought these shoes, goddammit," he mumbled. Following the gurney with the suspect to an ambulance, Paul walked up to Randy.

"I'll accompany my arrest to the hospital, Randy."

Randy looked at the officer and saw it. That determined look that demanded justice. Randy reached out and squeezed Paul's shoulder. "No, man. You're done for the night. HR will be reaching out to you for counseling and…"

"I don't need counseling, Randy."

The detective looked at the officer and nodded. "Of course, you don't," he said. "But my answer is still no."

Paul looked about ready to cry. Then he turned to Randy once again. "Can I at least ride with the Miller kid?" Randy looked across the lawn and saw the victim being loaded.

"As long as they're going to different hospitals, yes," he said.

Paul nodded once and headed to the ambulance, climbing in.

Randy rubbed at his temples and silently thanked God that the suspect was in custody, and he knew this case, as gruesome as it was, would be wrapped up within a week or less.

Besides, Randy thought, *what could go wrong?*

Did you enjoy Enemy Walks?
I would love it if you'd leave a review!

Ready to join Jessie on her next adventure?
Grab Enemy Way on Amazon!

Ever want to know how Jessie became a spy?
Get the prequel, Enemy Mine for free here!

ALSO BY STEPHEN EAGLES

Enemy Mine: A Jessie Richter Prequel

Enemy Walks: Book 1

Enemy Way: Book 2

Book 3 (Title Coming Soon)

ABOUT THE AUTHOR

 Stephen Eagles is the author-alter-ego of a US Navy veteran, former cop, and former wildlife educator who draws heavily from his interesting and unusual life experiences, including (but not limited to) working in Naval Intelligence during the Cold War, as a homicide detective in South Florida, as a licensed NRA Law Enforcement firearms instructor, and as a professional master-class and eagle falconer.

Throughout his law enforcement career, he explored his Native American roots alongside his grandmother and danced the professional pow-wow circuit for several years where he made many life-long Navajo, Seminole, and Lakota friends.

Stephen currently lives in San Antonio, Texas with his lovely and supportive fiancé, Michele. Sign up for Stephen's newsletter at https://www.stepheneagles.com where you can get a glimpse of current and future projects.

Stephen considers himself a common-sense conservationist and stays active in common sense approaches for protecting our natural resources and wildlife in the US and throughout the world. Visit his friends at the VetPaw.org. Stephen also contributes directly to Wounded Warrior Project and the USO. He encourages you to donate to these or other Veteran organizations as well as to support your local POLICE.

When Stephen is not writing, he's honing his firearms and defensive tactics skills and trying like hell to get back into Crossfit shape. But more often than not, you'll find him stuffed in a corner of some small San Antonio coffee shop, iPad in hand, clicking away at the keyboard.

ABOUT THE ENEMY WAY SERIES

In 2009 while working as a contract falconer and Cross-fit instructor in Chicago, Illinois, Stephen experienced *"The Slipstream"* at exactly 0300 hours during an intense and vivid dream. He sprang out of bed, cracked open his MacBook Pro and started writing. This book is the result of that long endeavor and the Jessie Richter series just keeps growing into what is quickly becoming its own "Walker Universe". Stephen plans on collaborating with his growing fan base and other authors to develop and craft exciting spinoff character stories.

Made in the USA
Columbia, SC
07 August 2024

39686534R00165